ALSO BY MARY GAITSKILL

Because They Wanted To
Two Girls, Fat and Thin
Bad Behavior

Veronica

Veronica

Mary Gaitskill

PANTHEON BOOKS, NEW YORK

Copyright © 2005 by Mary Gaitskill

All rights reserved. Published in the United States by Pantheon Books, a division of Random House, Inc., New York, and in Canada by Random House of Canada Limited, Toronto.

Pantheon Books and colophon are registered trademarks of Random House, Inc.

An excerpt of *Veronica* appeared in a different form in *Poz*.

Owing to limitations of space, permission to reprint previously published material may be found following the acknowledgments.

A Cataloging-in-Publication record has been established for this book by the Library of Congress.
ISBN 0-375-42145-9

www.pantheonbooks.com

Printed in the United States of America

First Edition

9 8 7 6 5 4 3 2

For B.C. and R.D.

Veronica

W hen I was young, my mother read me a story about a wicked little girl. She read it to me and my two sisters. We sat curled against her on the couch and she read from the book on her lap. The lamp shone on us and there was a blanket over us. The girl in the story was beautiful and cruel. Because her mother was poor, she sent her daughter to work for rich people, who spoiled and petted her. The rich people told her she had to visit her mother. But the girl felt she was too good and went merely to show herself. One day, the rich people sent her home with a loaf of bread for her mother. But when the little girl came to a muddy bog, rather than ruin her shoes, she threw down the bread and stepped on it. It sank into the bog and she sank with it. She sank into a world of demons and deformed creatures. Because she was beautiful, the demon queen made her into a statue as a gift for her great-grandson. The girl was covered in snakes and slime and surrounded by the hate of every creature trapped like she was. She was starving but couldn't eat the bread still welded to her feet. She could hear what people were saying about her; a boy passing by saw what had happened to her and told everyone, and they all said she deserved it. Even her mother said she deserved it. The girl couldn't move, but if she could have, she would've twisted with rage. "It isn't fair!" cried my mother, and her voice mocked the wicked girl.

Because I sat against my mother when she told this story, I did not hear it in words only. I felt it in her body. I felt a girl who wanted to be too beautiful. I felt a mother who wanted to love her. I felt a demon who wanted to torture her. I felt them mixed together so you couldn't tell them apart. The story scared me and I cried. My mother put her arms around me. "Wait," she said. "It's not over yet. She's going to be saved by the tears of an innocent girl. Like you." My mother kissed the top of my head and finished the story. And I forgot about it for a long time.

I open my eyes.

I can't sleep. When I try, I wake after two hours and then spend the rest of the night pulled around by feelings and thoughts. I usually sleep again at dawn, then wake at 7:30. When I wake, I'm mad at not sleeping, and that makes me mad at everything. My mind yells insults as my body walks itself around. Dream images rise up and crash down, huge, then gone, huge, gone. A little girl sinks down in the dark. Who is she? Gone.

I drink my coffee out of a heavy blue mug, watching the rain and listening to a fool on a radio show promote her book. I live right on the canal in San Rafael and I can look out on the water. There're too many boats on it and it's filthy with gas and garbage and maybe turds from the boats. Still, it's water, and once I saw a sea lion swimming toward town.

Every day, my neighbor Freddie leaps off his deck and into the canal for a swim. This disgusts my neighbor Bianca. "I asked him, 'Don't you know what's in there? Don't you know it's like swimming in a public toilet?'" Bianca is a sexy fifty-year-old, sexy even though she's lost her looks, mainly because of her big fat lips. "He doesn't care; he says he just takes a hot shower after." Bianca draws on her cigarette with her big lips. "Probably get typhoid." She blows out with a neat turn of her head; even her long ropy neck is sort of sexy. "I hate the sight of him flying through the air in that little Speedo, God!"

Sure enough, while I'm looking out the window, Freddie, all red and fleshy, with his stomach hanging down and his silver head tucked between his upstretched arms, vaults through the air and—*wap!*—hits the water like a bull roaring in the field. I can just see Bianca downstairs muttering "Shit!" and slamming the wall with her fist. He's a big fifty-something, with a huge jaw and muscles like lumps of raw meat just going to fat. His round eyes show one big emotion at a time: Joy. Anger. Pain. Fear. But his body is full of all those things happening at once, and that's what you see when he's swimming. He attacks the water with big pawing strokes, burying his face in it like he's trying to eat it out. Then he stops and treads water, his snorting head tossing and bobbing for a second before he turns and lies down in the water, like a kid, with total trust—ah!—face to the sky, regardless of the rain or turds.

Even though he's big, Freddie's got the face of somebody who's been beat too many times, like his face is just out there to be beat. He's also got the face of somebody who, after the beating is done, gets up, says "Okay," and keeps trying to find something good to eat or drink or roll in. He likes to end stories by saying, "But they'd probably just tell you I'm an a-s-s-h-o-l-e," like, Oh well, what's on TV? That's the thing Bianca hates most, that beat-up but still leaping out into the turds for a swim quality. Especially the leaping: It's like a personal affront to her. But I like it. It reminds me of the sea lion, swimming into town with its perfect round head sticking up—even though the lion is gliding and Freddie is rough. It's like something similar put in different containers. Sometimes I want to say this to Bianca, to defend Freddie. But she won't listen. Besides, I understand why he disgusts her. She's a refined person, and I like refinement, too. I understand it as a point of view.

The writer on the radio is talking about her characters

like they're real people: "When you look at it from her point of view, his behavior really is strange, because to her, they're just playing a sexy game, whereas for him it's—" She blooms out of the radio like a balloon with a face on it, smiling, wanting you to like her, vibrating with things to say. Turn on the radio, there's always somebody like her on somewhere. People rushing through their lives turn the dial looking for comfort, and the excited smiling words spill over them. I drink my coffee. The novelist's characters dance and preen. I drink my coffee. People from last night's dream stumble in dark rooms, screaming at one another, trying hard to do something I can't see. I finish my coffee. Water is seeping in and soaking the edge of the carpet. I don't know how this happens, I'm on the second floor.

It's time for me to go clean John's office. John is an old friend, and as a favor, he pays me to clean his office every week. Into my patchwork bag I pack the necessaries—aspirin, codeine, bottle of water— then I look for my umbrella. When I find it, I realize it's broken, and I curse before I remember the other one, the red one from New York that I never use. I got it at the Museum of Modern Art gift shop when I lived in Manhattan. It has four white cartoon sheep, plus one black one, printed on its edge, along with the name of the museum. The decoration is precious and proper, and it reminds me of Veronica Ross. She is someone from my old life. She loved anything precious and proper: small intricate toys, photographs in tiny decorated frames, quotes from Oscar Wilde. She loved MoMA and she loved New York. She wore shoulder pads, prissy loafers, and thin socks. She rolled her trouser cuffs in this crisp way. On her glass-topped coffee table, she had miniature ashtrays, gilt matchboxes, and expensive coasters decorated with smiling cats.

When I go out into the hallway, Rita is there in her housecoat and slippers, holding a little plate of fried chicken livers. She offers me some, says she made too many last night. They smell good, so I take one and eat it while I talk to Rita. She says

that last week "that son of a bitch Robert" fired up the bar-
becue again, on the puny deck right under hers, sending up poi-
sonous charcoal fumes, which, she has explained time and
again, are terrible for her hepatitis.

"I knew he still had that grill out there, and sure enough,
the sun came out and I heard him mobilize it. I heard the charcoal in the bag. I heard him slide the lid off. I sat down and I
meditated. I asked for help. I asked, What is the most powerful
force in the world? And the answer came to me: Water."

Rita has hepatitis C; so do I. We don't discuss it much; she
doesn't remind me that codeine by the fistful is like dropping a
bomb on my liver. I don't remind her that while charcoal smoke
is not a problem, her fried-food diet is.

"I filled every pot, every pan, every jar, glass, and vase,
and I set them all out on the edge of the deck. And as soon as he
fired it up—"

"You didn't!"

"I did. I doused the grill, and when he cursed me out, I
doused him. He just stood there a second, and then you know
what? He laughed! He said, 'Rita, you are a pisser.' He liked it!"

We talk a minute more; I laugh and say good-bye, step
outside onto the wooden stairs. I snap open the umbrella and
remember the last time I visited Veronica. She served me
brownies in pink wrapping paper, fancy cheese, and sliced fruit
she was too sick to eat. I remember the time I said, "I don't
think you love yourself. You need to learn to love yourself."

Veronica was silent for a long moment. Then she said,
"I think love is overrated. My parents loved me. And it didn't do
any good."

My street is all functional apartment buildings set back
from the sidewalk. White plus a few black people live here. Two
blocks down, it's semifunctional buildings and Mexicans. Turn
the corner and it's warehouses, auto-body repair shops, and a
bar with music coming out of it at 8:00 in the morning. Blunt,
faceless buildings that are too much trouble to tear down. Grass

and weeds and little bushes silently press up between the buildings and through every crack in the concrete. At the end of
the street is a four-lane highway that you can walk along. Big
businesses live here—car dealerships, computer stores, office
retail—and things I can't identify, even though I walk by them
almost every day, because the bigness makes me feel mute. The
mute feeling isn't bad. It's like being a grain of dirt in the
ground, with growth and death all around. A grain or a grass or
a stone, a tiny thing that knows everything but can't say anything. It isn't just the bigness of the businesses. It's the highway,
too, all the hundreds of cars roaring in the opposite direction
I'm walking, the hundreds of heads blurrily showing through
hundreds of windshields.

This happens sometimes when I walk along here; my
focus slips and goes funny. I think it's something to do with
walking at a slow pace against the speeding traffic, and today
the rain blurs everything even more. It's like I get sucked out of
normal life into a place where the order of things is changed;
it's still my life and I recognize it, but the people and places in it
are sliding around indiscriminately.

A fat white man pedals gravely past on a green bicycle,
one hand guiding the bike, the other holding a small half-
broken umbrella over his head. He examines me; there's a bolt
of life from his hazel eyes and then he's gone.

A dream from last night: Someone is chasing me, and in
order to reach safety, I have to run through my past and all
the people in it. But the past is jumbled, not sequential, and
all the people are mixed up. A nameless old woman who used to
live next door is reaching out to me, her large brown eyes brimming with tenderness and tears—but my mother is lost in a
crowd scene. My father is barely visible—I see him by himself
in the shadows of the living room, dreamily eating a salted
nut—while a loud demented stranger pops right up in my face,
yelling about what I must do to save myself now.

Meanwhile, a middle-aged Mexican woman is kneeling

on the sidewalk, patiently replacing the clothes that apparently spilled out when her big red suitcase broke open. She has no umbrella and her hair and clothes are plastered to her body. I stop and crouch, trying to help her. With an impersonal half glance, she shakes her head no. I straighten and pause and then stand there, holding my umbrella over both of us. She looks up, smiling; I'm invoking civility on this concrete strip between roaring and hugeness, and she appreciates it. Her smile is like an open door, and I enter for a second. She goes back to her nimble packing. She picks freshly wet little blouses, underwear, baby clothes, and socks up off the sidewalk. She retrieves a clear plastic bag of half-burned candles and a T-shirt that says 16 MAGAZINE! on it. She shakes out each thing and refolds it.

Toward the end, Veronica's shoulder pads used to get loose sometimes and wander down her arm or her back without her knowing it. Once I was sitting with her in a good restaurant when a man next to us said, "Excuse me, there's something moving on your back." His tone was light and aggressive, like it was him versus the fashionable nitwits. "Oh," said Veronica, also light. "Excuse me. It's just my prosthesis."

Sometimes I loved how she would make cracks like that. Other times it was just embarrassing. Once we were leaving a movie theater after seeing a pretentious movie. As we walked past a line of people waiting to see the other movie, Veronica said loudly, "They don't want to see anything challenging. They'd rather see *Flashdance*. Now me, if it's bizarre, I'm interested." There was a little strut to her walk and her voice was like a huge feather in a hat. She's not like that, I'd wanted to say to the ticket holders. If you knew her, you'd see.

But she *was* like that. She could be unbelievably obnoxious. In the locker room of the gym we both went to, she was always snapping at somebody for getting too close to her or brushing against her. "If you want me to move, just tell me, but please stop poking me in the bottom," she'd say to some openmouthed Suzy in a leotard. "Fist fucking went out years ago. Didn't you know that?"

The Mexican woman clicks her suitcase shut and stands with a little smile. My focus snaps back to normal, and the woman slips back into the raining hugeness. She smiles at me again as she turns to go, returning my civility with rain running down her face.

In the dream, it's like the strangers are delivering messages for more important people, who for some reason can't talk to me. Or that the people who are important by the normal rules—family, close friends—are accidental attachments, and that the apparent strangers are the true loved ones, hidden by the grotesque disguises of human life.

Of course, Veronica had a lot of smart cracks stored up. She needed them. When she didn't have them, she was naked and everybody saw. Once when we were in a coffee shop, she tried to speak seriously to me. Her skin was gray with seriousness. Her whole eyeball looked stretched and tight; the white underpart was actually showing. She said, "I've just got to get off my fat ass and stop feeling sorry for myself." Her tough words didn't go with the look on her face. The waitress, a middle-aged black lady, gave her a sharp, quick glance that softened as she turned away. She could tell something by looking at Veronica, and I wondered what it was.

Veronica died of AIDS. She spent her last days alone. I wasn't with her. When she died, nobody was with her.

I'm feeling a little feverish already, but I don't want to take the aspirin on an empty stomach. I also don't want to deal with holding the umbrella while I get the aspirin out, put it back, get the water, unscrew it, squeeze the umbrella with one arm, the one that's killing me. . . .

I met Veronica twenty-five years ago, when I was a temporary employee doing word processing for an ad agency in Manhattan. I was twenty-one. She was a plump thirty-seven-year-old with bleached-blond hair. She wore tailored suits in mannish plaids with matching bow ties, bright red lipstick, false red fingernails, and mascara that gathered in intense beads on the ends of her eyelashes. Her loud voice was sensual and rigid at once, like plastic baubles put together in rococo shapes. It was deep but could quickly become shrill. You could hear her from across the room, calling everyone, even people she hated, "hon": "Excuse me, hon, but I'm very well acquainted with Jimmy Joyce and the use of the semicolon." She proofread like a cop with a nightstick. She carried an "office kit," which contained a red plastic ruler, assorted colored pencils, Liquid Paper, Post-its, and a framed sign embroidered with the words STILL ANAL AFTER ALL THESE YEARS. She was, too. When I told her I had a weird tension that made my forehead feel like it was tightening and letting go over and over again, she said, "No, hon, that's your sphincter."

"The supervisor loves her because she's a total fucking fag hag," complained another proofreader. "That's why she's here all the time."

"I get a kick out of her myself," said a temping actress. "She's like Marlene Dietrich and Emil Jannings combined."

"My God, you're right," I said, so loudly and suddenly that the others stared. "That's exactly what she's like."

I cross a little footbridge spanning the canal and pass a giant drugstore that takes up the whole block. There's an employee standing outside, yelling at someone. "Hey you!" he yells. "I saw that! Come back here!" Then more uncertainly: "Hey! I said come back here!"

Hey you. Veronica sat in a doctor's office, singing, "We've got the horse right here; his name's Retrovir" to the tune of a big *Guys and Dolls* number. The receptionist smiled. I didn't.

Come back here. Veronica burst into laughter. "You're like a Persian cat, hon." She made primly crossed paws of her hands and ecstatic blanks of her eyes; she let her tongue peep from her mouth. She laughed again.

More employees come out of the store and watch the guy; he just keeps walking. It's obvious why. The police can't get there fast enough and these employees are not going to fight him, because he'd win. This animal reality is just dawning on the employees. It makes them laugh, like an animal shaking its head and trotting away, glad to be alive.

I pass the bus depot, where people are hanging out, even in the rain. I pass closed restaurants, Mexican and French. The knot of traffic at this intersection always seems a little festive, although I don't know why. The bus depot changes: Sometimes it's sad, sometimes just businesslike, sometimes seems like it's about to explode. John's office is in the next block. He shares it with another photographer, who mostly shoots pets. He seems to be better off than John, who sticks to people.

I let myself in and sit down behind John's desk for a ciga-rette. I know I should be grateful to John for letting me clean his office, but I'm not. I hate doing it. It depresses me and it tears up my arm, which was injured in a car accident and then ruined by a doctor. John shares a bathroom with the pet pho-tographer, who has filthy habits, and I have to clean up for both of them. I used to know John; we used to be friends. Even now, he sometimes talks to me about his insecurities, or advises me on my problems—smoking, for example, and how terrible it is.

I have some codeine to prep the arm, then walk around the office smoking. I look at the photographs on the walls; John's got pictures from three decades. The ones from the sev-enties are the best. The models aren't professionals; they are just people John knew. They are male and female and they are all naked except for boots or a hat or underpants, something to give them style. Most of them don't have good bodies, but they are looking at the camera like they are happy to be naked, either just standing there or posing in the combination of relax-ation and sexual nastiness that people had then. They all look like people whose time had given them a perfect style suit to wear, a set of postures and expressions that gave the right shape to what they had inside them, so that even naked, they felt clothed.

I drop ash into the potted plant by the desk and rub it into the dirt with my finger. I get up and go into the bathroom for the cleaning supplies, a yellow bucket full of rags and spray bottles of cleaner so potent, I once killed a giant spider with it. I put the bucket in the sink and run water into it. I spray the mirror with cleaner and fine blue poison twinkles into the filling bucket, bright ammonia and dull smell memories of cafeteria food and public piss, my mother kneeling and cleaning. I wipe the mirror with a store-bought rag and drop it in the bucket.

There is always a style suit, or suits. When I was young, I used to think these suits were just what people were. When styles changed dramatically—people going barefoot, men with long hair, women without bras—I thought the world had changed, that from then on everything would be different. It's understandable that I thought that; TV and newsmagazines acted like the world had changed, too. I was happy with it, but then five years later it changed again. Again, the TV announced, "Now we're this instead of that! Now we walk like this, not like that!" Like people were all runny and liquid, running over this surface and that, looking for a container to hold everything in place, trying one thing, then the next, incessantly looking for the right one. Except the containers were only big enough for one personality trait at a time; you had to grab on to one trait, bring it out for a while, then put it back and pull out another one. For a while, "we" were loving; then we were alienated and angry, then ironic, then depressed. Although we are at war with terror, fashion magazines say we are sunny now. We wear bright colors and choose moral clarity. While I was waiting to get a blood test last week, I read in a newsmagazine that terror must not change our sunny dispositions.

Of course, there is a lot of subtlety in all this, and complexity, too. When John took those naked pictures, the most

popular singer was a girl with a tiny stick body and a large def-
erential head, who sang in a delicious lilt of white lace and
promises and longing to be close. When she shut herself up in
her closet and starved herself to death, people were shocked.
But starvation was in her voice all along. That was the poi-
gnancy of it. A sweet voice locked in a dark place, but focused
entirely on the tiny strip of light coming under the door.

I drop the rag in the bucket and smoke some more, ashing
into the sink. A tiny piece of movie from the naked time plays
on my eyeball: A psychotic killer is blowing up amusement
parks. At the head of the crowd clamoring to ride the roller
coaster is a slim, lovely man with long blond hair and floppy
clothes and big, beautiful eyes fixed on a tiny strip of light that
only he can see.

Lift up the toilet lid—filthy again—and drop the cigarette
in. Turn off the water and lift the bucket down. I set my teeth as
pain tears a hole in my shoulder and I get sucked inside it. The
roller coaster roars and everybody screams with joy; the blond
man screams in terror as his car flies off into the sky and
smashes on the ground. White froth gently disperses on the stirring bucket water as I set it down.

It's not an easy thing. If you can't find the right shape, it's
hard for people to identify you. On the other hand, you need to
be able to change shape fast; otherwise, you get stuck in one
that used to make sense but that people can't understand anymore. This has been going on for a long time. My father used to
make lists of his favorite popular songs, ranked in order of preference. These lists were very nuanced, and they changed every
few years. He'd walk around with the list in his hand, explaining
why Jo "G.I. Jo" Stafford was ranked just above Doris Day, why
Charles Trenet topped Nat King Cole—but by a hair only. It
was his way of showing people things about him that were too
private to say directly. For a while, everybody had some idea
what Doris Day versus Jo Stafford meant; to give a preference

for one over the other signaled a mix of feelings that were secret and tender, and people could sense these feelings when they imagined the songs side by side.

"Stafford's voice is darker and sadder," he said. "But it's warmer, too. She *holds* the song in her voice. Day's voice is sweet, but it's heartless—she doesn't hold it; she touches it and lets go—she doesn't mean it! Stafford is a lover; Day is a flirt—but what a cute flirt!"

"Um-hm," said my mother, and she gritted her teeth on her way out of the room.

But my father didn't see my mother's teeth. He was too charmed by Day singing "Bewitched." *He can laugh, but I love it. Although the laugh's on me . . .*

My father was right. If Jo Stafford sang that song, you would feel the pain of being laughed at by the one you love, and still you would love. When Doris Day sang it, the pain was as bright and sweet and harmless as her smiling voice. *I'll sing to him, each spring to him. And long for the day when I cling to him. . . .* My father smiled and imagined being the one she painlessly longed to cling to; then he went home—to Jo. She sang, "But I miss you most of all, my darling," and hurt was evoked and tenderly held and healed, again and again, in waves.

But eventually those feelings got attached to other songs, and those singers didn't work as signals anymore. I remember being there once when he was playing the songs for some men he worked with, talking excitedly about the music. He didn't realize his signals could not be heard, that the men were looking at him strangely. Or maybe he did realize but didn't know what else to do but keep signaling. Eventually, he gave up, and there were few visitors. He was just by himself, trying to keep his secret and tender feelings alive through these same old songs.

I thought he was ridiculous. But I was only a kid. I didn't see that I was making the same mistake. He thought the songs were who he really was, and I thought the new style suit was who I really was. Because I was younger, I was even more naive:

I thought everything had changed forever, that because people wore jeans and sandals everywhere and women went without bras, fashion didn't matter anymore, that now people could just be who they really were inside. Because I believed this, I was oblivious to fashion. I actually couldn't see it.

I remember the first time I was made to see it. It was the first time I met a fashion model. Strangely, it was also one of the first times I saw someone for who she really was inside.

I was sixteen when this happened. I had run away from home, partly because I was unhappy there and partly because running away was what a lot of people did then—it was part of the new style. This style was expressed in articles and books and TV shows about beautiful teenagers who ran away even when their parents were nice; the parents just had to cry and struggle to understand. The first time I left, I was fifteen. My parents had fought and refused to speak to each other for three days; I slipped out through the silence and hitchhiked to a concert in upstate New York. United by my disappearance, my parents called the police, who picked me up in a shopping mall a week after I'd returned of my own accord. Daphne said that while I was gone, our mother acted like somebody on one of the TV specials about runaways—always on the phone talking to her friends about it. "I think she enjoyed it," said Daphne.

But our mother said she did not enjoy it. "We won't let you put us through that again," she said. "If you leave now, you're on your own. We won't be calling the police."

So a year later, I left again. I packed right in front of them. I said I would just be gone for the summer, but they assumed I was lying. "Don't call here asking for money!" shouted my father. "If you walk out that door, you are cut off!"

"I would never ask you for money!" I shouted back.

"She thinks she won't need it," said my mother from the couch. "She thinks being pretty will make her way." Her voice was angry and jealous, which made me think that leaving must be something great.

"She thinks she's going to make her way in the world," she said. But this time her jealousy was touched with wistfulness. She could've been talking about a girl in a fairy tale, walking down a path with her bundle on a stick.

I lived from apartment to apartment, sometimes with friends, sometimes strangers. I got a ride to San Francisco and stayed in a European-style hostel, where you could stay a limited number of nights for a fixed fee. It was a large dilapidated building with high ceilings and sweet, moldy drains. The kitchen cabinets were full of stale cereal, the kind with frosting or colored sweet bits made to look like animals or stars. You had to chip in for food staples. You weren't supposed to bring in drugs; people did, but they were moderate and they shared. The man who ran it, a college student with a soft stomach and a big ball of hair on his head, even kept a record player in one of the common rooms, and we gathered there at night to share pot and listen to playful elfin songs about freedom and love. These songs had the light beauty of a summer night full of wonderful smells and fireflies. They also had a feeling of sickness hidden in them, but we didn't hear that then.

For the first few days, I was one of two girls, the other being a little fifteen-year-old with suspicious eyes and a sexuality that was sharp and raw as her elbows. But she was with a boyfriend in his thirties, the kind of guy who put on airs about his clothes and manners even though he looked like shit. I tried to be friends with her, but she acted like I was beneath her, maybe because she had an older boyfriend who bought her dresses. The only time she was friendly with me was when she let me see her dresses, pulling them out of a canvas bag and laying them across her arm, smoothing them with her free hand and telling me where and how Don had gotten each of them for her. Otherwise, when we were in the kitchen with the others, she'd roll her eyes when I talked. The boys were nice to me, though; it was a treat for them to have a single girl around. Even

18

the older boyfriend was secretly nice to me. He told me I'd be beautiful in ten years if I "cleaned up." But in ten years, I thought, I'll just be old.

Then a German woman came to the hostel. She was already old; she was thirty-one. But the boys were stunned by her. Even before they said so, I could tell. When she came in the room, they looked alert and dazed at the same time, like the beautiful night world of the music had appeared before them and begun swirling around their heads. When she left, they all said, "She is so beautiful!"

I didn't understand; she just looked like a girl to me, only old. Then someone said, "She used to be a model," like that explained everything. "She was very famous ten years ago," he added.

The feeling of dazzlement increased. The next time she appeared, conversation stopped, and people were self-conscious about starting it again. The fifteen-year-old girl didn't even try. She just sat there smoking and staring, not even suspicious anymore, like finally here was something that was exactly what it was supposed to be. She didn't even care that her boyfriend was staring at this woman like he was in love with her. She looked at the model as if she were a glimmering set of dresses, like she'd drape her over her arm and stroke her if she could.

Every day, the German woman would walk into this reaction, eating her cereal, taking her turn at the toilet, sometimes joining in a smoke around the stereo. If she walked into the kitchen, carrying a book: What was she reading? Oh really! And what did she think of it? The German woman answered thoughtfully and pleasantly, but also stiffly, like she was trying to pass a test.

I still didn't understand. I didn't think she was beautiful and I didn't care that she had been a model. This is probably hard to believe. It is hard for me to believe. Now everybody knows models are important; everybody knows exactly what beauty is. It is hard to imagine that a young girl would fail to recognize a former model with full, perfectly shaped features as beautiful. It wasn't that I didn't care about beauty; I liked beauty as much as anyone, but I had my own ideas about what it was. This woman didn't look like anything to me. Now I would be staring at her like everybody else. But back then, I was the only person in the house who did not react to her appearance. The few times we were alone in the kitchen together, we made small talk, and I didn't think she was paying me any more attention than I paid her.

I left the house after a week. I moved into a rooming house with an older boyfriend who made a living handing out flyers on the street. One day in the fall, I was walking down the street, doing nothing, when suddenly the German woman was there—so suddenly, it felt like she'd leapt out from around a corner.

"Oh!" she exclaimed. "It's so great to see you! How are you doing? I was wondering what happened to you!"

Under her friendliness, her face was wild, like something inside her was crashing together and breaking, then crashing together again. Her voice was pleasant, but she did not look pleasant, or thoughtful, or like she gave a fuck about passing a test.

I told her about my boyfriend, with whom I now lived. "That sounds wonderful!" she said. "I have my own place just a few blocks away from here. Would you like to come visit?" Then, seeing my expression, she added, "Or maybe just go for a coffee now?" I stood there, nervous and speechless. She frowned, peering at me slightly, maybe noticing finally that I was just a kid. "Or, or . . . an ice cream! Would you like an ice cream?"

"Yeah," I said. "But I don't have any money."

"It's all right," she said, already leading me away without checking to see if I was following. "It's my treat." From the side, her eye was glassy and hard. Gingerly, I fell in with her.

We must have looked strange together. I was tall, but she was taller, and her high heels made her taller yet. Her burgundy dress was silken and plain, and it flattered the cutting, angular quality of her body. She wore sparkling earrings and eye shadow, lipstick and nail polish. It was hot and she was slightly wet under the armpits, but still she gave an impression of dryness and gleaming. I wore sneakers, jeans, and a T-shirt, with no bra underneath. My hair was unkempt and I wore no makeup. I didn't wear deodorant or bathe often; I might actually have smelled. She did not seem to notice any of this.

She took me to a very stylish and expensive place with little white tables covered by green-and-white-striped umbrellas. A year later, I would know enough to be uncomfortable sitting in this place looking like I did then. But at that time, I only felt bewildered; we didn't need to go there to get ice cream. I stared at the menu, dimly aware of the crudeness of my person for the first time. We ordered our ice cream. She looked at hers dully and began to eat as if she couldn't taste.

As we ate, a man in a suit came to our table and spoke to her in a foreign language. His voice was soft and he spoke briefly, but what he said enraged her. She did not act enraged, but I could see it, first in the muscles of her jaw and neck, then in her eyes. Rage was leaping from her eyes, but she answered him with a politeness so bitter, it seemed a kind of despair.

"What did he say to you?" I asked, thinking it must have been very obscene.

She literally clenched her teeth and said, "'You are very beautiful.'" Hatred illuminated her face like a bright flare and then went out. She returned to her ice cream.

I was even more bewildered; I had known many girls who, when men flirted with them, would pretend to be offended and disgusted, but it was clear that this woman was not pretending. I looked at her, really curious now why people thought she was beautiful and why it made her angry that they did.

But I didn't ask her what I wanted to know. We talked

awkwardly for about half an hour and then got up to go. When we returned to the street, she said we should get together again—tomorrow. Did I want to come to her apartment and listen to records? Another flare lighted her face; it was need, not hate, but it was as strong as the hate had been. I was very uncomfortable now, and felt that she was, too. But her need flared unabated, like a pounding drum that pulls you along to its beat and overrules your own emotions. I said yes, I would drop by her apartment at eight o'clock the next evening.

But I didn't. When I talked to my boyfriend about her, I said she was weird. "Then don't go," he said. "I have to," I replied. "It would be mean not to." But I sat there in the kitchen with my boyfriend, eating cheesecake from a tin and watching his huge black-and-white TV until I sank into a torpor. From there, the German woman's loud drum was hard to hear. I pictured sitting with her on a nice pillow in front of her stereo. Lots of records would be scattered about—she would have a huge selection. She would go through them with her long manicured hands and then put one on and listen to it dully, like she couldn't hear. Just picturing it made me feel heavy and tired. The gray figures running around on the TV screen made me feel heavy and tired, too, but in a comforting way. Eight o'clock came and I thought I'd sit in my heavy comfort just ten minutes more and then go. At 8:30, I pictured her sitting alone, going through her records, need and hate surging under her stiff face. She would still be waiting for me to arrive. By nine o'clock, I realized I wouldn't go. I felt bad—I felt like I was deserting a person who was sick or starving. But I still didn't go.

About six months later, I saw her on the street again. I was dressed better then; I'd streaked my blond hair platinum and wore platform shoes. Maybe that's why the German woman didn't recognize me, or maybe she pretended not to see me, or maybe she didn't see me. She didn't seem to see anything. She was walking alone, her arms wrapped around her torso. Her clothes were ill-kempt and didn't fit her right because she had lost a lot of weight. Her eyes were hollow and she stared fixedly before her, as if she were walking down an empty corridor. I wanted to stop her, but I didn't know what to say.

I had seen loneliness before that and had felt it, too. But I had never seen or felt it so raw. Thirty years later, I still remember it. Only now I am not bewildered. Now I understand that a person can be wild with loneliness. I understand that she wanted so badly to talk to me exactly because she sensed I was the only person in the house who was indifferent to her appearance. But it didn't work because she didn't know how. She had put on the suit of "model" many years before and now she couldn't take it off, and it hurt and confined her.

What's funny about this story is that a year after I met her, I became a model.

"Maybe she recognized that in you. Maybe she wanted to warn you." That's what Veronica said about it. We were sitting at a little table under the striped awning of an outdoor café, having gelato and espresso. It was the first time we'd met outside the office and it felt funny. "But I think you were right not to meet her. She sounds crazy, to be that aggressive with a young person."

A car rolled up and got stopped in traffic in front of us. Music poured from the radio, carrying a voice that was all smooth and elegant, except burps and grunts kept popping out of it, like a baby trying to talk. "She says I am the one," it sang. The music was a dark bubble in which the singer danced and twitched. An arm came out of the backseat and a hand pointed at me; a voice yelled, "You! You!" and the car roared off.

N ow time for the windows. I only do them once a month because it hurts my arm to reach over my head, which means by the time I do clean, I have to press hard, which also hurts my arm. Every now and then, John gets mad at me for not doing the windows every week and we have a fight. He stands there yelling, "What sense does it make to put it off? You're telling me it hurts when you press hard? Spray it and wipe it every week and you're fine!" He's a short guy with a big head on a long rubbery neck that operates like a rotating turret, and words spray from his mouth like bullets. "Do you even think?" he'll yell, and I'll go into my thing of how I have to spare my shoulder, how much it hurts, and he'll yell about why don't I go to the doctor, why don't I get physical therapy, and I'll remind him of how hard it is with my insurance, how I have to get all these forms, and how it never helps anyway. Crying will come into my voice and he'll get this wet, harried look in his eyes, and the turret will work uselessly, not knowing what to shoot at.

You. You. When I knew Veronica, I was healthy and beautiful, and I thought I was so great for being friends with somebody who was ugly and sick. I told stories about her to anybody who would listen. I can just hear my high, clear voice describing her antics, her kooky remarks. I can hear the voices of people congratulating me for being good. For being brave.

I drag the bucket across the room. Rain hits the dirty windows in great strokes. The people outside are blurred and runny: a middle-aged woman trying to pull a teenage girl under an umbrella, the girl pulling back and yelling. A car swishes around the corner, filling a fat wet drop with a second of head-light. The girl breaks away and runs into the rain. I think of the Mexican woman with rain running down her face. I spray the window and rub.

Now I'm ugly and sick. I don't know how long I've had hepatitis—probably about fifteen years. It's only been in the last year that the weakness, the sick stomach, and the fever have kicked up. Sometimes I'm scared, sometimes I feel like I'm being punished for something, sometimes I feel like I'll be okay. Right now, I'm just glad I don't have to deal with a beautiful girl telling me I have to learn to love myself.

I stretch up to the top window and breathe into the pain, like it's a wall I can lean against.

When I say that the songs we listened to at the hostel had a feeling of sickness in them, that doesn't mean I don't like them. I did like them, and I still do. The sick feeling wasn't in all the songs, either. But it was in many songs, and not just the ones for teen-agers; you could go to the supermarket and hear it in the Muzak that roamed the aisles, swallowing everything in its soft mouth. It didn't feel like sickness. It felt like endless opening and expansion, and pleasure that would never end. The songs before that were mostly about pleasure, too—having it, wanting it, or not getting enough of it and being sad. But they were finite little boxes of pleasure, with the simple surfaces of personality and situation.

Then it was like somebody realized you could take the surface of a song, paint a door on it, open it, and walk through.

The door didn't always lead to someplace light and sweet. Sometimes where it led was dark and heavy. That part wasn't new. A song my father especially loved by Jo Stafford was "I'll Be Seeing You." During World War II, it became a lullaby about absence and death for boys who were about to die and kill. *I'll be looking at the moon, but I'll be seeing you.* In the moonlight of this song, the known things, the tender things, "the carousel, the wishing well," appear outlined against the gentle twilight of familiarity and comfort. In the song, that twilight is a gauze veil of music, and Stafford's voice subtly deepens, and gives off a slight shudder as she touches against it. The song does not go any further than this touch because beyond the veil is killing and dying, and the song honors killing and dying. It also honors the little carousel. It knows the wishing well is a passageway to memory and feeling—maybe too much memory and feeling, ghosts and delusion. Jo Stafford's eyes on the album cover say that she knew that. She knew the dark was huge and she had humility before it.

The new songs had no humility. They pushed past the veil and opened a window into the darkness and climbed through it with a knife in their teeth. The songs could be about rape and murder, killing your dad and fucking your mom, and then sailing off on a crystal ship to a thousand girls and thrills, or going for a moonlight drive. They were beautiful songs, full of places and textures—flesh, velvet, concrete, city towers, desert sand, snakes, violence, wet glands, childhood, the pure wings of night insects. Anything you could think of was there, and you could move through it as if it were an endless series of rooms and passages full of visions and adventures. And even if it was about killing and dying—that was just another place to go.

When I still lived at home, I had to share a room with my sisters, Daphne and Sara. Two of us would share a huge bed with a giant headboard, and the third had one-half a bunk bed to herself on the other side of the room. We rotated to be fair. The good thing about the single bed was that it felt more mature, and that the wall above it had special cardboard cutouts our mom had made of huge-eyed dancing teens in short skirts and boots. Plus, you could masturbate privately, without having to carefully lift the blankets off your working arm and stiffen up to keep the mattress from shaking—and still wonder if your sister knew what you were doing. But if you shared the big bed, there was the fun of shutting out the third, giggling and whispering secrets under the blankets while the loner hissed, "Shut up!" Sometimes it felt better not to have to touch legs and butts together. Other times it was good to have your back right against your sister's back, especially if she was asleep and you could feel her presence without her feeling yours.

We also had to take turns sharing the record player. Daphne and Sara didn't like the music I liked—they still liked the old kind recorded on 45s. They'd pretend to be go-go dancers, dancing on the tiny green chairs we'd sat in as little kids to eat peanut butter from teacups. Sometimes when they danced, I'd roll my eyes and hunch up over a book or storm out. But sometimes I'd jump up on a green chair and yell, "I'm Roxanne!" after the most beautiful dancer on *Hullabaloo*. Daphne would yell, "I'm Linda!" and Sara would yell, "I'm Sherry!" even though whenever Sherry came on the TV, my father said, "There's that big fat girl again." Then we'd go wild dancing for as long as the record lasted.

My music was more private, and I didn't play it loudly. I crouched down by it, sucking it into my ears, tunneling into it at the same time. Daphne sprawled on her bed, reading, and Sara maybe played one of her strange games with miniature animals, talking to herself softly in different animal voices. Downstairs, my father watched TV or listened to his music while my mother did housework or drew paper clothes for the cardboard paper dolls she still made for us, even though we no longer played with them. I loved them like you love your hand or your liver, without thinking about it or even being able to see it. But my music made that fleshly love feel dull and dumb, deep, slow, and heavy as stone. Come, said the music, to joy and speed and secret endlessness, where everything tumbles together and attachments are not made of sad flesh.

I didn't know it, but my father was doing the same thing, sitting in his padded rocking chair, listening to opera or to music from World War II. Except he did not want tumbling or endlessness. He wanted more of the attachment I despised—he just didn't want it with us. My father had been too young to enlist when World War II started; his brother joined the army right away. When my dad was finally old enough to enlist in the navy, he sent his brother a picture of himself in his uniform with a Hawaiian girl on his lap; he wrote, "Interrogating the natives!" on the back. A week before the war ended, it was returned to my father with a letter saying his brother was dead. Thirty years later, he was a husband, father, and administrator in a national tax-office chain. But sometimes when I walked past him sitting in his chair, he would look at me as if I were the cat or a piece of furniture, while inside he searched for his brother. And through his brother, his mother and father. And through them, a world of people and feelings that had ended too abruptly and that had nothing to do with where he was now. He wasn't searching for memories; he already had them. He wanted the physical feel of sitting next to his brother or looking into his eyes, and he was searching for it in the voices of strangers that had sung to them both a long time ago. I was so attached to my father that I felt this. But I felt it without knowing what it was, and I didn't care enough to think about it. Who wants to think about their liver or their hand? Who wants to know about a world of people who are dead? I was busy following the music, tumbling through my head and out the door.

. . .

My parents were right: When summer ended, I did not go back home. At seventeen, I lived with twelve other kids (sometimes more slept on the floor) in a three-story purple house that listed to one side. I worked for a florist, selling flowers in the bars and outside go-go clubs in North Beach. The bars were little hump-backed caves with bright liquor bottles and sometimes a glowing red jukebox inside. I went in with my basket, and drunk people would dig around for money. Spirits swam in the cloudy mirror behind the bar, rising up and sinking away. The go-go clubs didn't let me in, but I could hang out in front, talking with the bouncer and warming myself in the heat from the door. Men would say, "Here's the Little Match Girl!" and drop bills in my basket without taking anything. There were huge neon signs above us, a big red one of an apple and a snake and a naked woman with big tits.

When we were done, my friend Lilet and I would meet in a coffee shop to count our money and have pie or fries. Then we'd take a late bus to Golden Gate Park and get high. At night, the park was thick with the smell of flowers and pot, wrapped in darkness and smells, hidden, so you could find it only if you knew the right way in. People sat in clumps or flitted in and out of the trees with night joy in their faces, sporting hot-colored hair dye and wearing zebra prints and pointy-toed boots. Sometimes I'd meet a boy and we'd walk so far up in the hills, we could see the ocean. We'd look up and see the fog race across in the sky, then look down and see trees, houses, knots of electric lights. I'd feel like an animal on a pinnacle, ready to leap. We'd kiss and put our hands down each other's pants.

Or Lilet and I would join a group and go to a crash pad, usually a cheap apartment, but sometimes a house with a lot of people in it. Everybody would be high and there'd be music filling the rooms with heavy, rolling dreams. Some people found a private spot in a dream, curled into it, and slept on the floor. Some people made it a dream of kissing and touching; peering into a dark corner, you could see a white butt humping up and down between open knees. Guys would talk loudly to one another about whatever they were thinking about or things that they did. I remember a guy talking about a girl he'd gotten pregnant. He'd told her to get on the ground and eat dirt first, and she did. "And then I fertilized it!" he said. The guys laughed, and the girls watched with intent, quiet eyes. I went out on the fire escape with Lilet and we sat with our legs dangling down, somebody's lilac bushes between our feet.

I wanted something to happen, but I didn't know what. I didn't have the ambition to be an important person or a star. My ambition was to live like music. I didn't think of it that way, but that's what I wanted; it seemed like that's what everybody wanted. I remember people walking around like they were wrapped in an invisible gauze of songs, one running into the next—songs about sex, pain, injustice, love, triumph, each song bursting with ideal characters that popped out and fell back as the person walked down the street or rode the bus.

I saw Lilet surrounded by music. She was seventeen and, like me, she'd left her family. She was blond, with wide cheekbones and pink skin that shone with the radiant grease of hormonal abundance. She fed the engine inside her with zest, gobbling stuff—big sandwiches and ice cream in paper dishes and French fries and bags of hot cashews from vendors—with both hands while we stood on the corner chatting, our baskets on our hips. She wore tight clothes that showed her stomach sticking out under the cheap cloth. She wore thick high heels and she walked proudly, thrusting out not only her breasts, which most girls did, but her stomach and her jaw, too, like they were also good. She walked like a dog—aggressive, interested, and curious, strutting alongside people with her basket, saying, "Buy a flower for the lady?" We'd meet for breaks in front of a club called the Brown Derby, which had a big derby sign outlined in sputtering gold bulbs, and she'd eat with both hands and talk about men. She was always with older men, not rich guys, but truck drivers and bartenders, drifters. They were almost never handsome, but she seemed to think they were. She was always excited about stuff they gave her, or did with her sexually. I remember a guy who came by for her one night; he was walking a Doberman on a long leash. His face was heavy and caved in, like somebody'd crushed it, but his eyes were shiny and fierce as his dog's. They stood together and laughed, Lilet petting the dog's glossy black head and letting it lick her hand with its dripping pink tongue. When he left, she told me she'd let him butt-fuck her. "Did you get on your elbows and knees?" I asked. "No!" she said. "That's not the only way to do it—you lie on your back and he pushes your legs up." Right away, I pictured it—her head raised a little so she could watch him, and her stomach sticking up in a mound. In my picture, her stomach was radiant in the same way as her greasy pink skin, with gold rays coming off it. I understood pornography then, how men could look at actual pictures like this and feel things. Sexual, but also the way you feel when you hear songs on the radio—the joy in knowing everybody's listening to them and understanding them.

I saw music, too, in the people I got stoned with in the park or saw dancing at parties or bars. I remember this boy and girl I saw dancing at a crash pad once. They didn't touch or act sexy, but they looked at each other the whole time, like they were connected through their eyes. They didn't pay any attention to the rhythm of the music. They danced to its secret personality—clownish and gross, like something big and dumb stuck in a tar pit and trying to walk its way out with brute force. Like being stuck and gross was something great.

In my mind, models and stars didn't have any of this. Though I remember once seeing a picture of one who almost did. She was shot so close-up, you could barely see what she was wearing (crumpled lace); her lipstick was smeared and a boy mussed her hair as he pressed a joint to her open dry lips. Her eyes rolled unevenly in her head, so that one stared blankly at the camera and the other shimmered near the top of her eyelid.

I looked at her for a long moment; then I tore her picture out of the magazine and tacked it up on the wall of my room. I didn't understand why I liked it. Even if the girl really was stoned, it was just a pose. Mostly, these poses were like closed doors I couldn't open, and this one was, too. Except that you could hear muffled sounds coming from behind it, voices, footsteps— music.

You see a lot more pictures like this in magazines now. Fashion has linked itself to music and so it, too, seems to expand forever into room after room. Maybe it does. But it's nothing compared to those people dancing, or even to Lilet wolfing her food on the street corner.

Because we sold flowers outside bars and go-go clubs, prostitutes were some of our best customers; the nice ones bossed their johns into buying from us. Most of them weren't beautiful girls, but they had a special luster, like something you could barely see shining at the bottom of a deep well. They treated us like little sisters, and we were tempted to join them when men came around looking for "models"—which everybody knew meant stripper or whore. Mostly, we would indignantly say no, but sometimes somebody would say yes. I said yes a couple of times. Why I picked those times to say yes, I don't know. One was an old fat man with a spotted face and pale, aggrieved eyes. He ran some kind of business, maybe postcards or comic books. He leaned on a counter in the back room of his store and blinked his pale eyes while I took off my clothes. When I was naked, he looked awhile and then asked if he could look at me from behind. I said okay; he walked around me in a circle and then went back behind the counter again. "You have beautiful hips and legs," he said. "Beautiful shoulders, too. But your breasts are small and they're not that good." He talked to me about the kind of work I might do while I put my clothes back on.

"You mean porn?"

"Sure, we do some porn. There's more money for the girls

that way. But we do seminude art, as well." His eyes became more aggrieved. "Do you care what the other girls do?"

I shrugged. Outside the window, electric music cork-screwed through the air. If he hadn't insulted my boobs, I might've tried it out. But I just said bye and left.

Like a cat in the dark, your whisker touched something the wrong way and you backed out. Except sometimes it was a trap baited with something so enticing, you pushed your face in anyway. Once when I was out with my basket, a short man with a square torso said, "Hey, hot shit—you should come work for me." He bounced a rubber ball on the pavement, caught it, and bounced it again. "I'm a pimp." His face was like lava turned into cold rock. But inside him, it was still running hot; you could smell it: pride, rage, and shame boiling and ready to spill out his cock and scald you. I stared in fear. He just laughed and bounced his ball; he knew that for somebody what he had was the perfect enticement. The street was full of these enticements, always somebody grabbing you or trying to get something, and us, the girls, proud of our refusals, and sometimes proud that we went ahead with it.

Some of the kids I knew didn't have parents, or didn't know them, but most of us did, so barely in the past that it was like they were in the next room. I still felt their breath and the warmth of their bodies, but I so took it for granted, I didn't know what I was feeling. I had walked out through the gauze veil of the song, not into killing and dying, but into colored lights, hunt and escape. But my parents were still there, like the wishing well and carousel, hidden in shimmering spots. "She's going to make her way in the world," said my mother. She stood at the counter, stirring a bright bowl with her brisk arm. She opened a book on her lap, and read a story about a wicked girl who fell down among evil creatures. My father wandered off into his music, but he came back in the cloudy bar-room mirror to watch over me. *I'll be looking at the moon, but I'll be seeing—*

I'm finishing up the windows when John comes in, dripping wet and obviously thinking about everything that's already gone wrong so far today.

"Hey, Allie," he says, and holds up the box of doughnuts he's gotten from the grimy take-out store. I climb down from the ladder, making pain noises and exaggerating how hard it is.

"Hey, John. How's Lonnie?"

"She's okay."

"How's the baby?"

"Cried all night. Lonnie was up and down all night."

His wife, Lonnie, is a sweet, chunky woman with flabby arms. When she holds their baby, he plays with her flab and he loves it.

John takes off his coat with angry jerks and sets down the doughnuts the same way. He moves like he's being yelled at by invisible people whom he hates but whom he basically agrees with. He smooths his hair like somebody just yelled, "And *look* at that *hair!*" Still smoothing, he turns around in a tight circle, sniffing the air, the contents of his whole head suddenly quivering on the end of his nose. Somebody must've just yelled something else. "Alison? Alison, have you been smoking in here?"

"John—"

"You have! Don't bother to lie! Jesus! How many times do I have to tell you? If you want to kill yourself, do it at home! I know there's no audience there, but it smells like a cheap motel in here, and the people who come here don't want to smell that!"

"It smells because I did the windows and tore up my arm."

"I'm not talking about your damn arm, which wouldn't hurt if you'd even try to take care of it. I'm talking about smoking in my office, which I've—"

"John. John?" A whine comes into my voice, like an animal showing its ass. "I always smoke one cigarette, one, because that's what it takes to clean the windows. I'd smoke more, but I don't because—"

"Don't run that number on me!" He is yelling now, but his eyes are sad and hard. "All I'm asking for is basic respect of my place! Respect and honesty and no bullshit manipulation!" Why is it like this? asks his voice. Why is it like this?

"You don't know." I speak quietly, looking down. "You don't know." I'm humiliated. He's angry. That way, we touch together. Tears come into my eyes. I look up; John looks away.

"Just open the window," he says. "I'll make us some coffee."

It really *does* hurt to open the window, but I don't say anything. The bush outside is live and wet, a green lung for the sluicing wind and rain. John's putting out doughnuts and coffee for us. The invisible people are looking away.

A long time ago, John loved me. I never loved him, but I used his friendship, and the using became so comfortable for both of us that we started really being friends. When I lost my looks and had to go on disability, John pitied me and then looked down on me, but that just got fit into the friendship, too. What can't get fit in is that sometimes even now John looks at me and sees a beautiful girl in a ruined face. It's broken, with age and pain coming through the cracks, but it's there, and it pisses him off. It pisses me off, too. When we have these fights and he hears crying and hurt in my voice, it's a different version of that ruined beauty, except it's not something he can see, so he can't think *ruined* or *beauty*. He just feels it, like sex when it's disgusting but you want it anyway. Like his baby plays with the flabby arms, not knowing they're ugly. I can't have a baby and we're not going to fuck, but it's still in my voice—sex and warm arms mixed with hurt and ugliness, so he can't separate them. When that happens, it doesn't matter that I'm not beautiful or even pretty, and he is confused and unhappy.

I always had that, but I didn't know it until now. It's the reason somebody once thought I could be a model, the thing they kept trying to photograph and never did. When I was young, my beauty held it in a case that wouldn't open. Then it broke open. Now that I'm almost fifty, it's there, so much so that even John feels it without knowing what it is. It's disgusting to whore it out in a fight over cigarettes, but that's life.

One night on the street, a small man wearing a red suit bought a yellow rose from me. I remember the color of the rose because I looked down at his feet and saw he had yellow socks on. The rose matched his socks! He said he ran a modeling agency and that I could be a model. He handed me a card with gold lettering on it. I took it, but I kept staring at his eyes; his expression was like somebody giving his hand to an animal so it could sniff, and holding back the other. He said, "Very nice." He put the flower back in my basket and walked away like he was tossing and catching a coin, like the pimp bouncing his ball, except he didn't have anything to bounce. The card said "Carson Models, Gregory Carson."

Carson Models was up a staircase between store windows full of cheap sassy clothes and glaring sun. I noticed a bag of shocking pink fur with a smooth gold clasp, and then ran up the cool stairway. Gregory Carson was waiting for me with a photographer who had a large head and the eyes of a person looking from far away at terrible, beautiful things. He took my hand and looked at me. His name was John. He was the only other person there because it was Saturday; Gregory Carson had wanted me to come on a weekend so that he could give me his full attention.

Gregory Carson said the same thing about my boobs as the fat man, but not right away. First, we drank wine while John set up his camera. Gregory paced, as if he could barely contain his excitement. He talked about how important a model's personality was. He talked about sending me to Paris. When I asked what Paris was like, he cried, "You're going to find out!" and leapt straight up and did a jig, like a chipmunk scrambling in the air. I glanced at John. He looked like a cardboard display of a friendly person. Gregory went into a corner and flicked a switch; music came on. It was a popular song with a hot liquid voice. "Ossifier," it sang. "Love's desire. High and higher."

I didn't know how to pose, but it didn't matter; the music was like a big red flower you could disappear into. The sweetness of it was a complicated burst of little tastes, but under that was a big broad muscle of sound. It was like the deep feeling of dick inside and the tiny sparkling feelings outside on the clit. Except it was also like when you're in love and not thinking the words *dick* or *clit*. Gregory Carson watched ecstatically, a tiny complicated thing looking for a big broad thing to hold him. "Doesn't she remind you of Brandy G.?" he cried. "Do you remember her, John?" John said yes, he did, and Gregory leapt up and scrambled again. I pictured him tiny, scrambling on a giant clit. I giggled, and Gregory said, "That's right! Have fun!"

So I did. It was like the first time I made a sex noise, and instead of being embarrassing, it was great. It was like being with people I didn't know and making them stop so I could go in a store and buy chocolate milk, instead of worrying they would think I was a baby or a pig—and it tasted great. It was like eating pudding forever, or driving in your car forever, or feeling the dick you love forever, right before he sticks it in. Far away, my dad was playing songs for men who thought he was crazy. I was going to be a model and make money walking around inside songs everybody knew.

Then Gregory said he had to see me naked. "We aren't taking any more pictures," he said. "No one ever shoots you nude. I have to look at you because I'm the agent." He went to turn the music off, and suddenly John was in the room. He looked at me so hard, it was like a meaty head zoomed out of his cardboard body. His eyes were different: There was no BS about beautiful and terrible things. He was saying something— what was it? The music shut off. "All righty!" said Gregory. John's head got pulled back into the cardboard. He smiled and said he hoped he'd see me again. Gregory walked him to the door. When he came back, I was naked. The stereo was still making an electrical buzz. The big broad thing had sucked the music back inside it.

Gregory looked at me. "You're five pounds overweight," he said gently. "And your breasts aren't that good." He touched my cheek with the back of his hand. "But right now, that doesn't matter." Ossifier's bright red voice sang in my head: *Don't hesitate 'cause the world seems cold.* "Alison," said Gregory Carson, "I'd like you to tell me about the first grade." He said "first grade" like it was something wonderful to eat, something he hadn't had for a long time. He looked like he might jump up and dance on the clit again. I looked down and felt my face frown. In the first grade, Miss Field was my teacher. She taught me how to write in big black letters. Ossifier stopped singing. Miss Field sat at her desk and folded her hands. A terrible feeling came over me. I felt like she was there, getting sucked into the electrical buzz. I didn't want her to be there. I didn't want her to be eaten.

Gregory reached out and took a tear out of my eye right as it fell. He put it in his mouth. He was tasting the terrible feeling and his eyes were full of pity. He had come to the deep liver place, where I was still a child attached to my family. He recognized it and he respected it, a little. "It's okay," he said. "You don't have to say." He reached down and held me between the legs. Here it was. Ossifier. Miss Field floated in a bright, distant oval. He watched my face as he rubbed me with his hand. He didn't care if he was a pig or a baby. The chocolate milk was delicious. His face came close and his one eye grew giant. Miss Field's bright oval winked shut and she was gone. Gregory Carson's eye said, After you, baby! and then we got sucked into the electrical buzz together.

. . .

One night at work, Veronica asked me how I got into modeling, and I said, "By fucking a nobody catalog agent who grabbed my crotch." I said it with disdain—like I didn't have to be embarrassed or make up something nice, because Veronica was nobody—like why should I care if an ant could see up my dress? Except I didn't notice my disdain; it was habitual by then. She noticed it, though. The arched eyebrows shot up and the lined, prissy face zinged out an expression sharp and hard as a bee sting. This ugly little woman had a sting! I would've stung back, but I was suddenly abashed by her buzzing ugliness. But then her expression became many expressions, and when she talked, her voice was kind.

"Every pretty girl has a story like that, hon," she said. "I had that prettiness, too. I have those stories."

I looked at her and my face must've said, Like what?

"I once had an affair with a man I worked with. It was a dull job doing market research—I had to do *something*. Anyway, it was toward the end of the relationship, not much excitement left, when he remarked that he'd never had anal sex. I said, 'Really? I'll do it with you.' He said, 'Are you sure?' And I said, 'Certainly!' Like I was performing a public service.

"Well, he was ecstatic. He told me later that during an office party he related this event to one of his friends from a visiting organization and that the guy insisted on knowing who I was. He pointed me out—discreetly, he assured me—and, according to him, the guy said, 'Why, she's cute!' Amazed apparently that I didn't look like some desperate slut, but I was quite flattered."

"You *were?*"

"Yes! The only time I was not flattered was a year or so later. It was during the Christmas party, after we had broken up; each department was nominating people for best smile, best legs, best ass, and so forth. I asked him if he'd nominated my ass and he said no. I sulked for the rest of the night."

She drew on her cigarette, blew out. "Of course, you're a lot prettier than I was—you'd have won the contest hands down!" She laughed. "But prettiness is always about pleasing people. When you stop being pretty, you don't have to do that anymore. *I* don't have to do that anymore. It's my show now." She said these words as if she were a movie star walking past me while I gaped.

"I wasn't trying to please anyone," I said uncertainly.

"No?" She stubbed out her cigarette in a bright yellow ashtray. "What were you trying to do?"

Imagine ten pictures of this conversation. In nine of them, she's the fool and I'm the person who has something. But in the tenth, I'm the fool and it's her show now. For just a second, that's the picture I saw.

Fucking Gregory Carson was like falling down the rabbit hole and seeing things flying by without knowing what they meant. Except I *was* the rabbit hole at the same time, and he was stuffing things down it like crazy, just throwing everything in, like he couldn't get rid of it fast enough. And I could take it all. I was on my back and he on his knees; he grabbed my ankles and spread my legs up over my head until my pelvis split all the way open. I pushed myself off the floor with both hands and rose up to face him. His small chest swelled as he reared above me; his stomach stuck out like a proud drum and I could feel his asshole alight and tingling on the end of his spine. His face looked like he was saying, Remember this when they're taking your picture. Remember *this*. Like he was stuffing me full of him so that any picture of me would be a picture of him, too, because people who looked would see him staring out of my eyes.

When it was over, I went down the stairs like I was sliding down a chute and came out the other end of the rabbit hole.

On the street, it was business as usual. There was no secret language of little complicated things. The fog had come in and the store windows had gone dull. It was cold and I was hungry. I found a diner, where I had a piece of blueberry pie with two creamers poured over it, then tea with sugar. Across from me, a meager girl with raw bare legs was crying against a big older woman in a rough coat. Flares kept going off in my body, rushes of strange, blank sensation, like bursts of electricity. Gregory Carson had given me cab fare, but I kept it and took the bus. It soothed me to sit with so many people and to rock with the movement of the bus creaking up hill after hill. The flaring subsided and my body quieted; with listless wonder, I realized that the song had not really said "ossifier." It had said "hearts of fire," which I thought was not as good.

I called Carson Models twice after that, but nobody called me back. Then a woman with an accusing voice called and told me I had a go-see South of Market. I asked if I could talk to Mr. Carson and she said he was busy. Would I go or not? she asked. I went and sat on a long stairway with a line of other girls. We rolled up the stairs on our bottoms like a caterpillar moving along in sections, each section a girl stuck to another girl. The one in front of me rocked back and forth, whispering, "Shit! Fuck! Shit! Fuck!" The one behind me held her pretty chin in her hand and read a paperback that had a screaming woman raised off the cover in bright colors. At the top of the stairs was a large room with two men in it. They wore beautiful clothes and they whirred like little machines that somebody wound up every day.

"Where's your book?" asked one.

"Book?" Confusedly, I glanced at the girl with the paperback.

The whirring stopped. A human head popped out a little shuttered hole in his mechanical head and glared at me in disgust.

"She's one of Gregory's," whispered the other.

"Oh." He mildly rolled his eyes and withdrew back into the mechanical head. The whirring continued. "Walk a little; then turn to face me," he said.

I walked a foot and he said, "Thank you. Next!"

The next week when a roommate yelled up the stairs that "somebody model agency" was on the phone, I said, "Tell them to fuck off!" and he did, loudly.

Weeks passed; it got cold and the park emptied. The smell of flowers was gone and by itself the pot was a thin and ragged wrap. Even in the dark, you noticed garbage. You saw shadows running out of the corner of your eye. Gangs of bikers came, huge men with a feeling of piled-up corpses inside them. One of them had a puppy with a dirty rope around its neck. Its eyes were full of misery, and when I petted it, it felt dead inside. It was like it had been killed while it was still alive. The guy holding the rope smiled maliciously. Very slowly, I turned and walked out of the park.

It got too cold to sell flowers outside. Lilet went to Las Vegas with a guy who had bought her an orange fake-fur coat. I got a dress at the Salvation Army and interviewed to be a file clerk. I still sold flowers, but instead of going to the park after, I went to my room and wrote poems. I was going to go home, go to community college and learn to be a poet. I fantasized about becoming famous, but I couldn't picture what famous poets did. I could only imagine walking around while people photographed me. I could imagine Gregory Carson's tiny hands clutching the glowing rim of my world, and his tiny, longing head peering over it. I imagined that over and over when I lay in bed at night.

I was going to call my family and tell them I was coming home, but before I could, Daphne called and said our mother had just moved out and gone to live with a guy from the car repair place. "Daddy feels like everyone's leaving him," she said. "He cries at night, Alison. It's horrible." I asked her to put him on. I felt like a hero, telling him I was coming home to go to school. He asked when. I said in a few weeks—when I had the airfare. He said he'd send me the money, and I felt proud refusing it. I didn't wonder how he felt offering it. He was quiet and then he said, "Just get here as quick as you can. I love you a whole lot." When Daphne came back on the phone, I asked her if he'd really cried.

"Just once that I heard," she said. "But I think it's been more."

She waited for me to say something, but I didn't know what to say.

"I think maybe if you come back, Mother will, too," said Daphne.

I still didn't say anything. I was remembering something that happened when I was ten. I was walking with my parents in an underground parking lot and my mother tripped and fell on her face. She went straight down on the concrete, then lay there with her mouth wide open, arms bent and palms flat, like she wanted to push herself up but couldn't. She lifted her head and made a long, low moan, like a cow. Her body had protected her face, but her breath had been knocked from her. I didn't know what to do. I turned to my dad, who was just behind us. He was smiling, like it was really funny to see my mom fall on her face and make a stupid noise. When he came close, he hid the smile; it amazed me how fast he hid it. "Lord," he said. "Are you all right?" He helped her up, and it turned out she was okay. But I still hated him for smiling. I remembered it now, and I tried to work up anger at him again. But all I could think about was him alone, crying.

I didn't get the file clerk job, so I sold flowers outside the stripper bars until late, when men would come out drunk and give me bills. At the end of the night, I'd go home to count it out on my bed and then I'd store it in a pair of folded socks in the back of the drawer. I'd sit on my bed in a T-shirt and underwear, writing poems while voices went past my window on clomping feet. I'd sleep at dawn to the sound of garbage trucks and wake to music from the weird-ass guy in the basement, the sound coming up through the heat vent like a haint.

I had enough to buy my ticket when I saw John in the park. I didn't recognize him until he walked up to me and started telling me he was sorry. He said, "We were in the same position that day, you and I." That's when I first noticed his neck, tense and rubbery, already angry and ready to torque around. "Gregory plays that game with girls all the time, and I go along because he gives me work. But I hate it, and after that day with you, I walked out and said, 'Fuck it. I'm not doing this again.'" I tried to act like I'd known what was going on, that nobody had fooled me. And he let me act that way—his eyes did not say, Come on, girl, you know you got took!—maybe because he was kind, maybe because he didn't notice I was acting. "But with you, he was also stupid," he continued. "Because you really could do it. I saw it right away." He wanted to send my pictures to a magazine modeling contest, and he needed me to fill out a contest form. He needed my address so he could let me know what happened.

Imagine ten pictures of me at Carson Models. In nine of them, I'm a real stupid girl, but in the tenth, I'm somebody who could be a model. John was looking at the tenth one, and because he was, I did, too. I said okay and gave him my parents' address in New Jersey. The next day, I got on the plane and flew home.

It's weird for me, too, looking at John and seeing a young guy turned into a twitchy middle-aged man being chased around his own office by invisible people; it's like an emotional funny bone. The terrible, beautiful things zoomed up close, flattened us, and sped off. Well, they flattened me. Him they just sped past. Which was lucky for him. Now he actually has something good, when he can stop twitching long enough to enjoy it. He has a house with a family and he has an office, a nest of past and present, where a remnant of everything he thought he wanted comes and cleans his toilet for him. He can yell at it and be yelled at by it and the invisible people go quiet and fade away. Then there's doughnuts with colored icing—pink, lavender, white with little hairs of coconut—and talk about the new baby he's had at fifty-two with a woman fifteen years younger.

"He just grooves on everything, Alison, and when he looks at me I do, too. To bring home food to them, to be the provider—I can't tell you how it makes me feel."

He doesn't have to tell me. I can see it in his face: Happiness shines on his dullard sadness and makes it scratch its head and blink with wonder.

"But sometimes I feel shut out, you know? Lonnie and Eddie are so bonded, so physical, it's like I'm a total third wheel, like this . . . utility unit. And I wonder, What about my dreams? You know?"

"John, when I was eight, I dreamed about being a ballerina. It was a good dream for an eight-year-old."

"What about now? What are your dreams?" A sly, sad look comes out of his eye like a tiny eye on a stalk, and he's behind the camera again.

"My dream is being able to sleep and to stop my arm from hurting." To stop traveling through the endless rooms that don't have music or people in them anymore. "But John, you've got your dream; you're living it. I can see it in your face!"

And he can see it, too, now that I say it. It's something I can give him, something I hold out in warm arms. He talks about Lonnie and the baby again, how sometimes he's scared he won't make enough money for them, how he doesn't want them to see he's scared. Except he doesn't come right out with that last part. I have to say it; he denies it, then says, "Maybe," and looks off to the side, chewing.

"I just want our house to be a house of love," he says.

"It will be," I say. As long as you quit going mental about shit like one cigarette! I don't say. We sit there together like satisfied animals, full of doughnuts. Maybe he hears what I don't say and maybe he even listens; he pays me my hundred bucks for the month without checking to see what kind of job I did on the toilet. I say bye and walk out into the rain.

The air smells of gasoline, dirt, and trees; cars farting out of hot iron stomachs; and the fresh BO of nature. Down the street, there's still a picket line out in front of the Nissan dealership, people standing in mud-colored rain slickers, their faces looking like crude sketches under their dripping hoods: brows, nose, lips, jowls. Clear plastic bags are tied over their signs, which read DON'T BUY FROM NISSAN. DON'T BUY FROM SCABS. Most of them trudge in a circle, like they are trudging through a ritual they no longer remember the meaning of but which they dimly believe is their only hope. Two others stand outside the circle, their plastic hoods thrown back, talking and laughing furious, face-crushing laughter as the rain pours down on their heads. They've been there a month. I try to catch somebody's eye to wish them luck, like I usually do. But nobody looks up in the rain.

The endless beautiful rooms inside the songs—wander through them long enough and their beauty and endlessness become horrible. There is so much, you always want more, so you keep moving, traveling ever more quickly, until you can't stop. Ten years ago, I used to see these kids running around in white makeup, sleeping in phony coffins, and paying dentists to give them vampire fangs. It was stupid, but it made sense, too. You want the endlessness to end; you want to go home, but there is no home. You despise the tender attachments of the liver and the body, but you also crave them; you bite other people in an attempt to find them, and when that doesn't work, you bite yourself.

Veronica and I went once to see an exhibit of photographs by Robert Mapplethorpe. She wore a bright red leather jacket with buckled pockets, and she promenaded through the gallery in it, making loud approving comments on the work. She was talking so loudly, she didn't notice the two giggling boys who followed us for a good half minute, mocking her officious gestures. We lost them in front of the famous self-portrait, in which Mapplethorpe crouches naked, his back to the camera, a bullwhip coming out of his ass like a tail, his face turned round with a triumphant leer. A woman standing behind us said in a voice of thrilled dismay, "I didn't need to see that!" and Veronica turned on her like the Red Queen. "Then why did you come?" she snapped. "*I* certainly didn't need to see *or* to hear you." The woman nearly stumbled trying to hide behind her husband, who was trying to hide behind her.

But when we walked out of the museum, Veronica began to cry incoherently. "Everything we did is being erased," she said. "They're denying it all. They're taking it all away." I was embarrassed; I didn't understand. Now I understand.

So one minute I'm standing outside a strip bar with my basket, flickering in the marquee light, on and off, like a ghost trying to be real. Women's naked asses, men's naked faces. The bouncer hugs himself against the cold and says he'll buy me some hot cashews. Then I'm in an airplane hurtling through gray clouds. The plane rattles like it will break, and the woman in the next seat moans with fear. Then I'm in the living room with my father. It's like I crashed out of the clouds. Sara is upstairs, yelling at someone on the phone, and Daphne is in the kitchen, making dinner. We crash into one another; everything rattles and shakes like the airplane, only more, and we can't hear one another even though we're shouting.

When they picked me up in Newark, my father's eyes were inward and methodical. He did not show the love he'd talked about on the phone. I didn't, either. All the emotion was in Daphne's eyes, big and shimmering, with so much hope in them, I wanted to punch her. Sara looked at me and then looked away quickly. She was getting fat. She was disappearing in plain sight. Her look made sure I was okay, then went back to concentrating on whatever she was hiding. When she turned in profile, I saw her nose had been broken. "How'd that happen?" I whispered to Daphne. "I don't know. I don't know when it happened. I just noticed it one day, and she yelled, 'I don't wanna talk about it!'" Daphne made Sara's voice like a monster's, like a stupid, crazy monster.

We drove home through a whooshing tunnel of traffic. It was dark, with bright signs and lights flying by. Daphne sat up front and talked light and fast, turning her head to scatter her words in the backseat and out the window, into the whooshing tunnel. Quarters, halves, whole squares of light flew through the back window and ran over her soft hair. Even when she talked to me and Sara, I felt a strand of her attention stay on our dad, like she was holding his hand. Sara sat deep inside herself, her hands together in her lap, holding the secret of her broken nose. Her calm animal warmth filled the backseat.

When we got home, my mother called. She said she was so happy to know I was there. Her voice ran and jumped, as if it were being chased by a devil with a pitchfork. "When are you going to enroll?" she cried. "I have to take the GED first," I said. "I have to study." "Well, I just think you're great," she said. She sounded like she was about to cry. My father stood in the next room, ramrod-straight and straining to hear.

Daphne made a special dinner of kielbasa sausage and

baked beans, which I used to love but which now seemed so sad, I didn't want it. But I ate it, and when my father asked, "Do you like it?" I said, "It's good." Sara picked out the sausage, glaring at it like she was really pissed. She ate the beans and went upstairs. "She's a vegetarian now," said Daphne. "Probably stuffing herself with candy," said my dad. Van Cliburn played Tchaikovsky in the next room; in the dining room, the TV was on mute. The months in San Francisco were folded up into a bright tiny box and put down somewhere amid the notices and piles of coupons. I was blended into the electrical comfort of home, where our emotions ran together and were carried by music and TV images. Except for Sara's—she couldn't join the current. I don't know why, but she couldn't.

The next day, Daphne and I drove to meet our mom at a coffee shop in White Plains. We got there first and waited for her. It was a family place with tiny jukeboxes on the tables. Daphne turned the knob on our box, dully flipping through the selections—"You Are Everything," "I Had Too Much to Dream," "Incense and Peppermint," "Close to You"—each a bit of black print inside a red rectangle. The people behind us picked one: "Can't Take My Eyes Off You." The singer's voice was light and gloppy at the same time, like a commercial for pudding. It had been popular when we were in elementary school, and the old recording gave off a dark, enchanted crackle. It made me think of teenage girls in bathing suits, lying in lawn chairs beside the public pool, eyes closed, breasts perfectly and synthetically cupped. Each blue wave sparkled with light. Boys shook water from their hair and looked at them. Daphne ran past, joyfully waving an inflated toy.

A car pulled up to the curb. We glimpsed our mother's boyfriend as he dropped her off—a dark mass of lust and need who kissed her in the car and drove away. *Don't bring me down, I pray.* My mother came in wearing a pantsuit that was too short for her high heels. Her eyes looked like her leaping voice, and

she walked like she was trying to go three ways at once. Here
was the jealous, furious one: She was wearing big earrings and
lipstick, and when she hugged us, sex came off her like a smell.
Her jacket flapped open, showed hide with bristles on it, then
flapped back: Here was the one who lay where she fell, moaning like a cow.

But then she sat down and crisply opened the plastic
menu, and here was the true one: Mom, boss of food and treats.
Our minds went blank and our bodies remembered when we
were little: She was the one who bought us our first milk shakes.
She carried them out to the car, holding all four huge shakes
squeezed together in her hands. The four of us sat drinking the
shakes in deep silence, until we had to get the last bit up from
the bottom; then we all slurped together. The warm, close air of
the car on our skin, cold sweetness in the mouth: It was a wonderful reversal of warm breast milk and cool air, and this was a
breast we could all experience together. Just seeing her open the
menu brought that feeling back without us knowing it. *You're just
too good to be true.* A slim white arm stirred the gold pudding. We
went into a trance, staring at the things on the menu.

But then there were the three directions and the bristling
hide. As soon as we got our food, she started talking about how
hard she knew it was. How hard it had been for *her* not knowing
whether I was alive or dead for weeks on end and getting no
support from our father. She ate her rhubarb pie. She had tried
her best to understand that things were different now, and she
hoped we would, too.

"Do you want a divorce or not?" asked Daphne.

Inside our mother's eyes, an expression opened like a
mouth and then snapped shut while her normal mouth prissily
ate the pie. "It takes time to know something like that," she said.
"A relationship of so many years is complicated." She ate with
her prissy mouth. The bristling hide swelled out.

"It's not fair," said Daphne.

She sat up. Under the earrings and lipstick, she was a plain woman, and she knew the dignity of plainness. "Do you judge me?" she asked quietly.

Yes, said Daphne's face. I judge you and I hate you.

In my mind, I looked over my shoulder and pouted at a camera while the song played. *Can't take my eyes off you.* Invisible eyes on me were like an endless ribbon of sweet music. I don't know what my face said.

"No," said Daphne. "But I want to know if this is permanent, and so does Daddy."

"So do I," said our mother. "So do I." And she looked sad. Her entire body looked sad. Daphne could do nothing against this except be sad herself.

The waitress came by with a sound of rasping and rubbing underclothes. She left the check on the table and disappeared through a swinging door. I glimpsed a bustling kitchen of steel tables and orderly movement, sandwiches and dishes laid out. A sharp-eyed little man in an apron suspiciously returned my look. What would it be like to work there?

Our mother opened her frayed wallet and wondered aloud how I'd make a living while I was writing poems.

"I could work in a restaurant. Or maybe I could be a model."

"Right." She sighed, got her wallet out and counted the bills carefully, figuring the tip on her fingers. "That sounds like a beautiful life."

Inside Daphne, I felt something tremble like it would break, then hold steady.

Then came routine. My father drove Daphne and Sara to school on his way to work. I slept until noon, then got up and drank tea for hours. It was late November and light moved from room to room with the active silence of a live thing. The cat lifted her head and blinked the deep black slits, the active green of her eyes. I paced from light to shadow, feeling my way back into the fleshy place I'd torn myself from. When I got there, I'd sit in the dining room and study for the GED with the TV on the rerun channel, volume off. I used to watch these shows with my family. The black-and-white people were so full of memory and feeling that they were like pieces of ourselves, stopped in a moment and repeating it again and again, until it became an electronic shadow of the fleshy place. Sunlight ran over the table and onto the floor. I've touched you all day, it said, and now I have to go.

Sara would cut school and come home early, then leave. I'd see her outside, kissing some boy who'd slap her ass when he said good-bye. Or whispering to another chunky girl with saucy goblin eyes, who offered her tits to the world in a sequined T-shirt. In the street, boys rode their bikes in slow swooping curves and called to one another. I'd strain to hear them; I was afraid they were jeering at Sara. But she'd come in like a cat, with an air of adventure about her, inwardly hoarding it. She'd get some food and sit in the room with me, watching TV with one big leg slung over the arm of her chair. She didn't ask questions about anything that had happened while I was away. She looked at me like she already knew and that it was okay. It felt good to be with her.

Once I asked my dad about her nose, and he said, "It's *broken?* Are you sure?" He seemed shocked, and then he said, "Are you sure it hasn't always been that way?" Maybe he felt like everything was broken and he didn't have time for one more thing. Maybe that's why Sara was so mad at him. When he would ask her to help Daphne make dinner or clean up, she'd yell, "In a minute!" and then she wouldn't do it. Or she'd yell, "We're not your wives, and it's not our fault if you don't have one!" Then she'd run upstairs, sobbing with rage, and our dad would stand there like she'd gut-punched him.

Daphne and I hated Sara for acting like this. But it was

hard to hate her all the way. Her rage was like gentleness trapped and driven crazy with sticks. It was flailing and helpless. It made Daphne's measured goodness seem somehow mean. Maybe our father felt this, too. He never chased Sara up the stairs to shout back at her. He just stood there in pain. Then later at night, I would walk by his room. He would be lying in his pajamas and Sara would be sitting on a chair at the foot of his bed, rubbing his feet. Even just walking past, I could feel her concentration; it was huge and fleshy, like her yelling. And his feeling for it was huge, too. Once I heard him say, "You have good hands, Sara. You should be a nurse." And she said, "Thank you," her voice small, like a child's.

I didn't tell them about the modeling contest. I only mentioned it to Daphne while we were driving to the store. She half-listened, because she was mainly concentrating on smoking her cigarette and dropping ash out the window. I lied and said the photographer was a guy I got high with, and it just flew by her as one more piece of sad crap.

I still thought about modeling, but it was like something I'd masturbate over without expecting it to happen: A door opened and I was drowned in images of myself, images strong and crude as sexual ones. They carried me away like a river of electricity. Electricity is complicated, but on direct contact, it doesn't feel that way. It just knocks you out and fries you. The door would shut and it would be gone, except for a fading rim of electric fire, an afterimage burning a hole in normal life.

But mostly, I studied, watched TV, helped with dinner, wrote, went for walks with Daphne, saw friends who were still in school. On the weekends, there were beer parties in apartments with older kids. My friend Lucia was beautiful, even though she had bad skin and bleached hair. She was three months pregnant. When she graduated, she was going to get married and work the cash register at a store where we used to steal candy. I didn't have disdain then, and so when I told her about the contest, I lied to impress her. I said I'd slapped Gregory Carson's face, and that John had followed me out, begging me to enter the contest. We were sitting on a concrete stoop outside an apartment complex, drinking beers and watching cars drive in and out of a strip mall across the way. She smiled without looking at me, and I knew she could tell I'd lied, and that she forgave me. Music and laughter tumbled from the apartment in a snarl. Headlights flew past Lucia's face and she gazed into nothing with a contentment that I didn't understand. *I saw it and I fertilized it.* For a second, I pictured her eating dirt. Then I went home and half-listened to my father talk about what had gone wrong with the marriage and what might be done to "bring it back together."

I took the GED in an old elementary school classroom in Hoboken. The desks were gray linoleum; the chairs were wood. The facilitator was a big, proud man with a bulbous, veiny nose, and he held his cheap jacket open to show his stomach. The other test takers were mostly middle-aged people with bodies curled like snails crossing a road. The only other young person was a girl wearing a skirt that showed the tops of her panty hose. She glanced at me with sullen camaraderie. Then we hunched over our tests. The facilitator watched us cross the road.

When my test scores came back, my father called my mother to tell her how well I'd done. She made her boyfriend drive her over and wait outside in the car while she kissed me. My dad yelled about "that bastard sitting out there where everybody could see," and Sara ran upstairs and slammed the door. My mother went out and told him to drive around the block. We all sat down and planned a budget for classes. I ordered course descriptions. I made ready to register. Then the letter from the agency crashed into the side of the house.

It has stopped raining. My sneakers are soaked, so I go ahead and walk through the puddles. Silver and black, full of sky and the solemn upside-down world. The bus shelter glides under my feet like a huge transparent fish. On the side of it is a model in a black sleeveless dress. An ad for perfume: WATCH OUT, MONSIEUR. She has a neat, exquisite face, deep, dim eyes, and a sensitive, swollen mouth. Her slight body is potent and live, like an eel. I like her. I am on her side to destroy monsieur. She makes me remember Alana, another small eel girl.

I walk through black shadows, across the inverted sky. I met Alana at a benefit show put on to support and celebrate the renovation of an ancient Parisian department store, the first of its kind in that country. I walked into the tiny dressing room and saw her standing naked in heels, picking through gorgeous gowns and yelling how her agent had made her get an enema that afternoon so she wouldn't look bloated. "Now Matmoiselle, ve vill unlock ze bowel!" She was cracking everybody up, talking about the crazy German who'd hosed her out. "Everybody" consisted of the seven models, four makeup artists, and fifteen hairdressers packed into a hot, narrow room that was all mirrors and countertop. Getting their faces made up, talking about enemas and shit: passing out in a nightclub and waking up in ruined panties; diarrhea attack during shoot; farting in boyfriend's face. The girls giggled hysterically; the hairdressers were getting in on it. They'd probably been up all night and didn't feel like doing this obscure show. I hesitated at the door; Alana saw me and pounced. "You look like you *need* an enema," she snapped. I blushed. The other girls tittered and quieted. Alana flounced into her chair and grabbed a handful of dark red cherries from a plastic bowl next to a mountain of hot hair-pieces. Slouching and chewing, she looked absently at her reflection: precise round forehead, nose, and chin. Hot eyes, dark, violent bloom of a mouth. White pearls in her clean little ears. If they wanted to find something wrong, they'd have to look up her ass. They went up there to serve perfection, and she mocked perfection with the shit that came out.

But—*Watch out, monsieur*. On the runway, she was a bolt of lightning in a white Chanel dress. She turned and gave a look. Thumping music took you into the lower body, where the valves and pistons were working. You caught a dark whiff of shit, the sweetness of cherries, and the laughter of girls. Like lightning, the contrast cut down the center of the earth: We all eat and shit, screw and die. But here is Beauty in a white dress. Here is the pumping music, grinding her into meat and dirt. Here are the other girls coming in waves to refill Beauty's slot. And here is little Alana, shrugging and turning away. Everyone applauded—and no wonder.

I walk past old homeless people huddled together under the dripping awning of a record store—three of them, like bags of potatoes with potato faces looking out of the bag to see what's going on. They look like they know me. Maybe they do. Alana disappeared almost as fast as I did. If I saw her sitting on the street like this, it wouldn't surprise me.

"You take the food out of my mouth and I'll kill you!"

Veronica had screamed that at a homeless guy once. We were walking down the street together and she was talking to me about how she had to hide her HIV from her coworkers. She was eating a bagel and this beggar made as if to grab it from her hand. The rage came up in her like fire; she turned with a scream and hit him in the face. He bolted and she whipped around to me. "They're trying to take the food from my mouth. Just let them try. Anyway, hon—" Her eyes were still wild with screaming, but she didn't miss a beat. For her, it was part of the same conversation.

She was like Alana that way: elegance and ugliness together. She'd take a sip of tea, properly dab her lips, and call her boyfriend a "cunt."

I stop to give change to one of the women huddled on the sidewalk. She looks up at me and it's like seeing through time. A young girl, a woman, a hag, look at me through a tunnel of layered sight; three pairs of eyes come together as one. We let our hands touch. She's given me something—what is it? I walk past; it's gone.

Veronica's boyfriend was a bisexual named Duncan. She'd go to a party with him and he'd leave with a drunk girl on his arm, looking like he was taking her out to shoot her. He'd come to dinner with a lovely boy who had bad table manners and a giant canker on his mouth. He'd go to a cruising ground in Central Park called the Ramble, where he'd drop his pants, bend over, and wait. "See what I mean?" she said. "A real cunt."

"Why do you stay?" I asked.

She tipped her head back and released a petulant stream of smoke. She righted her head and paused. "Have you ever seen *Camille*?" she asked. "With Greta Garbo and Robert Taylor?"

Camille is about a beautiful prostitute who dies of tuberculosis—a despised woman who is revealed to be better than anyone else, including the aristocrat who loves her but can't admit it. Veronica and Duncan purchased a VCR as soon as one was invented, so that they could watch a tape of it constantly. They watched it on the couch, lying in each other's arms under a blanket. They watched it eating dishes of expensive ice cream or chocolates in a gold box. They could speak the lines with the actors. Sometimes they did it for fun. Sometimes they did it while they cried. "At the end, we cry together," she said. "It's gotten so I cry as soon as the credits roll." She shrugged. "Who else could I do that with? Only a cunt would understand."

My mother was going for elegance and ugliness when she dressed her adultery in earrings, fancy pantsuits, and heels. But she couldn't do it right. It was at odds with the style of her time. Her generation distrusted the sentimental thrill of putting beauty next to shit. They didn't want to be split down the center—they figured they'd see what was there sooner or later anyway. They understood the appeal—of course they understood it! They'd made *Camille*. But you were supposed to know that was a movie.

My parents went with me to the agency in Manhattan. They were not going to put me on a plane to a foreign country just because I'd won some contest. They were going to ask questions and get the truth. They put on their good clothes and the three of us took Amtrak into the city to a building of gold and glass. In the elevator, we stared silently at the numbers above the automatic door as they lighted up and dimmed in a quick sideways motion. For the first time in years, I could feel my parents subtly unite.

The agency person was a woman with a pulled-back, noisy face. Her suit looked like an artistic vase she'd been placed in up to her neck. When she smiled at me, it was like a buzzer going off. I could tell right away that my parents didn't know what to do.

"Can you assure me that our daughter will be taken care of?" asked my mother.

"Absolutely!" said Mrs. Agency. She spoke of roommates, vigilant concierges who monitored the doors, benevolent chaperones, former models themselves.

"Aren't there a lot of homosexuals in the fashion industry?" asked my father.

Mrs. Agency emitted a joyless laugh. "Yes, there are. That's another reason your daughter will be as safe as a kitten."

My father frowned. I felt forces vying in the room. He sighed and sat back. "I just wish you didn't have to interrupt your school," he said. And then I was on another plane, humping through a gray tunnel of bumps. I stared into the sky and remembered Daphne at the airport, closing her face to me. She hugged me, but there was no feeling in it, and when she pulled away, I saw her closed face. Sara didn't hug me, but when she turned to walk away, she looked back at me, the sparkle of love in her eye like a kiss. Droning, we rose above the clouds and into the brilliant blue.

When the plane landed, it was morning. Invisible speakers filled the airport with huge voices I couldn't understand. I walked with a great mass of people through a cloud of voices, aiming for the baggage claim. I was distracted by a man in a suit coming toward me with a bouquet of roses and a white bag that looked like a miniature pillowcase half-full of sugar. His body was slim and his head was big. Deep furrows in his lower face pulled his small lips into a fleshy beak. His lips made me think of a spider drinking blood with pure blank bliss. Suddenly, he saw me. He stopped, and his beak burst into a beautiful broad smile that transformed him from a spider into a gentleman. "I am René," he said. "You are for Celesté Agency, no?" Yes, I was. He took one of my bags and handed me his roses. He took my other bag, put it on the floor, and kissed my hand. In a flash, I understood: Seeing me had made him a gentleman and he loved me for it. I liked him, too. "It is Andrea, yes?" "No," I said. "Alison."

His car was sleek and white and had doors that opened

upward, like wings on a flying horse. We got inside it. He opened the bag (which was silk) and scooped the cocaine out of it with his car key. He placed the key under one winged nostril and briskly inhaled. I thought of the time my father was insulted by a car salesman who said, "All you want is something to get around in!" For a week after, my father walked around saying, "What do you do with it, you son of a bitch? Screw with it?" We passed the key back and forth for some moments. Finally, he licked it and put it in the ignition. He said, "Alison, you are a beautiful girl. And now you are in a country that understands beauty. Enjoy it." He started the car. The drug hit my heart. Its hard pounding spread through my body in long dark ripples and for a second I was afraid. Then I stepped inside the electrical current and let it knock me out. We pulled out of the lot and into the Parisian traffic.

I had read about Paris in school. It was a place where ladies wore jewels and branches of flowers, even live birds in tiny cages woven into their huge wigs. The whipping boy sometimes played chess with the prince. The Marquis de Sade painted asylum inmates with liquid gold and made them recite poetry until they died. Charlotte Corday stabbed Marat butt-naked in the tub. I looked at the car speeding next to us; a plain girl with glasses on the end of her nose frowned and hunched forward. She cut us off and René muttered a soft curse. American pop music came out of her car in a blur. *Ossifier. Love's desire.* Huge office complexes sat silent in fields brimming with bright green desire. The queen knelt before a guillotine. Blood shot from her neck in a hot stream. The next day, her blood stained the street and people walked on it; now her head was gone, and she could be part of life. René asked what I wanted to do. I told him I wanted to write poetry. Cancan girls laughed and kicked. In paintings, their eyes are squiggles of pleasure, their mouths loose-shaped holes. On the street, people waiting for the light to change frowned and glanced at their watches.

René waited for me in the car while I went into the agency. It was a medium-sized building with a shiny door on a cobbled street. The doorman had mad blue eyes and beautiful white gloves. The halls were carpeted in aqua. Voices and laughter came from behind a door. It opened and there was a woman with one kind eye and one cruel eye. Behind her was a man looking at me from inside an office. His look held me like a powerful hand. A girl's small white face peeped around the corner of the same office. The hand let go of me. The girl blinked and withdrew. "Where is your luggage?" asked the double-eyed woman. "With René, outside," I replied. *"René?"* She rolled her eyes back in her head. When they came forward again, they were both cruel. "Very well. Here." She handed me a piece of paper. "This is a list of go-sees for tomorrow and Wednesday. I suggest you use a *taxi* to get to them. Now tell René that Madame Sokolov says he must take you straight to rue de l'Estrapade."

"Ah," said René. "Madame Sokolov is not always aware." He tapped his head with two fingers and drove us to a dark door squeezed between a tobacco shop and a shoe store. The concierge was an old woman with a brace on her leg. She led me slowly up the dingy stairs, with René following, bags in hand. We moved slowly to respect the brace. Each short flight of steps came to a small landing with ticking light switches that shut off too soon. *"Merde,"* muttered the old lady. The light had turned off while she was looking for the key to my room. In the dark, I felt René's hot breath on my ear. "Take a nap this afternoon, eh? I'll be by at eight." He bit me on the ear. I started and he disappeared down the stairs. The old lady pushed open the door; there was a weak burst of light and television noise and a high, cunty voice: "But don't you see, I want you here *now*. Two days from now will be too late!" My roommate, in bra and underpants, sat cross-legged on the sagging couch, the phone to her sulky face. She acknowledged me with a look, then rose and walked into a back room, trailing the phone cord. She carried her slim butt like a raised tail and her shoulders like pointy ears. When the old lady left, I sat on the couch and picked at a bowl of potato chips on the side table. Out a window, enamel rooftops with slim metal chimneys were bright against the white sky; a shadow weather vane twirled on a shadow roof. I watched it until my roommate got off the phone and I could call my family.

When René came, I told him I wanted to go someplace that had pie. He laughed and said, "You will have French pie!" We went to a patisserie with cakes that looked like jewelry boxes made of cream. I ate them, but I didn't like them. They had too many tastes, and I wanted the plain chemical taste of grocery store pie. But the tables were made of polished wood and the people sitting at them were drinking coffee from tiny white cups. A woman next to us took a cigarette out of a case and lit it with a silver lighter. And because René asked him to, the waiter sang to me. The song was about little boys peeing on butterflies. *Papillon, pee, pee, pee. Papillon, non, non, non.* The waiter bent down to the table and sang softly. His pocked face hung in bristly jowls and I saw he was missing teeth. But his voice opened the song like a picture book with feelings and smells in it. Blue flowers bobbed on the wind and butterflies dodged the piss of laughing boys. Mothers called; the boys buttoned their flies and ran home. I had awakened in New Jersey with my parents and I was going to sleep tonight with my French lover.

And so we lay naked on his rumpled bed. I was dimly aware that my body was exhausted and bewildered, but that didn't matter. I was in an upper chamber, far above those feelings, eating sugar with both hands. The silky sheets were scattered with white powder, mixed with granules and little hairs that were pleasant to feel. A brown moth flapped around a rose-colored lamp shade. Cold air from an open window stirred the papers on the night table. René held me in his hairy arms and sang the pee-pee song. He said, "You fuck humpty-hump, like a little witch riding her broom!" I smiled and he stroked my hair. "That's right, is good. I love my little witch! Riding humpty hump in the night!" Then he jumped up and said he wanted to go to a nightclub. But I had go-sees the next day! He laughed and said, "Don't think like a shop girl! Think like a poet!"

The nightclub was dark and had hot laser lights speeding through it. The music was like something bursting and breaking. People's faces looked like masks with snouts and beaks. But I knew they were beautiful. If the German ex-model I'd met in San Francisco had walked in, I'd have known she was beautiful, too. But I didn't remember her. My eyes and ears were so glutted I had no room for memory. I didn't sleep, but René was right: It didn't show on my face. I got a job for an Italian magazine and left for Rome the day after. Little witch riding humpty-hump in the night.

Riding still, out of the roaring night into a pallid day of sidewalks and beggars with the past rising through their eyes. Shadows of night sound solemnly glimmer in rain puddles; inverted worlds of rippling silver glide past with lumps of mud and green weeds poking through. The past coming through the present; it happens. On my deathbed, I might turn toward my night table and see René's rose-colored lamp shade with the brown moth flapping inside it. My sisters could be blubbering at my side, but if Alana walked in and stuck her tongue out at me, she'd be the one I'd see.

When my mother died, she talked to people we couldn't see while we sat there like ghosts. Once, she screamed in pain and the nurse came to give her morphine. She stretched her slack neck and raised her patchy, spotted face. She looked at the nurse, rapt with pain and straining to see past it. There was pleading in her eyes: Make it better, Mama. Then I said something. I called her "Mod"; that's what we called her for a while when we were kids. We didn't mean modern; we just meant plump and silly, tootling around the house in her short white socks and ponytails—*mom*, with the soft, stumpy strength of a *d*. All of that was gone on her deathbed, but I said it so she would know I remembered. In response, she dropped her eyes down to look at me and Daphne. Even on her sick face we saw her bewilderment. She looked back at the nurse—at Mama. Who were these big women on her bed? What was "Mod"?

I close my sleek wet umbrella, and the Museum of Mod. We stopped calling her that because other kids ridiculed us for it. They thought we were saying our mother was like girls in miniskirts, and they laughed at how stupid she would look dressed like that. We couldn't explain what we meant. Everybody knew you were supposed to say "Mom," and that was it. This was at the very end of the sixties, which people say was a very free time. But really the style suit was very strict then. It applied even to what children could call their mothers.

I turn off the main street and enter a residential zone. Well-tended houses sit in neat yards with trees. Yellow-and-white recycling buckets stand brightly curbside. Juice and jam jars for the kids, wine and fancy water bottles for the adults. My friend Joanne lives here. She and her husband, Drew, share a house with four guys in their twenties. Joanne was a teenager in San Francisco at the same time I was, but I only met her when I moved to Marin thirteen years ago. We met in a support group I used to go to for people with hepatitis C. She and Drew have hepatitis and AIDS. It's shitty, but the drugs are a lot better now and the virus is weaker.

In Paris, things happened fast. Two weeks after my first job, I met the head of Celesté. His name was Alain Black; he was a South African with a French mother. He was the man I had glimpsed on my first day there. He was lean and pale, nearly hairless. His eyes had thick, heavy lids. They were green, gold, and hazel, so mixed that they gave an impression of something bright swarming through his irises. Mostly, the swarming was just emotions and thoughts happening quickly. But there was also something else, moving too fast for you to see what it was. He asked if I had a boyfriend yet. When I said, "René," he laughed and said, "Oh, René!" Then he said I needed a haircut. Called a hairdresser, told him what to do, and sent me to the salon in a taxi. The salon was full of wrinkled women staring fixedly at models in magazines. When I walked in, they frowned and glared. But the girl at the desk smiled and led me through rows of gleaming dryers, each with a woman under it, dreaming angrily in the heat. The hairdresser didn't even need to talk to me. He talked to someone else while I stared at myself in the mirror. When it was done, I made the taxi take me back to the agency. It was closed, but the doorman with mad eyes knew to let me in. He knew where I was going and he knew who else would be there. Alain looked up and smiled. "Do you like it?" I asked. He stood and said of course he liked it, it had been his idea. Then he jumped on me.

I say "jumped" because he was quick, but he wasn't rough. He was strong and excessive, like certain sweet tastes—like grocery pie. But he was also precise. It was so good that when it was over, I felt torn open. Being torn open felt like love to me; I thought it must have felt the same to him. I knew he had a girlfriend and that he lived with her. But I was still shocked when he kissed me and sent me home. At "home," I wrapped myself in a blanket and looked out the window at the darkening mass of slanted roofs. René came by. I wouldn't see him. Darkness gradually filled the room. The phone rang; it was my mother—her tiny voice curled up in a tiny wire surrounded by darkness. I talked to her through clenched teeth. I told her she was a housewife who didn't understand anything about the real world. She told me I didn't know what I was talking about, but I could hear she was hurt. After I hung up, I could feel it, too. Her hurt was soft and dark and it had arms to hold me as if I were an infant. I sank into her soft dark arms, into a story of a wicked little girl who stepped on a loaf and fell into a world of demons and deformed creatures. She is covered with snakes and slime and surrounded by the hate of every creature trapped with her. She is starving, but she can't eat the bread still stuck to her feet. She is so hungry, she feels hollow, like she's been feeding on herself. In the world above, her mother cries for her. Her tears splash scalding hot on her daughter's face. Even though they are tears cried for love, they do not bring healing; they burn and make the pain worse. My mother's tears scalded me and I hated her for it.

My roommate came home and turned on the light, and—bang!—there was no mother and no demons. She clacked across the floor in her high heels, chatting and wiping her lipstick off. It was 4:00 in the morning, but when she saw how unhappy I was, she took out her tarot cards and told my fortune until it came out the way I wanted it. (Luxury. A feast. A kind, loyal woman. Transformation. Home of the true heart.) The sun rose; the enamel rooftops turned hot violet. I had just lain down on the couch to sleep when Alain called and told me I was going to be moving into an apartment on rue du Temple. The rent would be taken care of. Everything would be taken care of.

We met for champagne and omelettes in a sunny bistro with bright-colored cars honking outside. He talked about the Rolling Stones and his six-year-old daughter, after whom he had named the agency Celesté. He asked if I wanted children. I said, "No." He grabbed my nose between two knuckles and squeezed it. The omelettes came heaped on white plates with blanched asparagus. He hadn't kissed me yet. He spread his slim legs and tucked a cloth napkin into his shirt with an air of appetite. I wanted badly to touch him. Inside its daintiness, the asparagus was acrid and deep. He said, "The first thing we need to do is get you a Swiss bank account. All the smart girls have one. First, you don't have to pay taxes that way. Then they invest it for you. Your money will double, triple. You should see!" I loved him and he obviously loved me. Love like in the James Bond movies, where the beautiful sexy girl loves James but tries to kill him anyway. We would love each other for a while and then part. Years later, I would ride down the street in a fancy car. I'd see Alain and he'd see me. I'd smile on my way past. Sexy spy music rubbed my ear like a tongue; it rubbed my crotch, too. We finished quickly and went to my new apartment.

My new apartment had high ceilings and polished wooden floors. I entered it like Freddie leaping naked into turds. There was a sunken marble tub and a chandelier and a glass case of obscene figurines. There was a black velvet couch with a carved ivory back. I sat on it, smiling and trembling. Spy music blared. He knelt and took my hips in both hands. Brightness poured through his eyes in hot little pieces. I followed with my own eyes, thinking if I could stop one little piece and see what it was, I would find a whole world. But he never let one stop. He just showed glimpses. He knew that I saw this—not with my mind, but with my senses. I couldn't answer him because I was not his equal. But I could see it and he appreciated that. For just a moment, I saw something in his eye stop. It was like a window opening into space. It was dark and cold. Burning meteors fell in a bright, endless shower. He said, "Are you big shit? Or just cute little shit?" His voice was wondering and tender. The window closed. "Big or little?"

When we got to know each other better, we played like dogs, rolling and growling, pretending to bite. We'd make faces and chase each other around naked. If somebody knocked over a lamp or a pricey vase, it was okay. He'd caper and sing dirty French songs. I taught him "The worms go in, the worms go out, the worms play pinochle on your snout." He liked that a lot. He sang it, panted it while we were doing the "elephant fuck"—him holding my legs up from behind and me walking on my hands.

But when that was over, he'd be on the phone, pacing around naked, talking business and licking coke off his fingers. Someone would call and offer me a job and Alain would say, "No, not available." I would say, "I am too available!" He would say, "Shut up and wait!" They'd call back and offer twice as much money. He'd be happy and then he'd start calling around to check and see what people were saying about him. If anyone had said anything bad, he'd call around again and start plotting to get them back. "Blood will pour from his anus!" he'd say. I'd sit curled up in my white silk robe with the black dragons on it, smoking.

In the office, we had to pretend we weren't lovers. That was okay. I was a secret agent. I was an a-s-s-h-o-l-e. I saw his girlfriend with him at nightclubs, because we all went out together—I sat at their table with many other girls. She was stunning in magazines, but in person I thought she looked old. She had a long nose and a long tooth, and when she crossed her legs, her foot stuck out at a funny angle. But she was clever, I could see. She might have known about me. She'd run her eye over the table of girls and sometimes it would linger on me. She'd lean into him, sardonic and whispering. He'd laugh and look away, his eyes always moving and glittering.

I'd see René, too. He was always with another girl. Sometimes he'd come by the table to talk to Alain. He'd look at me and nod, a little bit of feeling for me still. His girl would blink and look around, scratch her arm. *Papillon, pee, pee, pee.* It was sad, but I was driving past.

Once, I asked René why he'd picked me up at the airport when he didn't know who I was. He said, "I knew who you were." And he had. He knew I would get into his car, and he knew I would go home with him. He knew I had a spider mouth, too. He knew that before I did. I couldn't see it because I was young and my lips were full and beautiful. But it was there.

The sidewalk climbs a hill. At the top, I see more hills, sky and trees. There is wind and the trees move with it, like it and they are part of the same body, breathing in and out; the wind sending, they receiving, passing it down into the ground. Joanne's house is at the bottom of the hill, a shambling one-story with a walkway lined with rocks painted by children. The garage is open, with work things and radio music pouring out. Joanne's husband, Drew, builds furniture and does odd repairs. He sometimes hires street people to help him. They are guys he's met at the men's shelter next to the church where the support group meets. He meets them standing outside for smokes. They come up to him for cigarettes, but they stand talking because Drew is like a warm stove of manness. He's huge, with a chest and back like an old brick wall on legs, a grumbling furnace stomach, and small thoughtful eyes in a fleshy red face. The intelligence in his eyes is warm, but it's not the love warmth of the heart. It's from the liver and stomach and glands, the busy warmth of function. He's slow to talk and he says "uhhhh" a lot. It doesn't make him sound stupid. It makes it seem like his thoughts are physical truths that have to come in noise form before he can get them into words.

Most of the guys he asks to work for him are okay. They're ex-junkies and fuckups, but they want to do better. Even so, their presence sometimes pisses the neighbors off. They come over to complain, and there's Drew: a wall with a furnace stomach and benevolent eyes looking out of a fleshy face. They'll talk to him about these unsafe people, these sad, ragged people appearing to bang around with hammers and wander the sidewalks. Drew will look into space and go, "Uhhh." There'll be a silence. Then Drew will explain why these men are okay. He'll point to a piece of work and say, "This man did that; that man did this. I need help; they can help." He'll make more "uhhh" noises. I believe it's the noises that get people. Takes them out of the world of words into practical thoughts: Things need to get built. Men need to earn. Neighbors have to be decent. The neighbors walk away confused, like they don't know what has happened.

A guy named Jerry is in the garage now, working. He looks high. He looks beat-up, worse than Freddie, beat-up inside and out. He looks like he still has goodness but that it doesn't help much. He looks like somebody wandering in a dark maze, clutching his little bit of goodness, knowing it's all he's got but not remembering what it is or how to use it. His body is empty, his face dull and numb. His forehead is a big soft knot of puzzlement. His puzzlement gives him just enough to keep him going; his puzzlement is where he's still alive. He's refinishing a chest of drawers. It looks like he's doing a pretty good job. I greet him. "Hey, Alison," he says. "Drew ain't home. Joanne is, though."

He doesn't look at me when he talks, but he sees me. It's like he's got an extrasensory system built into the side of his body. A lot of street people have this. So do a lot of fashion people. I stand there a minute, listening to the rap song coming out of the radio. A soprano voice peels out of the song, a flying red sound that ripples through the beat, then disappears under it. Somebody sampled the "Habanera" from *Carmen*.

I think of my first job in Rome. Huge open windows looked out onto the city. Long white curtains stirred in the wind. *Carmen* was playing on an old record player. We drank wine and flipped through an Italian comic book about a demon that lived in a pretty girl's cunt. He whispered to her clit as if it were an ear and said, "Do it with this one!" or "No, don't do it with that one!" When she did it with someone, the demon hid in her asshole and said, "Phew, it stinks in here!" I giggled, the photogra-

70

pher smiled, and the other model looked bored. The curtains streamed out the windows and Carmen sang of love.

I wonder if Jerry can see any echo of that moment when he scans me. If he does, he probably understands it better than most. The more withered the reality, the more gigantic and tyrannical the dream. From the dark hole of a bar on a street of sickness and whores comes a teeming cloud of music sparkling with warmth and glamour: *Sweet dreams of rhythm and magic*— Look in and see dark dead blurs slumped on stools.

"Joanne's in the kitchen," says Jerry pointedly. Still not looking at me, he puts down a can of varnish and studies the finish on the chest. "She with Jason's kids." He picks up the can again. He wants me to go away.

I say good-bye and cross the wet lawn. I open the door; a little girl stops running in the hall to look at me. Messy hair, small open mouth, aura of shy, senseless joy. "Joanne!" The girl runs again and disappears, waving the ribbon of her voice. "It's Alison!"

Jason is one of Joanne's roommates. In the blur of youth, he was married long enough to have five-year-old twin girls, who come to stay with him for a week here and there. Drew and Joanne take care of them while he's at work; mostly, that means Joanne. I come into the living room fast enough to see the kid dart around the corner into the kitchen. The living room is a bunch of slumping furniture, plants growing up to the ceiling, an electric guitar on the floor, cat dishes, the TV flashing cartoon pictures, and a huge fish tank bubbling against one wall. In the center of the floor is a chair, its orange seat back carved in the shape of flames—Drew's work. Also Drew's work is a bench on bird-foot legs, painted with peacock feathers. Beyond the living room, I glimpse the den, which is packed with Drew's work: a painted forest of legs and backs, the limbs of imaginary animals. Jason's little girls put their heads around the corner and giggle, then pop back into the kitchen.

"I'm in here, Allie," says Joanne from the kitchen.

"So he expects me—me with the bad back!—to carry two bags of clubs for this asshole," says another voice.

"Watch your mouth, Karl," says Joanne mildly. "Hi, Allie." She puts her cigarette out on a little plate and smiles. The girls smile, too—not only Jason's Heather and Joelle but also seven-year-old Trisha from down the block. They're at the table, drawing pictures. Another roommate, scrawny, pissed-off Karl, stands there bare-chested, raging about his golf course job. He's hunched over Joanne, sending small, concentrated rage at her, like she's standing there with a big bag to catch it. He looks at me, his raging head pulled into such a point, it's like his eyes are on the end of his nose. He says, "Hi," then continues his rant.

"I'm gonna tell that . . . that . . . pig, that fat pig—"

"Look," says Heather. "Look at my castle and my glass mountain!"

"I'm not gonna tell *him* anything! I'm gonna go to Loomis and tell him what's been going on in accounting! And then I'm gonna get Harris and get him together with—"

"Want some tea, Allie?" Joanne is sandy-colored, her skin and her hair. Her eyes are light brown, and they remind me of Alain's because they are sometimes filled with pouring movement. Except her movement isn't in pieces. It's continuous, like the movement of a plant or human cell fluxing with light or water or blood. Joanne is drinking from the world through her eyes, maybe even from beyond it.

"Look at my beach birds!" cries Joelle. "Look at my bird balls!" The children crowd around Joanne as she's trying to get up, loving what is in her eyes.

"I'll get the tea," I say, then realize I forgot to take off my wet shoes. I've tracked dirt through the house like a stoner or a senile old lady. Oh well. I bend to pull off my shoes. I feel my aging gingerly. I sit up. The children's faces are bursting with expressions, each gently crowding out the others. Karl looks at them, and his eyes go back where they're supposed to be. He turns around and gropes through a cabinet, pulls out a box of cereal with a cartoon tiger on it. The tiger roars as magic sugar flies over his giant bowl of cereal.

"Joanne, look! Look, Alison!" Trisha is dancing and waving her drawing. She is erect and seeking, and her white skin is as vibrant as color. Her brown eyes are radiant, but her small lips have a soft dark color that suggests privacy, hiddenness. Her dancer is red leaping on white, with wiggle arms and pointy yellow shoes on the ends of wiggle legs.

"Wow!" I say. "This is a real dancer. This is like real dancing!"

"Yes," says Trisha, "now look!"

Even Karl looks as Trisha stands exulting with her arms in the air. "All the way up to here!" She bends and puts her palms on the floor; her cartwheel is a quick, neat arc. "All the way down to there!" Her belly flashes its button. She laughs, cartwheels again, out of the kitchen into the hall. Heather and Joelle somersault after her, screaming, "Me, too! Me!" We applaud. I get a mug from the cabinet, brushing against Karl as I go past. His rage is still there, but it's inside now. I picture a little metal ball with spikes, rolling in one spot, tearing a hole in his heart while the rest of Karl holds it together, eating his cereal and thinking about other things.

"I'll get it." Joanne brushes past me, gets the kettle, runs water into it.

"It's total disrespect," says Karl. "He's shitting on me, and he's doing it so everybody else knows."

"Karl," I say. "I don't exactly know what you're talking about. But if you're talking disrespect at the workplace, I once worked with a photographer who told a girl to put her hand down her pants and masturbate."

"*What?*"

"He put it more nicely than that, but he meant, Stick your hand down your pants and masturbate. He wasn't kidding, either. And she was fifteen."

This happened in Naxos, Greece. The photographer was an American named Alex Gish. He was considered an artist. Whatever he looked at, he took apart and put back together with his mind, furious because he knew it would just go back to being itself as soon as he looked away. He was looking at me, this fifteen-year-old Brit named Lisa, and three local men his assistant had hired. He called the men "magnificent" and then gazed at them, rearranging. They gazed back, huge, bemused, squinting. One of them affably spat.

"So did she do it?" Karl pauses over his cereal, spiked ball on hold. He is curious. His eyes are a little turned on, but his small chest is soft and open. He has compassion. I get stuck on this for a second. If his compassion comes from the place where he's clawing himself, is it real? It seems mean to say no. But I wonder. One of the Greek men looked at Lisa with compassion, too. His look was not about something torn. He looked at her before she was disrespected. He looked like a kind dog might look at a nervous cat. Majestic wet tongue out, rhythmically inhaling the scent of feline. Store info in saliva, lick the chops, swallow it down. Blink soft, merciful eyes. Put tongue out again. Sometimes dogs are more dignified than cats. This man was probably sixty years old, and he was so beautiful, they wanted to put him in a fashion magazine.

"Yeah, she did it. He spent the whole day telling her she was bloated and fat. 'The lips are too thin, André. Can you work with that? And while you're at it, do something about those bags under the eyes.'"

"Pricks like that should just be killed," says Karl with feeling.

"I'll bet she was making a lot more than Karl is." Joanne's voice is careful and pointed. She pours the boiling water carefully. "And I'll bet she could've said no and not gotten fired."

"Yeah," says Karl. "It's not the same. But I still think the photographer should be killed. Along with—"

"I'm just saying, if you want to talk about disrespect . . ." I trail off. Joanne doesn't like it when I tell stories like this. She thinks I'm acting dramatic and victimized. But that's not how I feel. I feel like the bright past is coming through the gray present and I want to look at it one more time.

"My God!" cried Alex, throwing another Polaroid on the ground. "Can't you do better than that? Do you even know what fucking is?" I was drinking orange soda and giggling with a stylist. The shiny little picture flapped across the sand and got caught in some weeds near my feet. Lisa's mouth quivered. She *was* thin-lipped for a model. I tipped my head back to drink more soda and to look at the deep and bright blue sky.

"I still think you should try talking to him." Joanne's tuned into Karl. "Use the skills we went over. Always talk in terms of 'I.' Like, 'When you had me carry those bags, it made me feel—' "

Trisha's laughter sails into the room with a cloud of TV noise. They're playing with the channel changer. Zip—voices—zip—music—gray buzz—zip. Their laughter rolls together with the electronic babble in a dissolving ball of sound. Flesh and electricity gather and disperse.

"Okay." Alex sighed. "Look. We're going to be shooting from the waist up only. Just put your hand down your pants and make yourself feel good." One of the Greeks smiled nervously at me and kicked a little sand over my foot. The stylist threw me a hot smirk. Lisa's mouth was twisted with embarrassment. My heart beat. Tears shone on her face. I frowned and shook sand off my foot. "You haven't got the lips," yelled Alex, "so use your eyes! You've got the eyes! Use them!"

It was disrespect. But it was something else, too—something I would not be able to explain to Karl or Joanne. Afterward, we all went out for dinner and everybody was nice to Lisa. She sat there, tense and hunched under the niceness. The tension only heightened the beauty of her huge eyes and delicate movements. We ate lamb and sardines, tomatoes dripping with oil. We were sitting on an outdoor patio and the men went to piss in the darkness outside the strung ring of colored lights. It was warm. We could smell one another's sweat mingled with food and flowers. Alex sat across from Lisa. His face was naked and strange. He said something in a low voice, and for an instant her spirit showed itself—a bright orange pistil in a white flower. "There's a lady," he said, and his voice was warm.

Joanne puts her cigarette to her lips. Karl eats his cereal. His rage is quiet. His hurt is quiet. I have aspirin and codeine with my tea. Rain spatters the roof. We sit connected in a triangle. On television, haunted music tiptoes about. Animals bellow. Humans mutter. Comedy music bumps and stumbles. A voice says, "We are here to be the eyes and ears of God."

I think of Drew's room of furniture. Some of it he'll sell, but most of it will build up in that room and spread out through the house. He's building onto himself and out into the world at the same time. His furniture is for use. But whether anyone uses it or not, each piece adds to the huge place he's building inside—a place where the physical laws don't apply, where you can sit in orange flame and be okay. He's using physical tools to describe this place. He's leaving physical markers.

One night when I was here, I was alone in the kitchen for a minute and Drew came up behind and pressed against me. I could hear Joanne in the living room, talking to Karl over emergency music on the TV. Fear, pain, excitement, said the music. Sorrow, secret sorrow. We were all high on pot. I was standing at the counter, pouring apple juice. He came in and put one hand on my hip and one arm around my chest, as though to hold me steady. He crouched a little and pressed against me. He put his cheek against the side of my head. Joanne laughed in the next room. For a second, her laugh blended with his touch and I felt held by it. He pressed against my butt. I felt that soft noise feeling all through his body, insistent, warm, ardent, like a snuffling bear at a berry bush. His cheek against me ardent, too. Respecting the bush: May I? Before I knew it, Yes shot down my spine and lifted my tailbone slightly. *Ossifier, love's desire.* But silent now, huge and soft with sadness. I put my hand on his. "Stop," I said. "We can't." He held me long enough for me to feel his ardor turn to embarrassment, then sadness, then nothing. He let go, coughed, and opened the refrigerator. I went into the living room. A grim woman flew through gray traffic on a motorcycle. Triumph, said the music. Grim, lonely triumph flying through space. I imagined letting the feeling continue, letting it bend me forward. Open the door to the place where the huge things are. Let him stick it in. He sat far away from me, face blank, cheeks flushed. What would it have been like to open that door again? I might've done it, except for Joanne.

Karl puts his dish in the sink and disappears. Joanne takes my wet shoes and socks and puts them in the dryer off the kitchen. Gives me a pair of Drew's socks to wear. We make lunch—sandwiches and boiled eggs and carrots cut into neat strips. The girls run back in, clamoring for carrots and animal crackers. They sit and draw red animals, whole furious sheets of them. My shoes thud in the dryer. Roommate Nate comes out of his basement room in a pajama top and a cowboy hat. He works the night shift in the emergency room and he's training to be a fireman. He walks into the kitchen singing, "Move it in, pull it out, stick it back, and waggle it about, Disco Warthog!"

"One," says Joanne, "quit singing dirty songs. Two—"

The girls crowd around him with their drawings.

"'Disco Warthog,'" says Nate, pouring himself a cup of coffee, "is derived from the classic 'Disco Lady,' and is therefore not a dirty song."

"Nate," says Trisha, looking up, "warthogs *are* dirty. They're pigs with teeth!"

"Two. Could you and the girls go into the living room so I can visit with Alison?"

Nate leads the girls from the room, coffee cup aloft. "Let's go be clean lady warthogs!"

"And no disco whatever!" shouts Joanne. She turns to me and smiles.

Joanne is making a place inside her, too. She doesn't do it physically like her husband. She does it with thoughts and words. We move around the kitchen, and I can feel the building going on. She's talking about people we know at the support group. She's talking about a woman with hepatitis named Karen, who is superpissed about people who help her when she doesn't want their help. People who lecture her about her smoking and her soothing double vodkas at night, who harangue her about everything from interferon to Bach flower remedies, including yoga, root vegetables, and salmon. "'The worst thing isn't even being sick.'" Joanne imitates Karen's bitter, husky whine, so heavy, it's almost sensual. "'The worst thing is having some yoga-class, health food–eating, New Age therapist–going prick jam you about being a junkie. And like'"—with fine, hoarse disdain—"'I can afford salmon. Fuck you!'" We laugh because Karen is royal, with her long dyed black hair and jewelry, her harsh wild eyes with their ring of green around the gray. We laugh because she's an asshole. We also laugh because we know what she means about the health pricks, going to gyms, sitting in hot tubs, taking their stinking vitamins and antidepressants. "'Tellin' me what I need to do, what to eat, what to think about before I go to bed at night—because everybody has to be fucking perfect like they think they are. Because the reality that they can't control it, that people get sick no matter what they do, scares the shit out of them.'"

She's right about that, too. I think of the guy with hepatitis who was written up in the local paper as a success story last year; he thought he'd beaten the disease with a macrobiotic diet, Chinese herbs, acupuncture, and vigorous exercise. The son of a bitch ran five miles every day, then went home and sat in the hot tub he'd built himself. In the newspaper photo, he looked very pleased with himself; the caption under the photo said "In control." Then liver cancer squashed him like a mallet. He didn't know that high temperatures are very bad for the hepatic liver, and he'd apparently cooked the damn organ in his hot tub. Which is exactly what drives Karen crazy—his thinking that if only he did everything right, he might control mortality. His bossy little will with its nose in the air, up on a pedestal to be worshiped. Except she wants to put her sickness on a pedestal and worship it. She wants other people to worship it, too.

"Do you remember," I say, "all those spiritual healing books from the eighties? There was one that said HIV came to Earth because of shame. Do you know what I'm talking about?"

"Yeah." Joanne makes a carrot-strip sunburst on a yellow plate. "I think I read that one. Wasn't it by this grandmotherly old lady?" She goes to the refrigerator and comes back with handfuls of radishes. "There was an exercise you were supposed to do. I remember . . ." She stands at the sink, running the radishes under the water, quickly and lightly rubbing them.

"You were supposed to address each body part and tell it you love it, especially any part you felt shame about. A long time ago, I gave it to this woman named Veronica. She had HIV and I was desperate to give her something, even though she didn't want it."

"Like Karen talks about."

"Yeah, except she didn't get mad at me. She laughed instead."

Joanne cuts the radishes like my mother did, like her mother must've done—like flowers. I cut the sandwiches into triangles, like Daphne, Sara, and I used to have sandwiches. Like Trisha and Heather and Joelle might one day make sandwiches for children.

"She gave the book back and told me it was sweet. I asked if she did the exercise, and she said, 'Hon, I may not know much about love, but I know it's not an act of will.' She said picturing all those fags chanting 'I love my ass' made her laugh."

In fact, Veronica said she didn't know whether to laugh or cry. "Trying to put love up their asses like they used to put dick, under the benevolent ur-gaze of this grandmotherly 'healer,' like finally Grandma loves and accepts your ass—please. My shame didn't cause this and my love won't cure it."

"I remember she said, 'How do you think Stalin and Hitler wound up killing so many people? They were trying to fix them. To make them ideal.' She said, 'There's violence in that, hon.'"

"Yeah," says Joanne. "I see what she means. But I liked the exercise. I didn't expect it to fix me. I just found it comforting."

"Yeah," I say, "Me, too."

She drops a double handful of cut radishes in the center of the sunburst. Light comes through the window and shines on her hands; they are wet, rough, and slightly red at the knuckles. There's a torn hangnail on her thumb and chipped silver polish on her broken transparent nails. "Do you want apple juice?" she asks.

Heather and Joelle run through the room, using our legs to play hide-and-seek. Their young faces peep in and out of our aging limbs; their hands and eyes flash. I think of roses climbing a battered trellis.

"We've gotta get lunch on," says Joanne. "My radio program is gonna be on in forty minutes, and today it's the director of *Lost in Translation,* and I *loved* that movie."

The place Joanne is building inside has rooms for all of this. Not just rooms. Beautiful ones. For Karl and Jerry and Karen and Nate in his cowboy hat and the hot-tub guy and movie directors and old-lady healers and people trying to love their asses and people who think they're stupid for it. In these rooms, each thing that looks crazy or stupid will be like a drawing you give your mother, regarded with complete acceptance and put on the wall. Not because it is good but because it is trying to understand something. In these rooms, there will be understanding. In these rooms, each madness and stupidity will be unfolded from its knot and smoothed with loving hands until the true thing inside it lies revealed.

Joanne goes to get Jerry for lunch. The girls help me carry the food into the living room so we can eat it on a blanket while we watch *Animal Planet*. There're cheese sandwiches with lettuce, peanut butter and jelly ones, radishes and carrots, plus animal crackers and juice in little cartons. Joanne and I sit on the floor with the girls; Joelle sits between Joanne's spread legs, her plate balanced on Joanne's thigh. Jerry's next to Nate on the couch, laughing about something. The light from the fish tank glows behind them; fish traverse the rippling green.

On *Animal Planet*, people are putting computer chips under the skins of beautiful lizards in order to help save them from extinction. The camera zooms in on the writhing creatures. Their eyes bulge; their hinged red mouths fiercely gape. One strikes the air with a stiff webbed claw. Joanne presses the mute button to say grace. The bright and scalding past breaks through.

Toward the end, Alain would talk to people about me while I sat right there. I understood French well enough by then that I could understand most of what he said. "She's gone cold. Morbid, a little weird. She doesn't have the strength to carry that off. But you should have seen her when she first came." I just sat there, not saying anything. What shames me most about it is that by then I didn't even love him. I loved the rich things and the money and people kissing my ass. I loved the song I was living in, and he was the singer.

He still used the apartment for meetings and to hang out. He brought over girls and his beautiful friend Jean-Paul, an ex-model who smiled, dirty and sweet, when Alain called him "cunt face." He didn't have official parties there. That was for his real house, which he shared with his real girlfriend. But the apartment was set up so that little parties could happen if they wanted to. There were fresh flowers in freshly polished vases.

The pantry was stocked with wine and fancy nuts, big fat olives, figs, sugared almonds, and marzipan animals that I ate myself sick on when I was alone. In the refrigerator were salted fish, pâtés, cheeses. Also boxes of syringes filled with antibiotics for syphilis and clap. There was always cocaine in a big china plate on the mantel. Some nights, people would tumble in like they were being poured from a giant cornucopia, falling out on their royal asses, then getting up to dance and eat and strut. Some of them thought I was just a girl at the party. But lots of them knew this was actually my home. Alain insisted on keeping up the pretense of no sex, even though so many people knew. Once I did it with Cunt Face when people were over, to mock Alain and his policy. That's when I realized how many people knew. We came out of the bedroom and people looked at Alain to see what he would do. When he didn't do anything, they looked away. Little laughing people skipping and playing in the place where the huge things are.

But I wasn't a little person. I was huge. I was hugely drunk. I was a model and secret mistress of a powerful agent who could flaunt another lover in front of him.

I walked down a hallway crowded with gorgeous people. Lush arms, gold skin, fantastic flashing eyes, lips made up so big and full, they seemed mute—made not to talk but only to sense and receive. So much beauty, like bursts of violent color hitting your eye together and mixing until they were mud. I passed a bathroom and heard the sound of puking quickly covered by the music on the stereo. Rich, dreamy mud of sound. A girl met my eye and I was amazed to see her face emerge with such clarity. For a second, I was startled to think I knew her from childhood. Then I realized she was a movie star. I had watched her on TV with my family. She was looking at me curiously. I smiled and walked past. My father had loved her on TV. If he could see this, he would reach up and scratch his ear, not knowing what to say. Jean-Paul had scratched his ear just before he leaned in to kiss me. His kiss had been surprisingly sweet. I ducked into a bedroom to call my father and tell him about the movie star. I closed the door and sat with the phone cord wound against my chest, listening to the phone ringing in the dingy kitchen in New Jersey, my call hurtling through the night, over the cold ocean to land in that dingy phone.

I was going to show myself to my father, living big and bold. Mostly when I called him, I was stilted and hidden. Now I would show him something. I didn't know what. But I would show him. Jean-Paul had fucked me shallowly a long time before finally sticking it in. I was still drunk with feeling between my legs. The room blurred and swam in my eyes. I heard myself murmur, "I love you, Daddy." But when he answered the phone, I couldn't speak. His voice was a mild voice, tired and kind. There was nothing big in it. I didn't know how to speak to it. I was abashed before it. "Hello?" said the voice. "Hello?" Darkness spread around me, and in it I was tiny. "Hello?" Across the ocean, my father sighed. "Hello?" He hung up. Comforted, I went back to the party.

Sometimes, Alain and I still slept together. He would come into my room in the early morning, when it was still dark. He would bend over me and cover my face with tiny kisses, his rough coat brushing against me. He stroked my face with his cold hands and spoke so gently that I couldn't hear him. I thought I heard "I'm sorry, I'm sorry." He was so drunk, his eyes were finally quiet, swollen and rolled back in his head. He would lie beside me, and I would kiss his hands and his temples, shivering with the night air on his clothes. He would kiss me back and touch my body and then fall asleep. I would put my back against him, then pull his arm around me and hold it there. Little gusts of morning air made the shade tap against the window frame. Sunlight crept under the shade and across the floor. Strange to think it was the same sun the cat and I had watched on the dining room floor a long time ago.

But mostly, he didn't sleep with me. Sometimes he didn't sleep at all. Sometimes I'd wake up and find him in the living room with Jean-Paul and some girl, watching TV with red eyes and open dry mouths. Once I came out and saw Cunt Face bent over the kitchen table with his pants down so that Alain could give him a clap shot. Alain didn't look up. Jean-Paul smiled wanly, then winced when Alain jabbed him. He must've asked for the shot; Alain didn't give them away. Even friends had to pay.

Heather and Trisha are almost asleep before the TV. Joelle is standing at the sliding glass door, looking at the sky. The sun has broken through somewhere; the tops of the trees are glowing, almost gold with sunlight. Everything else is gray. A piece of rippling fish tank is reflected in the glass, like a mysterious heart in a gray body. A tiny fish flickers across it. Joelle stretches up a hand. "This is my eyes." She stretches up the other. "This is my ears."

Joanne stands beside her. The sun plays across her sideways face. I can see the white down on her skin. I can see the tiny crosshatch marks in the softness of her cheeks, the acne scars pocking one side of her face, the dark pouches under her eyes. Liver, weariness, bile. The weight of her cheeks just starting to pull her mouth into a severe shape. Sensitive lips now sensing death mingled with all the tastes of life. All her pores opened and saturated with waning life. Still sending out the message of Here I am. The little girl stretches her face up to receive it, drinking in with her own perfect skin what it is to be. Joanne turns to face me. Behind her eyes, she is going from room to room, turning on the lights.

"What are you thinking?" she asks.

That you are beautiful. That not everyone could see it. I almost became the kind of person who could not. I missed being that kind of person by a hair.

"About the way I used to be. Things I used to do. You know. Stuff I can't understand anymore why I did it."

The girl pricks up her ears. "What did you do, Alison?"

I turned into a puppet with a giant hand inside me. Not a particular hand. Just a hand. During a fitting, a client jabbed my crotch with her long nails. She was supposedly smoothing the wrinkles on some pants. She snapped, "You keep sweating!" then twisted my leg so hard, she hurt my knee. I went into hysterics and was fired for the first time. I insulted Alain in public and arrived home two days later, to find myself locked out of the apartment. I ran to the bank, but I was too late—two years too late. I could only get fifty thousand francs. The rest was in a Swiss bank account in the agency's name.

I look into the child's eyes. She meets my look, takes it in. She frowns and looks down, fiddling with the hem of her shirt. At that age, they know about doing things you don't know why you did. When I was five, I slammed Daphne's leg in the car door. We were having a fight and she said something I didn't like. I was in the car and she was just getting in and I slammed her leg. She screamed. My mother yelled, "Why did you do that?" I was too shocked to answer. I stroke Joelle's lowered head. The shine of the sun follows my hand on her gold-brown hair.

We were stupid for disrespecting the limits placed before us. For tearing up the fabric of songs wise enough to acknowledge limits. For making songs of rape and death and then disappearing inside them. For trying to go everywhere and know everything. We were stupid, spoiled, and arrogant. But we were right, too. We were right to do it even so.

Drew walks in. Rough face flushed and sensate. Eye sparkle rooted in the slow, low body. The spry feet of a dandy. Long graying hair fluffy and touched with rain. He stops and his eyes zero in on me. I sit down and take his socks off my feet. I have to go. Heather and Trisha wake for me to kiss their

cheeks. Trisha hugs my legs and shouts, "Good-bye!" I bend
and kiss her forehead. Ten years from now, I will be a kiss in a
great field of faceless kisses, a sweet patch of forgotten territory
in her inner country. Joanne hugs me, too, her heart against
mine. Nice to think that in her dreams Trisha might run through
that field and love it without knowing why. Drew puts out his
hand and I clasp it. There is a ball of heat and feeling in his
palm. The same feeling as when he pressed up against me that
time. If I asked him why he did that, what would he say? *I still
have this. Do you see? I am sick. One day, I could be very sick. But in the
meantime, I still have this and it's still good. Do you see?* I do see. It's not
just sex. It's why he can help other men without making them
feel like bums. Why people will listen to him when he's not saying words. *Yes, I see.* I tell him that with my eyes. He thanks me
with his eyes. He lets go of my hand.

The rain is out again, hammering the puddles full of holes,
pocking the black-and-silver world with shining darkness. Rain
soaks each leaf and blade of grass, bloating the lawns until they
seem to roll and swell. Houses recede. The wind rises. The eyes
and ears of God come down the walk.

    I should go home. I'm tired and weak. Should take the
bus. Should call my father. He is alone in an apartment with
junk mail and old newspapers spread all around. Looking here
and there in bafflement while dry heat pours out on him from a
vent in the ceiling. His radio with a bent antenna on the dining
table is tuned to a sports channel. People on magazine covers
smile up from the floor and tabletops—a flat field of smiles
blurred with slanted light from the cockeyed lamp. My father
doesn't listen to his old songs anymore. They finally went dead
for him. Instead, he has these people in magazines and on TV:
actors, singers, celebrities. He knows they are vessels for a

nation of secret, tender feeling, and he respects them. I think he tries to cleave to them. But I don't think he can.

Above me, the treetops wave back and forth, full of shapes, like the ocean. Wild hair, great sopping fists, a rippling field, a huge wet plant with thousands of tiny flowers that open and close with the wind. Form recedes. All the smiling television faces blend to make a shimmering suit that might hold you. I see my father trying to put one of them on. Reaching for it trustfully, noticing the poor quality but letting it pass. Smiling like he doesn't see when it falls apart in his hands. Still wanting to believe. Afraid not to.

Veronica had whole picture books of celebrities in her apartment, thick books by Richard Avedon and Helmut Newton, who were almost celebrities themselves. These books did not bewilder her; she understood them as vessels. I remember a picture of two slender, sinewy women in neon underwear, one bending over with perfectly straight legs and a perfectly straight back while the other one, perfectly erect and frontal, pretended to spank her with a paddle. Veronica's apartment was a condominium that she worked double shifts for a year to buy, and it wanted very much to be perfectly elegant. It was like an aquarium of gray and chrome waiting for something perfect to be placed in it. These pictures were the first perfect things.

When Alain locked me out and stole my money, I went back home. Eventually, I moved to New York; eventually, I returned to modeling. Eventually, I lived in a big apartment, too. I remember returning home to my big apartment alone and drunk. Moving through rooms, turning on the lights. The buzz of my own electricity loud and terrible in my head. Someday to be cut off. That doesn't happen when I go home to my place on the canal. I am glad to be there. I always turn on the space heater first thing, a wonderful humming box filled with orange bands of dry heat. Take off my wet shoes, sit in the chair, warming my wet feet. Look out the window, look at the wall. Travel slowly through the wall. My millions of cells meeting all its millions of cells. We swarm together like ants touching feelers. Now I know you. Good, yes, I know you. I have some coffee. Listen to the radio. This afternoon maybe I'll call my father.

But not yet; I won't go home yet. I'll take the bus and go someplace beautiful and I'll walk until I'm so tired that I won't be able to stay awake tonight. So tired that my sleep will not be pestered by dreams or fairy tales.

At the end of the Naxos shoot, Lisa was not crying. Her face was ravaged and fevered, but she was erect, and her eyes were full of dull flame. She looked like a different person. She looked amazing. Alex moved about her, quick and silent. If he spoke, he did so in a very low voice, so that only she would hear him.

Everyone was so busy watching that I was the only one who saw the old Greek man. He was staring at Alex with a face of astonished disgust. His expression made me blush, and he wasn't even looking at me. He took a step toward Alex, as if he meant to hit him. He stopped as if confused and wiped his mouth. He turned and walked away. He did not even come back to get paid.

Here's the main street. Here's the bus stop. Here's a retarded girl coming toward me in a yellow slicker and baggy corduroy pants. She is dainty and shambling, with her big body and small feet, her ragged hems crushed and muddy under her heels. She comes close. Her fat, soft face is thick with feelings too blunt for words. Soft like paws, not nimble like fingers. Paws can read the earth better than fingers. I can feel her reading me, running her senses over the invisible scars left by my appetites, vanities, and passive cruelties. Feeling my secret mouth—still there, even if the fangs have fallen out. Don't worry about me, I think at her. I am harmless. But she looks wary. She doesn't answer my hello. She keeps her eyes on me till she's passed.

When I returned home to New Jersey, everybody met me at the airport. My mother had a fake smile on her face, meant to shield me from her tears. Daphne did not smile. She looked at me calmly, except that her brow was knitted up so high, her eyes were almost popped. My father's face had the awful tact of a witness to an accident with bloody people sprawled out naked. Sara was the only one who seemed the same. She glanced at me to be sure I was still there, then went back into herself.

I sat in the backseat with my sisters, as if we were children again. For a second, they held apart from me and then we were joined together in the old membrane. My mother had come back to my father just weeks earlier, and the membrane was active and vibrating with recent vigor.

"Do you want anything special to eat?" My father raised his eyes in the rearview mirror but did not look at me.

"I've made spaghetti," said my mother.

"Spaghetti would be good," I replied.

We drove past low-built gray stores set back in lots half-full of cars and hunks of dirty snow. Their lights were starting to come on. The Dress Barn, Radio Shack, the 99-Cent Store. My mother began to cry; her tears scalded my face.

The bus is coming. I feel my fever subtly mount. A frowning young man, soft and slumped in his worn jacket, appears out of nowhere and flags the bus. It stops, popping open its door with a spastic rasp. The driver is small and bristling, with a lined face and jug ears. Hard and fiery, with a mouthful of spit waiting to be spat, he glares straight ahead as he pulls the door shut.

That night, I shared the big bed with Daphne. They had moved Sara into a small room in the basement, so we were alone. There was a desk where the maturity bed used to be. I piled my clothes on it until we could figure out what to do with them all. We brushed our hair and changed into flowered gowns. I walked around naked more than I had to. She looked away. We had emotions, but we held them back. Silence and stillness connected us. Silence and stillness were where we understood each other. We could still be children together there, and we were afraid to let adult emotions break it. We got into bed and shut off the light. I turned on my side. Silently, she put her arm around me. I took her hand and kissed it. We laced our fingers together and I kissed her hand again before resting it against my chest.

I sit next to a doughy girl with a stopped-up nose. Who's the nose of God? The girl sniffs so hard, her head squeaks; she breathes softly through her mouth. Maybe the animals are in charge of smell. Taking everything into their hairy nostrils and translating it with their bodies, patiently putting it through each cell, each organ. Sitting and mulling it over with half-closed eyes. Licking their paws and sending it upward in an invisible skein of knowledge.

. . .

I enrolled in the community college. Daphne was already there. Sara had dropped out of school and taken a job at an old people's home a few blocks over. She didn't yell anymore. There were no boys to slap her ass. She came home from work and went down into the basement. It was winter and we could hear her hacking cough rise all the way up to the second floor. It was winter and my mother's skin dried and her face grew thin and shrunken. I might look at her in her rubber boots and her wool cap pulled down over her forehead, the wool darkening with sweat as she worked to scrape ice off the chugging car, and I would think, No sexy pantsuit now. Nobody wants you now! And with that thought, my heart contracted and the world shrank around me so fast that I thought it would crush me. Every morning, my father got up looking like he felt the same way. The expression on his face said that the world shrank around him every day, so close in that it was hard to move. The expression on his face said that he pressed against the hard case of the shrunken world and pushed it back with every step. It was an expression I knew without knowing. I put my forehead down and I helped him push.

Our father dropped Daphne and me off at the college before he went to his job. He let us off at the end of the parking lot and we walked a long concrete path caked with blue-and-gray ice that gleamed on sunny days. The school was small and dingy. The people inside it stared at me like I was a stuck-up bitch. To get away from their stares, I climbed further up my stick. But I didn't feel stuck-up. I felt scared. I felt like I had to prove I was smart enough to go to college. I worked hard. I wrote poems. The poetry teacher was a little man with sparse hair on his dry head and spotted, trembling hands. But I loved him because he wrote "very good" on my poems. At the end of the day, Daphne and I would sit in the Student Union eating sweetened yogurt and dime doughnuts. Night students came and stood in the cafeteria line. At six o'clock, we walked back down the concrete to meet the car.

If we got home and our mother wasn't there, our dad danced around the house, pretending he was an ape. He did it to relieve tension. He'd run into the living room swinging his arms and going, "Ooooh! Oooh! Eeee eee eee!" He'd jump up on a chair, scratching his armpit and his head. Daphne and I did it, too; we ran around after him. It was like dancing on the green chairs, only it wasn't a song everybody knew. It came from the deep flesh place, except it was quick and alive and full of joy. Not that I thought of it that way. I just knew I loved it. If it had gone on longer, it would've been better than any song. But it lasted only a minute. Our dad would always call it; he'd suddenly go back to normal and climb down off the chair, his smile disappearing back into his face. "Whew!" he'd say. "I feel a whole lot better now!" Except once between ape and normal, he took my shoulders and hugged me sideways. "I'm proud of you," he whispered, and kissed my ear.

I was proud, too; I knew I was doing something hard. Sometimes I was even happy. But another world was still with me, glowing and rippling like a dream of heaven deeper than the ocean. I could be studying or watching TV or unloading clothes from the washing machine when a memory would come like a heavy wave of dream rolling into life and threatening to break it open. During the day, life stood stolid, gray and oblivious. But at night, heaven came in the cracks. I would want Alain, and want his cruelty, too. I would long for those cabinets of rich food and plates of drugs, for nights of sitting alone in the dark, eating marzipan until I was sick. For bitches who yanked at me and yelled at me for sweating. For nightclubs like cheap boxed hell, full of smoke and giant faces with endlessly talking lips and eyes and snouts swelling and bulbous with beauty. For my own swollen hugeness, spread across the sky. It didn't matter that I had been unhappy in the sky, or that I had been cheated and used. I cried for what had hurt me, and felt contempt for those who loved me; if Daphne had put her arm around me then, I would've clenched my teeth with contempt.

Then, lying next to her warm body was like lying in a hole with a dog and looking up to see gods rippling in the air of their hot-colored heaven. I wanted her to know that she was a dog, ugly and poor. I wanted all of them to know. I wanted my father to know that he would always be crushed, no matter how hard he pushed.

On the last night I saw Alain, he took a bunch of us to a sado-masochist sex club. It was a dump guarded by a fat tattooed man who smacked his blubbery lips at us. Inside the cave, there was a bar and a handsome young man pouring drinks behind it. Cheerful music played. Two middle-aged women with deep, sour faces sat at the bar wearing corsets and garter belts. Some people were dressed in costume like them; other people were dressed normally. One man was naked. He was skinny as a corpse—you could see his ribs and the bones of his ass. He had long matted gray hair and thick yellow nails like a dog's. He crawled on the floor, moaning and licking it with his tongue. The hair on the back of my neck stood up. Nobody even looked at him. He crawled to the women at the bar and got up on his knees. He moaned and pawed the air like he longed to touch them but didn't dare. Without looking, one of them took the riding crop from her lap and lightly struck him across the shoulders. "Va, va!" she scolded gently. He reached down and yanked at his limp penis. He yanked it hard and fast but also daintily. She returned the crop to her lap and he scuttled away, balls swinging between his withered thighs. She saw me staring and made a face, as if I had broken a rule. I looked for Alain and saw him disappearing into a crowded back room with his arm around a dimly familiar girl. "Don't worry." Jean-Paul was suddenly beside me. "It is harmless here." He winked at me. "Just a show, mostly. Unless you want to join." But I pushed through the crowd.

Sometimes the spell would break: I would look away from the terrible heaven and see my sister lying next to me, her neat, graceful form and her even breath beautiful and inviolate. If I put my hand on her warm shoulder, my thoughts might quiet; heaven would vanish and the ceiling would be there again, protecting us from the sky. I could lie against her and feel her breath forgive me. The day would come. My night thoughts would pale. My sister and I would go to school.

But sometimes I would barely sleep, then get up with heaven still burning my eyes. I would be full of hate and pain because I could not get back to it. On one of those mornings, I told Daphne the story of the sex club. We were moving around the room quickly, getting out of our warm gowns and into our cold clothes. I told her about the crawling man and the women at the bar. I could tell she didn't want to hear. But I kept talking, faster and faster. I pushed through the crowd. A hand reached out of it and grabbed my wrist. I took its little finger and bent it back. It let go. I threw my gown on the bed and walked across the room naked. Daphne turned her back, bent, and showed me the gentle humps of her spine. With dignity, she put on her pants.

In a reeking back room, I found Alain with Lisa from Naxos. Her sensitive little lips were tense and strange. They were watching a middle-aged woman climb onto a metal contraption so that a man could whip her. Daphne yanked open a drawer and slammed it shut. I brushed my hair with rapid strokes. Alain smiled at me. I told him I wanted to go home, now. "Then go home," he said. Lisa was not looking at me on purpose. Daphne pared her nails. She was not looking at me, either. The man with the whip was waiting for the woman to get settled into the proper knee and hand grooves. He seemed nervous; twice he moved his arm, like he was anxious to assist her, then moved it back. "I want to go home!" I nearly screamed. Both the man with the whip and the climbing woman turned to look at me; she brushed a piece of hair from her quizzical eye.

The people watching them looked, too. There was a crash; "Shit!" hissed Daphne. She had knocked a water glass off the bed table, splashing the mattress. Without looking at me, Alain took an ice cube out of his drink and threw it at my face. The woman settled her face into the metal headrest. I kicked Alain's shin and ran.

"That's poetry," I said. "Life and sex and cruelty. Not something you learn in community college. Not something you write in a notebook." Daphne slammed the glass back on the table so hard, I thought she'd break it. She went out of the room and down the stairs. She knew what I'd said was stupid, but she half-believed it, too.

I left the sadomasochist dump with a girl from the south of France named Simone. She was wearing a tight blue dress with red wine spilled down the front of it. She was so drunk, she didn't care. *"Fuck it,"* she kept saying in English, "you know?" The tattooed doorman called out an endearment to us as we emerged from his cave. "Fuck it!" she yelled. The club was on a tiny alley that smelled of interesting piss, but one block over, glamorous traffic ran biliously. *Papillon, pee, pee, pee.* We linked arms and walked. Simone was talking about her new boyfriend, but I didn't listen. I was thinking about Lisa's shame at Naxos, trying to gloat. But Alex was right: Even a young girl's shame can be beautiful. The naked man in the club crawled on the floor, looking for his shame, starving for it. Locked out of life and trying to crawl back through a tunnel made of shame. Yanking his dead dick in reverence for a life he couldn't have. I looked up at the sky. Gnats sparkled in the flickering light of a broken street lamp. Plunged into dark, then dancing for joy, over and over again. Alain hadn't even looked at me. Just flicked the ice in my face.

Simone raised her arm and stopped a taxi. The driver had

a great bony jaw and hairy brows and lightning coming out of his forehead. Simone gave the address of a nightclub and he drove like a charioteer, war arm manning the wheel. I sank back in the dark seat.

By spring, my father and I had succeeded; we had made an open space. I got *B*'s and even *A*'s. I spent more of my French money to take a class in the spring semester. I made friends with kids who liked it that I seemed stuck-up. They liked it even better that I was an ex-model who'd gotten kicked in the ass. "Models are stupid cows," said a girl named Denise, and I said, "Yeah, they are." She blinked her big heavy eyes and looked at me curiously.

Denise was even taller and thinner than I was. Her round face and huge frantic hair sat atop her fleshless body like a large flower on a drooping stalk. She acted like she was too good for everything. She acted like everything had hurt her and used her, and that this made her superior. But she was nice. She was the kind of person who'd hold your head while you were puking and not mention it later. She almost made me believe in living like music again, just because of the way she'd hunch and rock herself and slowly bring her cigarette hand from knee to lip and back; it was like acoustic guitar on a scratchy record. Her boyfriend, Jeff, was also slim and slouching with a friendly pouchy face and sweet little lips that he pursed and nervously bit. Then there was Sheila, small and royal, with lush bags under her bitter eyes, narrow hips, and tiny breasts. And huge square-shaped Ed, who'd first invited me to share a joint with them behind the Student Union.

Behind the Student Union were a field of blue weeds and a half-built playground made of a swingless swing set, a rotted little merry-go-round, and a plastic red cube with half the red worn off. Water flashed from a rusted pipe in a little ditch. There were fireflies in the deepening sky. The traffic droned in the distance. It was a place of effaced sweetness, and we went to it every day to smoke and talk. After dark, Ed drove me home in his rattling car with its mad turn signal and tape deck full of surly love. His tape sang about a bridge of sighs like a drunk giant pushing a boulder up a mountain. A weird thunder of bells rumbled in the valley. Clouds flew by. I sank back in the dark. In Paris, the taxi dodged cars, ran up over the curb, over the walls of buildings, through apartments, out the windows, up over the sky. A woman's voice unscrolled and made a road in the sky for us to ride on. It was *La Traviata* on my father's record player, flying across the sea to carry me.

A dark blur sails over thought. Veronica emerges. Is she here simply because now I am sick and alone? Yes—no. Candles burn behind her. A small plate of half-eaten cake sits before her. *Rigoletto* is playing. "He wasn't a cunt," she says. "He was a Ganymede. A beautiful boy, a jester." Duncan bends over, reaching back with both hands to show his butt hole, naked except for little belled slippers and a striped belled hat. He grins over one shoulder. "The *'Caro nome,'*" says Veronica. Tears run down her face.

I kissed Ed on the cheek and got out of the car. In the house sat my father, drinking beer and waiting for dinner. *La Traviata* was on the record player. I said hi and walked through the room. Sara was in the dining room, crouching an inch away from the TV, straining to hear over the music. My mother was in the kitchen, stirring a fragrant pot. How I loved her. How I didn't know. *La Traviata* filled the house with woman's love. My tiny father sat in his tiny chair while the singer's giant voice took over his house. She sang of suffering and abasement. She sang of strength and love. Her voice made these feelings into great complex waves that opposed, then joined, then opposed one another again with a force that would've torn a lesser voice to pieces. My father's eyes were glazed with concentration and his jaw moved rhythmically from side to side as his mind rose up the crest of one wave, then down the other, then back up, riding their impossible heights until they met in a crescendo of passionate joining. I padded indifferently through the room, on my way to the kitchen for something to eat.

The worms go in, the worms go out. Lisa had no voice, and she was not an artist. But she had done it, too. Alex had pried her open and bullied her, and somehow, she had caught the force of his bullying and joined it to her own force. She caught it at just the right moment, made it into something sexual. And she didn't even know what she'd done. This is what Alex meant when he called her a "lady." This is what Alain meant when he called me "cold." I couldn't do what Lisa had done. I was too hard. I walked through the room, glanced at my father's music, glanced away. It wasn't that I was stupid. I could hear what it meant. But I would not let it in. I would not let myself be broken.

"You're different now," said Sara. "You walk through the house like you're alone on a beach. Like nobody's there but you."

Simone yelled, "Arrête!" and we spilled out in front of the club. *La Traviata* vanished into the dark. A regal woman with a fierce dog face held off the crowd. Simone dug in her purse for the cab fare. Two dirty young boys sauntered past. They slowed down, looking at the crowd. They had craning necks and rubbery faces full of gawking scorn. Something in me lighted up at the sight of them; they were like New Jersey boys. The regal dog at the door glowered at them and one of them laughed and shouted, *"Kalaxonez ton con!"* Somebody laughed. "What did he say?" I asked Simone. The kid yelled again, *"Petez des flames!"* She said, "'Go honk your pussy.' And 'Go fart flames.'" The fierce dog waved to us and let us in.

At night, I went to strip-mall bars and apartment parties with my new friends. People crowded in, ready for anything. They yelled and drank and sang. Sheila turned into an imp, talking out the side of its mouth, her words a buzzing cloud that hovered above her like smoke. Jeff sat on the floor rolling joints and grinning and generally giving the impression that he was melting into a puddle of goo. Denise became the ringmistress, sitting spread-legged on the edge of the couch, cutting lines of coke with military precision. We drank and snorted until we turned into robots and root vegetables dancing and singing in little pointed boots. *Back from suffragette city!* A guy with the face of a bloated sweet potato sang, "Hey, don't lean on me, man," and leaned into me hard. "Want to dance?" he slurred, and I shrank away so stiffly that he almost fell. You can't afford the ticket, I thought, but he heard it like I'd yelled and he yelled back—"Oh pardonez bitch-ez!" *Hoo ha!* "With her lips that she's always kissing at people, and her hair that she cream rinses!"—until Ed punched him in the face. The guy fell with one foot twisted under his skinny calf. Denise stood up so fast, she knocked down a bowl of goldfish. People roared with pleasure. The punched guy stood and ground a little dancing fish into the floor. He rubbed his face. "I'm sorry, man," he said. "I just wanted to dance with her." "Shut up," said Ed. He turned to me. His dulled eyes and slack mouth came close. Beyond him was the body of the little fish, mashed except for its poor staring head. A girl walked by with a set mouth and fierce staring eyes with little wet blobs of makeup underneath. Was this where I belonged? "I love you," whispered Ed.

Go honk your pussy. I looked at the beautiful nightclub crowd, the smart French businesswomen with matching gold jewelry, the models, the slouching playboys, the pretty boys and girls darting like minnows, and that's what I thought. I thought it all night. I thought it at myself when I went to use the bathroom and saw my reflection in a mirror filled with female faces, eyes made up smartly, but stupid with drunkenness, though sometimes shining nonetheless with intelligence at the very center. Lush fruits jumping down off a branch in human form and sauntering off.

Because it was hot and crowded in the apartment, Ed and I took some couch cushions and a sheet out onto the fire escape. I woke with the sun warming my eyeballs through the lids. The inside of my mouth was sore and sweet with alcohol. Compared to Alain or Jean-Paul, Ed was a very clumsy boy. He said he loved me, and all I could think of was the one who called me "bitch-ez." But I said, "I love you, too." Below us, beyond us, all around us, traffic ran.

Alain and Lisa walked in just as Simone and I were walking out. I looked at Lisa and instead of thinking, Go honk your pussy, I shouted it. Alain glared after me as if his face might break. *"Petez des flames!"* I screamed. It was two days later that I got home from a job and found he had changed the locks. Fifteen months later, I sat in Ed's car in the A&P lot with a copy of *Vogue* on my lap, sobbing and clawing at it. Lisa was on the cover. She was stunning. "I hate her!" I screamed. "I hate all of them!"

Ed sneaked a hot slit-eyed look at Lisa. I screamed, tore the cover off the magazine, and threw it into the lot. A lumpy old man watched it scud across the asphalt. He gave me an irritated look. I hunched down in the seat and sobbed. Lumpy Man got in his car. Ed fiddled with his keys. "Why don't you go to New York and be a model?" he asked. "You still could."

"No," I moaned. "No, never."

"Then why don't you go be a poet?"

"I'm not a poet, Ed." I sat up and stopped crying.
"Then why don't you just go?"

The bus humps and huffs as it makes a labored circle around a
block of discount stores and a deserted grocery. As the bus leans
hard to one side, its gears make a high whinging sound, like
we're streaking through space. Looking beyond the stores, I
glimpse green hills and a cross section of sidewalks with little
figures toiling on them. Pieces of life packed in hard skulls with
soft eyes looking out, toiling up and down, around and around.
More distant green, the side of a building. The bus comes out of
the turn and stops at the transfer point. It sags down with a
gassy sigh. Every passenger's ass feels its churning, bumping
motor. Every ass thus connected, and moving forward with the
bus. The old white lady across the aisle from me sits on her stiff
haunches, eating wet green grapes from a plastic bag and peering out to see who's getting on. The crabbed door suctions
open. Teenagers stomp up through it, big kids in flapping
clothes with big voices in flapping words. "Cuz like—whatcho
look—you was just a—ain't lookin' at you!" The old lady does
not look. But I can feel her taking them in. Their energy pours
over her skin, into her blood, heart, spine, and brain. Watering
the flowers of her brain. The bag of green grapes sits ignored
on her lap. Private snack suspended for public feast of youth.
She would never be so close to them except on the bus. Neither
would I. For a minute, I feel sorry for rich people alone in their
cars. I look down on one now, just visible through her windshield, sparkling bracelets on hard forearm, clutching the wheel,
a fancy-pant thigh, a pulled-down mouth, a hairdo. Bits of light
fly across her windshield. I can see her mind beating around the
closed car like a bird. Locked in with privileges and pleasures,
but also with pain.

Just a week before I got locked out of the apartment on rue du Temple, I saw something I still don't understand. Without understanding, it has become the reason I can forgive Alain. It happened so early in the morning, it was still dark. I awakened to sounds from the kitchen—Alain's night voice, plus frying butter. I got up and went down the hall. Alain was at the stove, his back to me. At the table was the man I had seen licking the floor at the sadomasochist club. He was sitting in my place. He was naked except for Alain's coat, which was draped over him. Under the coat, he was like a skeleton with hair and dirt on it. I could see the bottoms of his filthy feet and the rims of his toenails, thick and yellow as a dog's. I stood at the door, invisible and dumb. He stared at me like he was staring into pitch-darkness. Alain turned from the stove; he held a plate with an omelette on it. He had made it with jam. He put the sweet plate gently before the skeleton. "There," he said tenderly. "For you!" He pulled a chair out from the table and sat in it. "Go on!" he said. Alone in the dark, the creature ate, quickly and devouringly. Watching him eat was almost like watching him crawl, even though you didn't have to see his balls or his ass. Like the German woman, he ate as if he could not taste. Lack of taste had made her indifferent to eating. It made him ravenous. It made him crawl on his hands and knees through the no taste, trying to find taste. Alain put his elbow on the table and leaned toward him, enrapt. He didn't see or care when I turned and walked away.

Later, I called Jean-Paul to tell him what I had seen. He would know who the skeleton man was, I thought, and he might know why Alain would take him home and put him in my chair. There was so much music and laughter on his end of the line that it took a while for him to understand me.

"Ah," he said finally. "It is hard to believe, but this man was once a very successful agent."

"A modeling agent?"

"A long time ago, yes. I've heard that he was a friend of Alain's father. But don't tell him I said so, okay?"

This incident was so peculiar to me that I didn't tell anyone about it for a long time. Veronica was the first person I told. We were working late in a conference room, wrapped in a membrane of office noise, the clicking and whirring of machines soothing and uniting like the rumbling bus.

"I understand now why you loved him," she said.

"You *do?*"

"Yes. He was willing to go places most people won't go. He was looking at himself, you know. Most people won't do that."

She was a fool to talk that way—"you know." Like she could know anything about Alain or where most people would go. One side of her lips curved up in a repulsive know-it-all style, sensual and tight. But her eyes were gentle and calm. I knew how trite and smug she was being, and I felt superior to it. But I didn't know the gentleness of her eyes. They were like windows in a prison cell—you look out and the sky comforts you without your knowing why. Unknowing, I took comfort and went back to feeling superior. Maybe I was able to feel the comfort because I half-despised it. I don't know. But it helped me to forgive Alain.

When I saw Jean-Paul next, I tried to ask him more about Alain's father. We were at a party, some kind of function. It was dark and crowded. Big plates of food soaked up the smoke in the air. Jean-Paul frowned and blearily leaned into me, trying to hear. The beauty of his eyes was marred by deep stupor. Rum-soaked spongy crumbs fell down his rumpled shirtfront. One hand drunkenly cleaned the shirt; the other loaded the wet mouth with more tumbling crumbs. An ass paraded by in orange silk. Half the crumbs went down the shirt. He did not know who I meant. His tongue came out and licked. "Alain's father," I repeated. "How did he know that man who crawls on the floor of that place?" Recognition lit his stupor and made it flash like a sign. "You believed that?" he cried. "Ha ha ha ha!" He threw his head back into the darkness of the room, rubbed with the red and purple of muddled sex and appetite, drunken faces smeared into it and grinning out of it. His handsome face was a wreck before my eyes. The smell of wreckage came out of his open jacket as he leaned over to cram more food in his mouth. Ha ha ha! Tiny humans lost in tiny human hell, with all hell's rich flavors.

We ride past precious stores for rich people. The Rites of Passage bookshop. A Touch of Flair. A French-style pastry shop painted gold and red, the window heaped with cakes. The bus flies over the cakes in a blur of windowpane light.

If I do see René's rose-colored lamp beside my deathbed, it will be beautiful to me. I will want to touch and linger on every thread of its carefully woven fabric, especially the bits of gold that you half-see when you lean up close to shut off the light and then forget. I will cry to think I ever forgot. I will cry to lose it. It will be the same if Jean-Paul appears before my bed in a dark nimbus of smells and party music. His oafish ridicule will be sweet, like wine. Because I won't taste it again. I'll wish I could hold his bloated, blinking face in both my hands and kiss it good-bye. I'll want to take back the curse I muttered as I turned away. Or maybe I won't. Maybe I'll miss that, too.

The bus stops at the light. Sun shines lovingly through the cloud cover and warms us through the dirty windowpanes. The bus hums in the light. We are all quiet in the warmth and the sound of the humming motor. I look outside and see a little budding tree, its slim black body shining with rain. Joyous and intelligent, like a fresh girl, the earth all new to its slender, seeking roots. I think of Trisha, erect and seeking with sparkling eyes. A fleshy nimble tree, laughing as it discovers the dirt. Stretching up its limbs to tell the sky what it's found.

This moment could come to me on my deathbed, too. If it does, I will love it so much that I will take it into death with me. Perhaps if I try, it will dissolve in my arms. But I will try.

The light changes. The bus chugs forward. Veronica's face floats in the window for an instant before blending with mine. She was right: Alain did go where most people wouldn't, though not because he willed it. He couldn't help it. The storm of movement was in him all the time. He lived in pieces, jumping from one falling meteor to the next, and going wherever it went. Of course, everybody has different directions in them. I saw three in my mother when Daphne and I met her in the family diner, and she had more than that. But she was not quick or flexible enough to jump from one to another. Even just to feel three at once made her awkward and confused. She didn't have the strength to hold that much opposition in one place. That's why she went back to my father. She still had all her different directions. She just chose to ignore most of them. She came back and became Mod again, *mom* with a hard *d* and a nasal *o*.

But sometimes the other directions took shape and ran against one another, filling the house with invisible war. At night, I sometimes started up with my heart pounding, scared not by a dream but by an image flying loose from thought, big and loud as a freight train: my parents in their room upstairs, their faces distorted with hate, screaming curses and lunging at each other with knives.

I yank the rope, signal the driver that it's my stop. His head is a human pellet against the wide gray windshield. Directions:

Mottled light and shadow go down; droning wipers go side to side; driver's head goes up.

Alain had the strength and the flexibility; that was his misfortune. I saw him with his daughter once on a windy street. I knelt to meet her; he knelt, too. He pressed her cheek to his and introduced her as "Tiny Duck." He didn't introduce me to her. She didn't mind. She laughed and put her hand on his head and said "Goose" in English. He laughed, and I saw his eyes were the same as they were with me. He could not stop, even for her. He could not stop even to be sad about it. Speaking English back to her, he said "Duck" in a mock-British accent and put his hand on her head. "Duck"; he put his hand on my head. "Goose," and she put her hand on him. She didn't look at me. She must've met a lot of girls named Duck.

We stop at the curb; the door suctions open. A mist of rain and traffic noise floats in and breaks apart. People stir and cough. I come down the aisle of heads. Duck, duck. The driver acknowledges me with the hard side of his silent head. Goose. His human hand squeezes and pulls; his crabbed wing of a door folds closed. The bus drives off with a loud swoosh, a gray rainbow of sound that twinkles and evaporates. In the distance, Alain and my mother sparkle and evaporate.

I turn off the main street and go down a wide road into a grove of giant redwood trees. It is a canyon at the foot of a mountain. It is a dignity preserve for rich people. Homes are set way back from the street or nested up on high hills with wooden stairways winding up their sides. Invisible children yell and run down an invisible path. The sun flashes in an attic window. The wet pavement is lush as a stone sponge. Giant trees grow up out of it and buckle it with their knotted muscley roots. Their bark is porous, like breathing skin. Through their skin you feel the beat of their huge hearts from deep in the ground. People drive slowly and weave around them, passing one at a time. I picture the lady I saw in the car with the bracelets driving through the trees, her mind fluttering against the glass.

When I first moved here, I lived in this town. I didn't live in the canyon, but I'd come to walk in it. I'd come especially when I felt afraid, knowing I had hepatitis but not feeling sick yet. I'd look at the big trees and the mountain and I'd think that no matter how big any human sickness might be, they were bigger. Now I'm not so sure. How much sickness can even a huge heart take before it gets sick itself? The canyon is full of dead and dying oaks. Scientists don't know why. It's hard to believe we didn't kill them.

The wind rises. The rain dashes sideways. Slowly, the trees throw their great hair. Their trunks creak and mull. My fever makes a wall in my brain. A door appears in the wall. It opens and another dream comes out. Is it from last night, or the night before, or every night? In it, a man and woman are on a high-speed train that never stops. Music is playing, a mechanical xylophone rippling manically up a high four-note scale again and again. *Bing bing bing bing!* It is the sound of a giant nervous system. The man and woman are built into this system and they cannot leave it. They are crying. Looking out the window, they see people hunting animals on game preserves. There are almost no animals left, so they have to be recycled—brought back to life after they've been killed and hunted again. Mobs of people chase a bear trying to run on artificial legs. It screams with fear and rage. The man and woman cry. They are part of it. They can do nothing. *Bing bing bing bing!*

My forehead breaks into a sweat. I unfasten a button and loosen my scarf. The air cools my skin; the fever recoils, then sends hot tadpoles wiggling against the cold. Drive the animal before you and never stop. Starve it, cut it, stuff silicone in it.

Feed it until it's too fat to think or feel. Then cut it open and suck the fat out. Sew it up and give it medication for pain. Make it run on the treadmill, faster, faster. Examine it for flaws. Not just the body but the mind, too. Keep going over the symptoms. It's not a character defect; it's an illness. Give it medication for pain. Dazzle its eyes with visions of beauty. Dazzle its ears with music that never stops playing. Send it to graze in vast aisles of food so huge and flawless that it seems to be straining to become something more than food. Dazzle its mind with visions of terror. Set it chasing a hot, rippling heaven from which illness and pain have been removed forever. Set it fleeing the silent darkness that is always at its heels. Suck it out. Sew it up. Run. When the dark comes, pray: I love my ass.

I button my coat and let myself sweat. I try to think of something else. I think of an interview I heard with a religious person who had two kinds of cancer. The radio host asked her if she'd prayed for God to heal her. She said that she had and that it hadn't worked. When she realized she was going to die, she asked God why He hadn't healed her, and He answered. She actually heard His voice. He said, "But I am."

I am not religious, but when I heard that, I said yes inside. I say it now. I don't know why. There's a reason, but it's outside my vision.

On the sidewalk, leaves dissolve into mud. Another door opens and Veronica comes out, exhaling her smoke with a swift, cool snort. "No, hon," she says. "That's your sphincter." The mud and leaves go into a slow churn, so slow that it's invisible to me, but I can feel it. I feel something rising from the churning, also invisible. Something we haven't killed and never will.

I went to community college two more semesters. Instead of poetry, I concentrated on word-processing classes. When I felt I was skilled enough to get a job, I quit. I moved to Manhattan when a friend of a friend told me about a friend (named Candy) who needed a roommate for a six-month sublet. My father said, "Why? You were doing so well." I told him, "Because I'm too bored to live here," and he just shook his head. "You always expected so much," said my mother. "You expect even more after what happened. You have to enjoy what you have." And I replied, "But I don't have anything here. I need to go where I can have something." My father looked down and left the room. I had hurt him, but he couldn't do anything about it—I still had what was left of the French money and I could do what I wanted.

Ed drove me to the city with some furniture, clothing, and a few plants. My sublet was a loft in the meatpacking district, a labyrinth of sleeping rough-faced buildings with sweet and rotting breath. We took my bags up in a clanking freight elevator with a frayed cable that you could see quivering tensely through the broken ceiling fan. When we reached the top, we emerged to find a stout gray-haired man in leather unlocking his door.

"We use that elevator to remove the bodies of our victims," he said. He spoke in an aggressive, fluting little voice. "Welcome to New York," he added, and shut himself in. The door across from him opened. "Don't pay any attention to Percival," said Candy. "He's just being silly again."

Candy was a pretty southern girl with a weak chin wearing pink paisley shoes. She smiled and led us down a long hall to a big living room lined with huge windows full of daylight. She made us martinis and said, "Don't you think we're special people to be in a loft in Manhattan, drinking real martinis?"

Late that night, the sleeping buildings woke and opened for business. I stood in a window as tall as a door and watched heavy trucks feed fresh-killed beef to an openmouthed warehouse across the street. The light from the open mouth shone on one and a half cows at a time, their bodies hanging inverted on the conveyor belt, heads wagging on fresh-cut throats, horned shadows nodding on the warehouse wall. The belt droned and the massed corpses danced with jiggling forefeet. The man operating the belt whistled a song. A snout and gentle brow was flung out, then rolled back into the mass. The man driving the truck joked with the man running the belt. I can accept this, I thought. I can live this life.

The next morning, I began interviewing for secretarial positions, including one at an intellectual magazine run by a tiny woman with a dry face. "I quite like you," said the woman. "There's something spooky and incongruous about you. You don't look like a girl from a community college in New Jersey, but unfortunately, that's what you are. Everyone else I've spoken to is more qualified than you—though likely you'd do the job better." She gave me an application and told me to call her in a few days.

"She must really like you," whispered her current secretary as I left the office. "She usually rolls her eyes at me when she's seeing people out."

"What the hell would you do in a place like that?" asked Ed. "It doesn't pay, and she's obviously a bitch."

"I could learn about editing. I could become an assistant and then something else."

He was visiting me for the weekend. We'd just seen a movie and we were walking to a Korean deli for bags of cherries and grapes. There were a lot of hookers standing around, flashing like something at the bottom of a deep well. A tall black girl and a little blonde came into the store behind us to buy cigarettes and two rolls of breath mints. The man behind the counter said, "Hey, slim" to the black girl. When we left, Ed said, "I saw you looking at them."

"So?"

"You look at those girls, those whores, like they're something great."

"It's just . . . those two in the store were really pretty. The black girl looked like a model."

"A model! Are you kidding me? She didn't look like a model. She looked like shit, because that's what she is."

"I know what a model looks like," I said sharply.

We went to the loft and ate our fruit lying in my bed naked, piling the cherry pits in a white Kleenex on the bedside table.

"You're not going to try to model?" he asked.

"No. And anyway, if you don't like whores, you shouldn't like models, either."

I reminded him of Lisa at Naxos with her hand down her pants. For the dozenth time, he asked me if I had ever done anything like that. For the dozenth time, I said no, because I was the mistress of the most powerful agent in Europe and I didn't have to. But a lot of girls did. We were quiet and I felt his discomfort. I stared at the ceiling, watching shadows come and go through a stretched square of light. Soon he would want to go, and I would let him.

I called the tiny dry editor. "Goodness," she said. "I had completely forgotten about you. I'm afraid this week's not so good after all. I still haven't looked at your application. Could you call next week?"

"Do you think she's serious?" I asked Candy.

"I don't know," she said. "She sounds like a bitch."

I registered at a temp agency with stick furniture and a thin carpet, the color of which made me think of cholera. When I walked in, the gimlet girl behind the desk sat up straight and stared. I remembered my fifteen-year-old enemy, one sharp elbow sticking out as she stroked the dresses that lay over her arm. I applied for a word-processing job and checked the box that said "night shift." She sent me to an advertising firm that evening.

The office was on the forty-second floor of a beautiful half cylinder of steel and glass. The word-processing room was large and curved, with whole walls made of enormous windows that had no glare on them. The supervisor showed me to my desk— a section of long table blocked off by low plastic barriers. Some day workers were finishing up a birthday party at the end of the table. There was laughter and crumbling cake. I turned on my machine, and a black square of infinity appeared, one flashing square star in its upper left corner. There was a burst of laughter. I glanced sideways and saw a strange little figure coming down the hall. From a distance, her whole face looked askew, puckered like flesh around a badly healed wound. She came closer. I saw the wounded pucker was a smile. She sat across from me. "Hi, hon," she said.

The mouth of the canyon opens to swallow the road. I walk down its slippery muddy throat. Old trees slowly tip into the ravine, gripping the crumbling pavement on one side, seizing fists of wet earth on the other. Their root systems come out of the soaked embankment like facial bones, clenched in unseeable expressions. At the bottom, their children—oak and madrone— stand close together and hold open their shining arms. They are covered to the waist with wet chartreuse moss; it grows away from the trunks in long green hairs that stand in the air like prehensile sense organs. I take off a glove and stroke the cold fur, then sniff my rank, wormy palm. I put my hand on the tree again to see my white skin against the green. When I was a kid, chartreuse was my favorite color. But I didn't think it was real.

Up close, she was not askew in any way. She was monstrously ordered. In her plaid suit, ruffled blouse, and bow tie, she was like a human cuckoo clock. She gave me a pursed smile, lighted a cigarette, and opened a magazine. We sat a long time with no work. I stared out the window. The East River became a dark length of flickering movement with a lit boat on it. In Queens, the neon sign of a sugar factory rose up, its script burning red and radiant in the night.

"Excuse me," said Veronica. "Have you spent time in Paris, hon?"

I was surprised, but I just said, "Yeah."

"I thought so. You have a Parisian aura." She turned her head sideways and worked her throat, head back, cigarette angled rakishly up and out. "I haven't been there for ages, but I do so well remember the Jardins du Luxembourg in autumn, with the yellow horse chestnuts in bloom."

We were paired again for the next three nights. I got used to the strange, strident pitch of her voice, even felt oddly caressed by its twists and changes. I talked to her about looking for a job. I told her about the editor calling me "spooky and incongruous."

"Really? Dorothea Atcheson called you spooky? How delightful."

"You *know* her?"

"Not personally. But I've read her publication."

"I filled out an application, but when I called her, she said she'd forgotten about me. Then she said to call back this week. Do you think she's serious?"

"No. Yes. Who knows if anybody's serious? But I can imagine Dorothea Atcheson would appreciate you."

Her voice on *appreciate* was like the rough tongue of a cat absently licking a kitten on the head. I could not help raising my head to meet it.

The next day, I called Dorothea Atcheson. "You're going to think I'm awful," she said, "but I've lost your application. Do you suppose you could run by the office and fill out another one?"

"*Well,*" said Veronica. She drew on her cigarette and tipped her head back; her throat beat like an intelligent heart. She exhaled and asked, "Have you ever seen *A Star Is Born* with Judy Garland and James Mason?"

I shook my head.

"It's worth buying a VCR for, but barring that, look for it late on the Movie Channel; they show it constantly." She smoked; her heart-throat beat. "It's about a girl whose dreams aren't big enough, who gets a break and becomes a star."

"My dreams aren't the problem. I'm looking for a job as a secretary and I can't get one because I'm not qualified."

"Judy Garland isn't qualified, either! But she meets someone who sees her qualities, who believes in her."

Another proofreader, a balding little queen named Alan, wheeled round in his frayed throne. "And then he kills himself because she's left him in the dust."

"'It's too late!'" cried Veronica. "'I destroy everything I touch. I always have! You've come too late!'"

"'No!'" fluted Alan. "'It's not too late, not for you, not for me!'"

"'Believe it!'" exulted Veronica. "'Believe it! Believe it!'"

In nine of the pictures, it was ridiculous and ugly. But in the tenth one, it was thrilling. I smiled.

Veronica exhaled her smoke and smiled back with fierce, fancy-twisted warmth. "You won't be here long, hon," she said. "Trust me."

I cross into the canyon on a wooden footbridge. The stream below is awake and rushing, light tossing on its cold flux. Silver wrinkles flow in a quick sheet, churn into foam, disperse and sink, flow up and wrinkle the water again. Bright algae, pebbles, and tiny fish stir back and forth. I step off the bridge; huge and calm, the landscape unfolds. Silent and still, it rings with force and hidden motion. The ringing strength is like blood singing in the body of the ground—passionate music you don't hear with your ear, but feel just outside your senses. Redwoods rise up straight; madrones elegantly wind. Soaked moss and brilliant leaves fill the air with green and tender feeling. Tenderness seeps into and softens my fever. The unfolding deepens.

I said I had not gone to New York to be a model, and I hadn't. I'd gone there for life and sex and cruelty. Not something you learn in community college. Not something you write in a note-book. The city was so big and bright that for a moment my terrible heaven paled, then went invisible. I thought it was gone, but what I couldn't see, I felt walking next to me in streets full of vying people. I felt it in their fixed outthrust faces, their busy rigid backs, their jiggling jewelry, their creeping and swagger. I

Mary Gaitskill

felt it in the office workers who perched in flocks on the concrete flower boxes of giant corporate banks, eating their lunches over crossed legs and rumpled laps, the wind blowing their hair in their chewing mouths and waves of scabby pigeons surging at their feet, eating the bits that fell on the pavement. I felt it in the rough sensate hands of subway musicians playing on drums and guitars while the singer collected money with his cup, still singing like he was talking to himself in a carelessly beautiful voice while riders streamed down concrete stairs like drab birds made fantastic in flight. I felt monstrous wants and gorgeous terrors that found form in radio songs, movie screens, billboards, layers of posters on decayed walls, public dreams bleeding into one another on cheap paper like they might bleed from person to person. I took it in and fed on it, and for a while, that was enough.

Then one day on my way to work, a cab stopped in front of me on a trash-blown street and Alana got out. I looked at her and my breath stopped. She slammed the cab door; her shining hair flashed about her face. I stood still while everybody else crossed the street. She walked lightly in neat white boots, but her eyes gave off the cold glow of an eel whipping through remote water. Down, down through the water floated a magazine picture of a girl in crumpled lace. A picture like a door with music behind it, rolling with the water and soon to be erased by it. "Alana," I said, but too softly. She walked past me without turning. My face burned. And I wanted heaven again.

But I didn't know how to get it. Before I had gotten it because a hand had picked me up and put me in the middle of it. Then I lost it because a hand removed me. I knew Alain's hand could reach across the ocean; I knew he was associated with two powerful New York agencies. Candy said he probably had too much on his mind to bother with me. But she hadn't seen him naked, with coke coming out his nose, pacing and yelling into the

116

phone, looking for people who might've said something bad about him just so that he could fuck them up. Years later and miles away, I still saw him. I saw my hands walking on rich red carpet like paws, me laughing at my legs in the air and his dick inside me. Or panting and openmouthed, a tiny strand of saliva glistening between me and the rug before it dropped.

I looked for another hand to find me. I walked the street, searching for men in beautiful suits, searching their faces for the lips of a spider drinking blood with pure, blank bliss. If I found one, I would look into his eyes, and usually he would look back. If he asked me for my number, I would ask him for his card. The first few times, I looked at the card, put it in my pocket, and mentally threw it away. The last time, I dropped it on the pavement and cursed the gentleman spider to his face.

I stopped looking for a permanent job. I went out whenever I could, under any circumstance. When Sheila's cousin in Brooklyn had a birthday party, I took the train out, only to stand in a sparsely furnished room with strangers. When a temp at the office gave a reading combined with a dance performance, I showed up to watch determined girls in leotards creep and crouch across a ratty stage drenched in nightmare orange. A friend of Candy's—a harmless girl I despised for being harmless—invited us to a bachelorette party and I went.

No matter how unfashionable the party, fashionable music was always playing. The fashion then was silly and sepulchral at once, with hopping, skipping beats playing off a funereal overlay. Somebody sang, "This kiss will never fade away," his voice like an oily black machine operating a merry-go-round of music flying on grossly painted wings. "It's about the bombing of Dresden," said a drunk boy. "Excuse me," I said, and walked away. Heat flared in the flying music, then died like an explosion seen from far away. People walked around smiling and talking while the music likened mass death to a kiss and gave silliness a proud twist to its head. *This kiss will never fade away.* Alain kissed me forever while I stood on the outskirts of parties, watching people who meant something to one another. A fat person with an out-thrust jawbone took someone's hand and squeezed it; there was a burst of goodwill. A woman with desperately bony calves, made stark by her big high heels, grinned at someone across the room, her grin a signal of deep things inside both of them that nobody else could see. Sometimes I saw the goodwill and the deep things and longed to know them. Sometimes I saw the thrusting jaw and the bony calves and turned up my nose. Because I could never fully have either feeling, I stayed detached. It was as if I were seventeen again and longing to live inside a world described by music—a world that was sad at being turned into a machine, but ecstatic, too, singing on the surface of its human heart as the machine spread through its tissues and silenced the flow of its blood. In this world, there were no deep things, no vulgar goodwill, only rigorous form and beauty, and even songs about mass death could be sung on the light and playful surface of the heart.

I didn't say any of this. I didn't even think it. But it was visible in the way I held my body, and in my bitter, despising eyes. Other people could see it in me as surely as I saw it in them. And so I was able to make friends. I went to nightclubs with an "actress" named Joy, who might've been a model if not for hips that would've been ungainly in a photograph, but which gave her living walk a pleasing, viscous reek. She worked as a hostess in a piano bar, where she got paid to drink and talk to lonely businessmen. She lived in a tiny shotgun apartment piled with dirty dishes, cat boxes, and open jars of clawed-at cold cream. Hurled pairs of pants tried to flee across the couch; wilted dresses snored on the kitchen chairs. The two cats tore the stuffing out of the couch and rolled toilet paper down the hall. During the day, Joy sat in this ragged nest like a princess, bathing in the kitchen with one gleaming pink foot perched on the edge of the tub, or sitting wrapped in a soiled comforter to drink coffee and eat cheesecake out of a tin. At night, she sailed out wearing absurd clothes as if they were Givenchy gowns. Once when I complimented her on one of her mismatched earrings, she pointed at the sky and said, "That earring means, Don't look at my finger; look at the moon."

Together, we were assured admittance to exclusive clubs where, lifted up and out of the hoi polloi and deposited at the entrance by the doorman's fastidious gaze, we handed our coats to a gaunt creature in a coat-lined cave, then walked down the glowing sound-chamber hall, where music, lightly skipping in the main rooms, here bumbled from wall to wall like a ghost groaning in purgatory. We turned a corner and the music showed its laughing public face. We entered the great night flower of fun, open and dark like a giant lily swarming with drunken fairies. Into the swarm we flew, Joy darting, hovering, seeking and finding the inevitable man handing out cocaine to girls.

Our conversation was so much torn paper on the surging current of our united forward intent. But at some point, she would lean with her hip against me, and her body would talk to me, light and charmingly, of earrings and the moon. And at some other point, I would emerge from the bathroom and she would be gone, leaving me to wander with drunken, burning eyes, seeking a way into heaven. Sometimes I would wake with a dry mouth in the dim apartment of a naked man who'd promised he was that way but whose snoring face now denied it.

If I called Joy, she would tell me of her own adventures, of this one's amazing kiss, or that one's art-world status. Otherwise, I didn't hear from her until she wanted to go out again; if I wasn't able to go out that night, she quickly got off the phone.

Then there was Cecilia, with whom I went to movies and coffee and sometimes dinner. She had meager beauty and magnificent style. Her face was made of such dramatic planes that I remember her with her big bossy nose on sideways, one intense little eye to the side of it and the other peering over its humped middle. She wore jewelry and hats and she sat in a sideways twist. She wrote plays. She had a rich family, who paid for her huge place; when she was depressed and feeling "trapped," she would check into a suite at the Plaza for the weekend and return feeling refreshed. Most of our conversations were ironic and lively on the first layer, blunt and fixed on the second and only layer down. But she once called me late at night, crying because she felt ashamed of her wealth and her privileged family. "We thought we were so great because magazines came and photographed our fucking unlivable living room. But we were shit! Alison, we were shit! I don't want to be shit! I want to be a real person!" I didn't know what to say; dimly I understood, and was moved. But when I called her the next day, she just talked about a party she was giving, one to which she had not invited me. "I need people who can talk about the arts and current events," she said. "It's that kind of party."

"That is so rude," said Candy.

But to me, it wasn't. I understood that Cecilia looked at me as an object with specific functions, because that's how I looked at her. Without knowing it, that is how I looked at everyone who came into my life then. This wasn't because I had no feelings. I wanted to know people. I wanted to love. But I didn't realize how badly I had been hurt. I didn't realize that my habit of distance had become so unconscious and deep that I didn't know how to be with another person. I could only fix that person in my imagination and turn him this way and that, trying to feel him, until my mind was tired and raw.

Heart pounding dully, I climb the outer ridge of a small but steep hill. I can smell my fever coming off me like mist. Tired and raw. My whole being is tired and raw. At the top of the hill are rotting trees, dying as they stand. I shouldn't be walking up this hill. I should be home in bed. With each step, I sway in my basket of tendons and bones, my mind too weak to turn anything any way. My mind can't protect me from feeling, and I'm glad for that. Sight and sound flow into it; feeling bleeds out of it. I walk up the mountain now because soon I may be too sick to do it. But still, I'm glad.

At the bottom of the ridge, dead oaks have fallen, blanched as old bones, dry even in the rain. Above me, living trees list and groan. I climb over the bones. The gray bark of the freshly dead is loose and cracked open; pale lacy whorls of fern cling to it in clumps, like tangled baby's hair. Sensitive and perseverant, they cling to and comfort death. Beneath the fern, the bark is mottled with light green mold, feeding lovingly. My thoughts dissolve in the gray and green, traveling from life to death to life.

I did not fix Veronica in my mind, or turn her this way and that, because I didn't care about her. But I was tolerant enough to take her in at the regular low decibel of work-time conversation. I was not interested in her, but I was curious about her, like I might be curious about an elaborate object. The cuckoo clock sounded the hour; the bird popped out. I listened to her talk about her movies, her six seal-point Siamese cats, and her bisexual boyfriend, Duncan. On either side of the clock face, tiny wooden doors sprang open and figures with blind eyes and puckered lips came whirring out to kiss.

She and Duncan picnicked in Central Park late at night, she in a white lace dress, he in gray flannel pants and a straw boater. They packed their basket with smoked salmon, white bread, pâté, olives, grapes, and deviled eggs. They lounged in the black and shadowed grass, drinking wine from the bottle. *La Bohème* played on a cheap cassette deck with spools that creaked and strained. *"Quando men vo soletta per la via,"* sang Duncan, *"la gente sosta e mira e la bellezza mia . . ."* A gang of tough black kids drew near, then withdrew in bewilderment, one of them looking wide-eyed over his shoulder as he went. Duncan said, "Just a minute," then got up and walked away. Veronica was left alone with love creaking and straining in the dark. An enormous cloud streamed across the sky, making the moon a radiant blur. It was beautiful, the voices coming out of the tiny machine to deepen a patch of night, a shimmering skin of eternal love cracked and strained, with mortality coming through. *"Così l'effluvio del desìo tutta m'aggira, felice mi fa, felice mi fa!"* Her heart beat. She was afraid. Some bushes stirred. Had Duncan gone to the wide-eyed boy? She sat up, heart pounding. But it was him, coming back to her—and with him were two ragged white children, a small boy and a smaller girl.

"Who were they?" I asked.

"They lived in the tunnels under the subways. They'd come up looking for food for their family. Duncan knew the boy somehow—not *that* way, he said."

The boy stood whispering to Duncan. The girl squatted next to Veronica, blinking curiously. Her clothes, her face, her hair were coated in oily gray dirt. When Veronica called her "hon," she bared her teeth, then smiled. Veronica wanted to take them to the police, but they shook their heads vehemently; the cops would take them from their parents, said the boy. Instead, they greedily ate the grapes and then the bread. Veronica wished they had cookies to give them; she wished she could comb the girl's hair. Duncan asked about somebody named Ray; in a careful voice, the boy said he was sick. They put the rest of the food in the basket and gave it to the children. They watched them carry it into the dark, each holding the handle like a modern Hansel and Gretel, filthy, sick, and innocent.

"Who was Ray?" I asked.

"I don't know. Another of Duncan's boys, I assume. Excuse me, hon." In a curve of light on the convex face of my screen, Veronica's tiny reflection approached the supervisor's tiny desk. The fun-house curve stretched her body pencil-thin, then mashed it, then pulled it grossly wide. I had a second of feeling—what was it? She came back, gross, mashed, elongated, then, stepping out of the curve, disappeared.

Another time, they went to the Museum of Modern Art, then returned to the park to ride the carousel, where stumbling security guards chased a shrieking homeless woman around the rising, falling ponies. They dined with an elegant old man, an author and lover of opera—"He once cared for Jean-Paul Belmondo's dogs, exquisite chows"—who called them "Lord and Lady Bracknell."

"To lose one's girlfriend is perhaps careless," said Lord Bracknell. "But to lose one's boyfriend is incorrigible."

"To lose one's boyfriend is also impossible," replied Lady Bracknell, "when one has so many."

"Ah, but so many is the same as one, my love, and their one is nothing to your two."

Lady Bracknell's words were elegant in fragrant shapely smoke fresh from her throat. The red impress of her striated lower lip was perfect on her Styrofoam cup. The sugar sign beamed its red message across the river. Safety, it said. Stillness. Sweetness.

Lord Bracknell's young lover arrived and there was a scene. He was a somewhat unclean but fetching boy with pocked skin and sullen, flashing eyes. He looked at Lady Bracknell and said, "Who's the fish?" "Better fresh fish than rotten meat," said she. "You don't look so fresh to me," he sniffed. "I'm still fresher than you smell, young man." Lord Bracknell laughed like a hyena in a lace ruff and kissed his lady good-bye, first on her lips and then her hand. He was off into the night with his pro-tégé. Veronica shared a cab home with the elegant and embar-rassed old man. The little wooden doors had whirred shut on the little kissing figures.

. . .

I stop to wipe the sweat gathered at my eyebrows. My bad arm twinges as I crush it against my side, pinning the umbrella in place while I get the aspirin and water bottle from my bag. I imagine massed atoms of gray and green rising from the ground in a moving cloud, twinkling like motes of dust, except alive, complex, full of joy and perversity. Alain's eyes—perhaps they were the human form of this. Perhaps Duncan was the human form of this in his entirety. I imagine myself blundering through a night haunt, amid plain people dressed so fantastically, they make my beauty trite—an enormous cloud streams across the room and there is Duncan, singing, *"E tu che sai, che memori e ti struggi da me tanto rifuggi."* I go into a bathroom, where the thudding music is dulled, and there a tinny thread of *La Bohème* flashes and disappears amid voices and rushing water—back to the enchanted park where Veronica and Duncan picnicked with their children. Walking home one morning—cold white sky with a thin aura of liquid gold quivering on buildings and roaring trucks—I saw a prostitute haggling with a john. Mockingly, she shouted, "Hey, blondie!" There was Duncan kissing Veronica in the street, and I did not care about heaven.

I smiled and said, "Good morning!" with such warmth that the prostitute looked abashed.

"Have you ever thought of modeling, hon?"

"I already was a model." I didn't take my eyes off the word processor.

"Really? What kind? Catalog or—"

"Print. Runway. Paris."

"And what are you doing *here*?" she asked.

"I'm here because I got cheated out of all my money and made bad enemies." I trembled inside to talk about it. My contempt rose up to steady my trembling. "It's a horrible business," I snapped. "I'd never do it again."

There was a wondering silence. Veronica smoked with her lips in a sideways purse so she could stare at me as she inhaled; her eyes flared with each tiny facial twist.

"How did you get into modeling to begin with?"

"By fucking a nobody catalog agent who grabbed my crotch."

I didn't have to be embarrassed or make up something nice, because Veronica was nobody. My disdain was so habitual, I didn't notice it. But she did. She said, "Every pretty girl has a story like that, hon. I had that prettiness. I have those stories. I don't have to do that anymore, though. It's my show now." And she turned into a movie star, strutting past me while I gawked.

It's raining again. I am deep in the unfolding. All around me living green opens and closes, undulating in ripples and great waves. The creek flashes, eager for the piercing rain, its hard, concentrated pouring. A slim tree naked of bark, ocher, smooth, comes out of the ground in a sinuous twist. A piece of fungus grows in a neat half wheel around a twig, like a hat on a lady with a long neck. I think of Veronica. I speak aloud. "I don't have to do that anymore. It's nobody's show now."

"Well, hon, if I were you, I'd try again. This is New York, not Paris." She lighted another cigarette. "But this time, don't let anybody grab your crotch." And she smiled.

One evening when I was walking in the East Village with Candy, we came on a party that had spilled out of an apartment building; people stood on the sidewalk, drinking from plastic cups, or lounged on the hoods of cars, like the girl in black laughing at the boy who tried to kiss the bottom of her silver shoe. Music fell out windows, splattered on the ground, got up, and walked away. Candy recognized somebody; he invited us into a tiled hallway (blue, gold, and ruined white) and up a linoleum stair to a large apartment sagging on its moldings and vibrating with many feet. Because I had to work that night, I drank orange juice straight and wandered through the party, bored by but still accepting the expression that rose on every face as I went past. "Beautiful." "Beautiful!" "Bee-oot-ee-fool." The expression might be formed with wonder or contempt or warmth or disinterest, but it was still the same coin I mechanically took and tossed on the pile. Half-looking for something else, I walked past a partially open door and saw a well-dressed boy sitting on a bed, gazing at the party with a look of intent, distant amusement. He held a worn toy dog on his lap, which he stroked as if it were a pet. There was something mocking in the gesture, as if it were meant to subtly ridicule anyone who saw it. When he saw me, his expression offered me the coin, but so casually that it fell on the floor before I could take it. He was very handsome himself. "Hello," he said, holding the toy dog up to his face. "Would you like to meet Skipper?"

His name was Jamie. His soft voice was desiccated and voluptuous at once. He said he was in his room because it was his roommate's party and he didn't expect to be interested in anyone there, and besides, he was shy. A fragile system of model airplanes hung from the ceiling over his bed, casting soft, gently stirring shadows. "These are beautiful," I said. I reached up to touch one; shyly, the system dipped and bobbed.

"Skipper likes you," he said.

We left the party and went for a walk. On the bottoms of his severely pointed shoes, Jamie wore cleats, which clicked loudly on the pavement. The only people I'd ever known to wear cleats were middle-school boys, who wore them so they could kick hard and make a lot of noise when they walked. I asked Jamie why he wore them, and he said, "I just like them." His words were modest, but they whirred with secret importance. He said everything that way. The British monarchy was very important; Prince Charles's recent marriage was particularly so. Ornette Coleman was the only good jazz musician. He approved of men's shoes on women. He approved of Buckminster Fuller and Malcolm McLaren. He approved of Bow Wow Wow.

His opinions were frivolous, fierce, and exact. He worked in a small graphics plant that made logos and labels for sundry products. But he was as proud and particular as any Parisian playboy. His favorite logo was the brand name of a line of white paper sacks commonly used by small grocers; I had never noticed, but TORNADO was printed in brown letters with a vibrant round *T* at the top of each bag. "It's so elegant," he said, and it *was*.

When I told him I had to go to work, he asked if he could see me again, and I said yes. He hailed me a cab and I got into it even though I could only afford to take it to the nearest subway.

I think of Jamie and silliness pops out of the ground in the form of a California hazelnut, bearing its tasseled foliage on each slim branch. Amid death and groaning wooden power and the wet complexity of moss and fungus and vines—from the same solemn pit, silliness pops up to dangle its tassels. Jamie. Alain. Joanne. We all came up out of the ground and took our forms. So much harder for us to have a form because we have one on the outside and too many inside. Depth, surface, power, fragility, direction, indirection, arrogance, servility, rocks, roots, grass, blossoms, dirt. We are a tangle of roots, a young branch, a flower, a moldy spore. You want to say, This is me; this is who I am. But you don't even know what it is, or what it's for. Time parts its shabby curtain: There is my father, listening to his music hard enough to break his own heart. Trying to borrow shapes for his emotions so that he may hold them out to the world and the world might say, Yes, we see. We feel. We understand. I touch the hazelnut bush gently as I pass.

I saw Jamie again and we went for another walk. We bought tinned sardines and potato chips and candy, then went back to his apartment to eat. His roommates weren't home. We finished our dinner and talked until it was so dark, we could see each other only as dim shapes. Jamie didn't turn on the light. Shadow airplanes appeared and disappeared as headlights swept the wall. "Would you like to take a bath together?" he asked.

In the claw-foot bathtub, I sat between his legs while he held me from behind. Out a low half-moon window was the back of an abandoned building and a piece of illuminated street: the deep gray stone of the building stippled with scars and holes, squares of sidewalk, a lip of curb, a groove of gutter, the melancholy gray of the street. On the street a dog came trotting, chin raised and tail up, all brisk paws, ears, and snout. Jamie laughed; laughing, I turned and he held my face in his wet hands and kissed my forehead, then my closed eyes.

He was gentle in a way that I had not experienced before. He touched me intimately but also somewhat impersonally. He was polite, yet dirty, too. He was covered with soft black hair, which seemed at odds with his sleek habits of dress; with his clothes off, he revealed his nature, without any cleats or clothes to hold it up, and it was wonderful to see, like the coarse little dog prancing down the street.

"You should model," he said. He was lying on top of me, feeling my eyebrows with his lower lip. "You could make money."

"I already did," I said. "I didn't like it."

"Class," he said warmly. "You have class."

But I was lying.

Candy didn't like Jamie because he was affected and because he was short and cold with her. "He makes such a big deal out of himself—those *stupid* cleats and that toy dog—and I don't think there's anything there."

But that wasn't true. There was something "there." Something so scornful that it willfully stunted itself just to withhold itself; something so scared that it blindly clung to objects like toys and cleats, pitifully trying to blossom, jealously nursing its own pathos and mocking it, too.

"It's glamour in its purest form," said Veronica. "I approve."

She spoke of fey youths she had known, of their clothes and hair, the petulant swing of their slim hips. Of one who tried to kill himself with pills and wound up curled in a corner of her apartment, alternately sobbing in her lap and barfing in her wicker basket.

"It's so moving, that artificiality," she said, "moving and wistful. Of course there's something there; unfortunately, there's always something 'there.' Something you will one day be sorry you ever saw. But my advice to you, hon, is not to go looking for it. You'll see it eventually." She exhaled a noseful of smoke. "Probably in your nice wicker basket."

Of course, she was wearing men's shoes. She was also wearing a cable-knit sweater with raised colored animal shapes knit into it: a cat, a dog, a rooster. Red, green, and orange on peach. Frivolous, exact, and fiercely ugly.

In September, the sublet with Candy ended. I found a new sublet, a tiny apartment in the West Village; I used the last of my French money for the deposit. It was a studio with a stove, a refrigerator, and a sink on one wall and a bed on the other, both walls boxed in by a window on one end and a closet on the other. The window was protected by a metal grid that had gotten stuck shut; to open it, I had to poke a broom handle through one of the grid's diamond-shaped gaps, manipulate the latch with it, and nudge the window open. Not much sun came in, but when it did, it made a wobbling grid of diamonds on the floor.

When Sheila came to visit from New Jersey, she said, "God! You have to do that every time you open the window?" She told me Lucia was pregnant again. She told me she had been promoted to store manager. We went to Central Park, where we rented a rowboat and rowed on the lake. She let her hand trail in the water and her face grew wistful and luminous. Her face was tense for a twenty-year-old girl. Heavy like her will was pushing down, trying to crush something deep inside her, tense like the crushed thing was pushing back. I thought, She is ugly already. As if she heard me, she frowned and drew her hand from the water. "Did you know Ed is seeing Denise?" she asked.

I didn't see Sheila or Candy again. I saw Jamie every night I could. We would go for walks and buy our dinner to take back home and eat. Sometimes he would take me to secondhand stores in the East Village and tell me what clothes to buy. Sometimes we would go to clubs and meet his friends, people with changeable hair and light, pointedly civil manners. One of them, a pleasant blond named Eric, with the faintly impossible air of someone who had never been hurt, told me I was stupid not to model. He worked at a magazine made up almost exclusively of pictures of models and actors. "Nobody likes it," he said. "It doesn't matter; you only do it a few years and make a lot of money." When I told him about Alain, he scoffed.

"Did you steal anything from him?" he asked.

"No," I said, "he stole from me."

"Then he doesn't remember you. Everybody knows he's crazy anyway."

Eric was only an assistant at the magazine, but he said he could introduce me to a photographer. "You just need pictures. Go to an agency; you'll be working again. Just lie about your age." He gave me his number. He smiled at the hunger that suddenly came into my eyes.

The photographer lived with his assistant in a loft in the flower district. It was cold and the flower stands were closed. Their rough doors looked boarded up; their dark windows were haunted by ghostly stalks and stems and cold, faint-gleaming pots. The photographer was three flights up. We sat in his kitchen smoking hash and drinking tea from china cups, talking about Paris. There was a big tub in the kitchen, an unhinged door on the tub and a dish drain on the door. Old trunks and makeshift wardrobes draped in musty clothes spilled in from the bedroom, and the assistant, a serious boy with the short, sweet legs of a child, deftly picked through them. They dressed me in a red jumpsuit with a white plastic belt and matching white boots. The photographer said, "You're a Bond girl!" From out of the past, spy music brayed. I grinned and, legs widely akimbo in my little boots, pointed my finger to shoot Alain through the heart.

. . .

"Do you think he was a real photographer?" asked Joy.

"Real, yes. Good, I don't know."

We were at her house, drinking red wine and half-watching a black-and-white movie on TV. Except for one little lamp draped with a shirt, the lights were off to hide the mess. In the gray glow of the television, Joy applied hot blue nail polish and talked about another audition that had gone badly. As she talked, a girl's face appeared on the television, ardent and soft, with millions of light cells flowing through it. Her dark liquid eyes were vulnerable, joyful and radiant with hope.

"Wait," I said. "Is this *A Star Is Born?*"

"No, it's Judy Garland, though. It's *Presenting Lily Mars,* which was before she got all pitiful. So anyway—"

Quick, smart, and tremulous, the girl's voice was full of hot life rising out of her own liquid darkness. In nine pictures, she was a charming actress at the top of her form. In the tenth picture, she was a child crying because she'd dropped her radiant hope into a deep pool, where everyone could see it but she could never feel it. *Believe! Believe! Believe!* I don't know what she was saying, but that is what I heard.

When I saw the contact sheets, my heart sank. But Eric said they were great, and so I went to an agency wedged between a discount furrier and a furniture outlet. Sweating men carrying a houndstooth sofa wrapped in flapping plastic gawked at me on their way to a gaping truck.

"Beautiful," said one.

I opened the shining glass door.

"Cold feesh," said the other.

The door closed behind me.

A Ms. Stickle stared at the contacts up close and at arm's length.

Voices rose over the cheap walls of her cubicle; one was

crass, one was rapid, and one was a child staring shyly at its lap. *So, sweetie, what's your bra size? . . . You don't know? Let's measure it. . . . Can you call your mother? . . . tape measure?*

"How old are you?" asked Ms. Stickle.

"Eighteen," I replied, lying.

"Hum." She pushed the pictures across the desk. "These photos are too downtown. See a real photographer and come back."

She says it's— My God, will you look at this?

"Can you recommend somebody?"

Ms. Stickle grimaced. Then she wrote a name and number on a scrap of paper and handed it to me without looking.

Well, she is a monster.

This photographer was a thin, small man with soft, sexy jowls and gloating eyes that made you feel like he was examining your ass even when he wasn't. He slathered hair gel on his hands and asked what sign I was. I said, "Scorpio."

"I thought so." He worked the gel into my hair so it stood up and away from my head. "I can tell you are strong." He stepped away and signaled his assistant. "But even so, I could dominate you completely."

That established, he photographed me in his bathroom, where I leaned into the mirror in an ill-used evening gown, then on the roof in a white shirt and black leather jacket.

I took the pictures back to Ms. Stickle. Once again, she sighed and stared as voices spoke into the air. "Don't know," she finally murmured. "I can't tell if I love you or hate you."

I went to another agent. He tapped his finger on the shot of me in the white shirt. "This one," he said. "This one almost makes me feel something."

"I thought you didn't want to do it," said Jamie.

"I need money."

We were on my bed, eating hot cereal, a box of sugar on the rumpled bedding between us.

"You could work at the Peppermint."

"I wouldn't want to be there all the time."

He carefully poured a layer of sugar on his cereal and ate it with shallow bites. "Where do you want to be?" he asked.

The season got cold and dark. When I arrived at work, people would be putting on their hats and tying their scarves; one girl, with wavy brown hair and a rosy, commonly pretty face, would tuck her chin against her lapel and button her coat with trustful, parted lips—her hands the mother, her body the tenderly buttoned child. Outside, night was already putting on its neon, and traffic was laying the streets with knotted jewelry. Veronica would come down the hall, her walk a waddle and a vamp, a bag of snacks bobbing at her side, her smile and waving hand stiff with routine.

Before she had been a proofreader, Veronica had been a secretary at a screenwriters' agency. She'd been an assistant script doctor for a television show that I'd never heard of. She'd written flap copy for a publishing house that had gone out of business. In college, she had been a social-work intern with a caseload in the worst neighborhood in Watts. Her first day, a young thug asked if she was the new social worker; she mimicked her own dumb grin and her "Yes." He asked if he could walk with her, and she said yes again. As they walked, he told her the previous social worker had been shot.

"Were you scared?" I asked.

"No, I was too stupid. Anyway, he walked with me long enough for people to see us together. Later I realized he was a member of the neighborhood gang and it was to my advantage to be seen with him."

"Did he come on to you?"

"No. He was protecting me. He was a gentleman." She turned sideways to smoke, and when she turned back, her mouth had a little sarcastic twist. But her eyes were wide and suddenly deep. She had been given something by this thug-boy gentleman, and she had kept it. She was showing me that with her eyes.

"What was it like being a social worker there?"

"I was twenty-three years old. I was ignorant. I came from a psychotic family. That's what it was like. Except for one thing." She put out her cigarette with a proud, bristling air, and told me the story of a cat named Baldie, a stray that lived under a table at the community center where some of her cases played pool. One day, she brought in a can of cat food for him.

"At first, I thought they were angry at me, the men. They glared and they said, 'He don't know what to do with that. He ain't never had anything that good in his life.' I said, 'Well, I'll just try,' and I opened the can. They stopped playing pool and they all watched when I put it down. And Alison, the way that cat buried his head in that can!" She thrust her head down, fingers splayed, her refined voice rolling and softly gobbling. "He looked up at us, and if cats could cry, tears would've been streaming down his face. Nobody said a word. Then one of the men crouched down and held the can so the cat could get to it better.

"Every day after that, I brought in a can of food and every day the men would gather to watch Baldie eat. It was probably one of the few times they got to see a righteous need completely satisfied. When I quit, I left a case of food. I like to think they kept it up. They were hard people, but they had real hearts." She shrugged. "That was the good thing that happened there."

I come to a clearing filled with little sticks poking out of the ground. Whatever they had been, somebody had chopped them off. Hard people, real hearts. So many of Veronica's stories were coarse and sentimental. Another time, she told me about being raped by a man who broke into her apartment. He said he was going to kill her, but she talked him out of it. "I told him, 'If you kill me, you won't be killing just one person. You'll be killing my parents. They're old and it would kill them to know their daughter died like that.'" She shrugged and held out her hands like a Borscht Belt comedian. "And he didn't!" She smoked luxuriously and leaned back in her chair, into the sky with red writ across it. "He was very tender." Her voice deepened; it became fulsome, indulgent, almost smug. "My rapist was very tender."

Smart people would say she spoke that way about that story because she was trying to take control over it, because she wanted to deny the pain of it, even make herself superior to it. This is probably true. Smart people would also say that sentimentality always indicates a lack of feeling. Maybe this is true, too. But I'm sure she truly thought the rapist was tender. If he'd had a flash of tenderness anywhere in him, a memory of his mother, of himself as a baby, of a toy, she would've felt it because she was desperate for it. Even though it had nothing to do with her, she would've sought it, reaching for it as it sank away in a deep pool. *I'll be looking at the moon, but I'll be seeing—*

I see myself, home for Christmas. There I am in the warm kitchen, seasonal music coming from the living room in great swollen chords. I see the red mixing bowl on the counter. I see the mixer, mashed potatoes stuck to its dull blades. My mother opens the oven; there is a golden turkey sweating juice. My father sits in his living room chair, his eyes like deep holes full of layered visions invisible to us. Good King Wenceslas looks down at pictures flashing on the mute TV. A local family is turned out of their apartment; alone and defiant, the mother leads her children down the hall, her eyes flaring into the camera. My mother stirs hunks of butter into the peas; she lays the pecan pies out on tattered pot holders. The local family finds shelter with a church group that has pledged to help them. Daphne decorates the tree with nimble, loving gestures. The children accept stuffed toys from strangers; their mother smiles and rapidly blinks. I light the red candles and put them on the dining room table. Rows and rows of wonderful cars are for sale. Santa takes aspirin for a headache. *So bring him incense, gold, and myrrh;* the music is deep and rich, with sparkling colors flashing in its depths. The TV station's logo opens and closes like an eye. A mute reporter talks into a microphone; rows of hands pull up rows of pant legs to show rows of lesions. "This is outrageous!" cries my father. "Showing this tonight!" Mute doctors talk and speculate. "Everyone knows they're diseased," says my father. "We don't need it shoved in our faces."

The rooms roll by. In them, there are plates heaped with apples and oranges, bowls filled with nuts in complex, perfect shells. There are stockings our grandmother made for us before she died, our names spelled in felt letters. There is a crystal dish of cranberry sauce, marked around its shiny middle with the circular impress of its tin. There is a feeling of fear. It connects and holds and flavors everything else like aspic. My father gets up and turns off the TV. It is not really fear of homosexuals. That is just something to say. The real fear is of things that can't be said. The fear shows through the purposeful expression in my mother's eyes as she carries the turkey to the table. It gathers in every corner of the house and pools in the basement, where Sara hides in her room, splay-legged before the TV, eating painkillers and hard candy by the handful. My father searches, but his brother has gone too far away to find in any song; when my father looks, he reaches into darkness and grasps nothing.

Against this darkness, our stockings were filled with candy canes and little toys; the table was laden and the tree—a real one my father held upright while my mother and Daphne struggled with the screws in the metal stand—was decorated with ropes of lights and tinsel and dear, strange ornaments—striped balls and snowmen and a silver peacock with its face worn away. How sad and weak these talismans seemed to me, like the music my father played for men who turned away from him. How weak against the fear and the terrible unsaid things.

At night, when the others had gone to sleep, Daphne and I went out and walked in the neighborhood. Street and star light made the shoveled walks gray corridors of soft white mass and softer black shadow, and the *crunch-crunch-crunch* of our boots played up and down them in the ringing dark. Across the billowing snow, gaunt trees signed in shadow language. Modest houses hung their squares and rectangles with lights the blunt sweet colors of happiness—secret delight hidden in the cold body of winter. Felt but unseen except for now, the deity's birthday, when people climb wobbling ladders to string symbolic lights on trees and around windows. *Crunch-crunch*. We used to run across these yards, shouting. There was a birdbath and a strawberry patch behind that house hidden in pine bushes, under a sloping roof swollen twice its size with snow. There was a little girl named Sheila Simmons, who sat on the sidewalk and played with a red rubber ball and a handful of shiny jacks. *Crunch-crunch-crunch*. In some glossy folded place, they were still there, unseen but felt. And so, unseen but felt, were the unsaid things.

"The thing is," said Daphne, "his father was a wife-abusing drunk who was killed in a bar. His mother was crazy and his brother was really the one who raised him. And then his brother got killed. But his father was also this delicate, poetic person who sang for a living—"

Giant figures came from their folded places and loomed about us. Walking among them with the hood of her parka over her head, Daphne spoke in a low and rapid voice, hectoring and beseeching them at once.

"—and his brother was also this big, powerful, pragmatic

jock type who didn't really accept Daddy because he was like *their* father, and probably Uncle Ray could see that even then, the emotionality, the love of music, the fights over nothing."

There was the Simmonses' old house. Pale television light flashed on their ceiling, then darted down to flash even paler on the banked blue-shadowed snow outside their window. I wondered if they still lived there. A face emerged out of the dark; an open mouth and eye holes strained against the porous membrane of present time.

"Daddy must've looked up to Ray so much, but he couldn't please him, and if he tried to emulate him, he'd have to fail. The one he could be like was his father, a dead failure, and he didn't want to be that. So he didn't have anyone to be."

Quick and incessant, Daphne went on telling me things I had already heard, trying to say the unsaid things, to say them and say them and say them.

"Except for his mother, who favored him and expected him to be like his dad, wanted him to be, including the abuse, including the drinking, sending double messages, like wanting him to win the statewide spelling bee, and being thrilled when he did, until the next day, when—"

Our father's father was a heavy drinker who, to supplement his income as a mail clerk, sang for tips at a local bar. One night, he got in the middle of a fight; a knife was pulled, and my father, ten, was orphaned because an ambulance blew a tire on a back road. (Somewhere the driver is still trying to change the tire while his rotating red light rhythmically drenches the dirt and sweeps the sky.) His brother, Ray, fourteen at the time, helped his mother support the family by going to work for a butcher. He enlisted in the army at eighteen and was dead at twenty-two. This we knew. The rest we had invented by looking at pictures of Ray and listening to things our mother had said in certain tones of voice. We'd gotten the story about the spelling bee from Daddy's great-aunt Claire, who'd been at the bank when Daddy had gone with his mother to deposit the fifty-

dollar prize he'd won. He told the teller about the spelling bee
and his mother snapped, "Stop bragging on yourself, you swell-
headed brat."

Daphne gave a tense, shuddering sigh; her breath then
was always high and strained. "Then Ray died in the war," she
said, "and he could be turned into the perfect brother who
loved Daddy as much as Daddy loved him." She finally fell
silent, trying to calm her breath. Colorless smoke billowed out a
chimney and rose churning into the sky. The folded place vanished. Our childhood slipped back through its private door.
There was nothing but breathing and the light rub and rasp of
our clothes. But somewhere, in the sky, in the snow, in a hidden,
folded place between them, was a perfect brother who loved as
much as he was loved.

When we got back, the house was warm and dark except
for the Christmas tree, its burning lights making glowing caves
in its branches, jeweled with soft colors and the lit intensity of
tiny needles. The blood tingled in our legs as we stamped our
feet on the front mat; dangling tinsel stirred with our motion,
ghost light alive in each strand. It was beautiful and brimmed
with love. Yet the unsaid things remained mute and obdurate.
As we went upstairs to bed, they stood like invisible stone tab-
lets, unreadable and indifferent to our words. When we lay
down, Daphne slept, but I turned back and forth between sleep
and wakefulness. It was there again, clanging between dream
and thought—the mental sensation that in the next room our
parents were screaming curses and attacking each other like
animals. I turned on the light and remembered them as I had
seen them earlier that day at the grocery store: an overweight
man and a tall pear-shaped woman with their glasses on the
ends of their noses, staring about them in mild confusion, their
carts full of bargain eggnog and candy canes. I remembered the
tree downstairs, the lights outside, and the sky.

. . .

Yes, we were stupid for disrespecting the limits placed before us; for trying to go everywhere and know everything. Stupid, spoiled, and arrogant. But we were right, too. *I* was right. How could I do otherwise when the violence of the unsaid things became so great that it kept me awake at night? When I saw my father sitting in a chair, desperate to express what was inside him, making a code out of outdated symbols even his contemporaries could no longer recognize? When I saw him smile because my mother fell on her face and then put the smile away like it was a piece of paper? When I heard him rail against dying men because otherwise he had no form to give his hates and fears? All the meat of truth was hidden under a dry surface, and so we tore off the surface with a shout. We wanted to have everything revealed and made articulate, everything, even our greatest embarrassments and lusts.

I walk faster and faster, apace of my chattering mind. Here is another slim ocher tree naked of bark. It is utterly smooth and, in the rain, so shiny that it looks almost plastic. It is twisted so elegantly, it is like an art object, made to suggest irony and hauteur. Veronica and Duncan didn't have to attack each other in the hidden world one glimpses before sleep. They were what they were in public. His lust and scorn, her abjection and bitterness—these were acted out on city streets in graphic, unapologetic form. Not merely unapologetic but ironic, elegant, and haughty. I take off my glove and stroke the tree trunk as I walk past. I wonder if it is diseased. *Everyone knows they're diseased.*

But we were not satisfied with revealing and articulating; we came to insist that our embarrassments and lusts were actually beautiful. And sometimes they were—or at least could be made to look it. The first high-end job I had in New York was with two other girls, one of whom was an unstable lesbian with dark, dramatic looks and a known hard-on for the other, a bland blonde from Norway who didn't speak English. The photographer had us pose at night against the chain-link fence of a deserted ball field. He put me and Ava, the Nordic girl, on one side of the fence and Pia, the dyke, on the other. He photographed Pia alone. He photographed Ava and me together, me slightly behind her to indicate my sidekick status. He photographed Ava and me holding hands while Pia pressed up against the fence. At the end, he had Pia strip down to her underwear and hurl herself onto the fence, like she was "trying to get to Ava," grabbing it with her hands and bare feet. Most models of Pia's stature would never have done that. But he knew she would. She was half out of her mind with lovelessness and rage, and she wanted people to see it—she wanted it revealed and articulated. She threw herself at the fence again and again, until her hands and feet were bleeding. That shot ran at the end of a three-page spread and it was a great picture; Pia's nakedness was blurred by the fence and by her motion, but her face and flying hair came at you like demon beauty bursting out of darkness to devour human beauty. Ava and I huddled together in our pale spring lace, two maids lost in a postmodern wood, she moving forward, me half-turning toward the demon who silently howled at us with her great gold eyes, her genital mouth and long flawless claws with just a hint of anguish in their swollen knuckles. Of course, you didn't see any blood. You didn't see human pain on the demon's face—or rather, you saw it as a shadow, a slight darkness that foregrounded the beauty of the picture and gave it a sort of luscious depth. It was a page-stopper. It restarted my career.

After Christmas, I went to see Jamie and found him making model airplanes with a fourteen-year-old girl. She had full deep-colored lips with no set to them yet, dark, snapping eyes, and gold skin intensely refrained in the fiery gold aura around her pupils. Her laughing eyes lightly touched mine on their way up and down my body; she was not as pretty as I was, but it didn't matter—she giggled behind her hand as Jamie giddily explained that she was his roommate's friend's daughter. I looked at him. The black and gold of her pupils saturated his eyes and shone from them, and in their light I was a mortal in someone else's heaven. I turned and walked away, while Jamie followed me to the door, protesting that he would call me, until I shut the door on his hand and ran down the stairs.

That night, Veronica wasn't at work, and for the first time I missed her. When the shift was over, instead of taking a taxi home, I walked blocks of asphalt glossy with yellow lamplight and streaming with yellow cabs, each with a hard nugget of human head inside. When the tears finally came, I sat on a bench in front of the Public Library and let them fall. A man with a face like the bottom of a broken shoe discreetly worked around me, slowly and painfully collecting cigarette butts off the ground and storing them in his pocket. He didn't look at me, but he sang a nasal, wordless song that touched me like calm hands.

The following morning, I was awakened by the agent who had "almost felt something"; I had a go-see. It was in a cavernous loft full of echoes that sprang from each scraping chair and clacking step, grew ceiling-high in one bound, bounced back, then subsided in sideways waves. Each girl rose from her chair and walked through her own rising echo into someone else's, until they all overlapped and I couldn't tell who might be chosen and who would not. The echo of a laughing eye lightly touched mine on its way up and down my body; long white curtains streamed out an enormous window on an ancient city; a demon whispered to a clitoris as if it were an ear; a girl laughed and ate cherries from a plastic bowl; I pounded a door closed to me forever. These and thousands of other bright-painted moments became tiny and featureless as grains of sand that whirled about me while I whirled, too, a tiny grain among grains, condemned to whirl forever. The booker looked at one page of my pictures, then turned to chat with his assistant while absently flipping through the others. "I can't work with any of these," he said. "They're not what I asked for at all."

"What's really sickening about it is, I'll bet she really was his roommate's friend's daughter. I don't think he went out to find her. She just appeared and he was charmed. That seems worse to me."

"It's awfully blithe," agreed Veronica. "Do you think he had sex with her?"

Her tone took me aback. I hadn't even asked myself that question. "Well, yeah. His eyes—yeah, of course. Don't you think?"

"Not necessarily. The way you describe him, he'd be enchanted just to kiss and cuddle with her."

"That's the same thing."

"Not in my book, hon."

Veronica had come back to work after being gone for an entire week. She and Duncan had broken up, too. He had promised, because of the new disease, that he wouldn't sleep with anyone but her. Two weeks later, he confessed to an affair with a minor soap opera actor and Veronica walked out.

"Are you worried?" I asked.

"I'm worried for him, not me. They say it's not a woman's disease."

"They don't know that for sure."

"Hon, it's been ten years. If I have it, I have it. There's nothing I can do."

I thought, Most men who call themselves bisexual are really gay. Duncan had probably had sex with Veronica infrequently, and it was true: Everyone acted like women couldn't get it. But why would Veronica have been involved with a gay man who could not desire her? How had she coded that humiliation so that it looked like something else? Perhaps to her, it had actually *been* something else. I pictured Veronica and Duncan side by side in a stifling pocket of refinement, dressed up to their necks in stiff Victorian clothing, their lips pursed, their pinkie fingers linked, viewing the world through tiny lorgnettes as they discussed Oscar Wilde and Jean-Paul Belmondo's dogs. Meanwhile, dirty anal sex was happening somewhere else, between someone else and a Duncan she never had to know. Trips to the art museum and weeping at *Camille* continued unabated. I could see it.

"He took custody of the two big seal-point brothers, which is very sad. Technically, they were his, but I've had them since they were kittens. Now I've got all girls. A harem of beautiful Siamese."

She put down her Styrofoam cup. The stirring coffee shone with oils from her lipstick. The side of the cup was marked with the impress of her lower lip. For a strange moment, I wanted to take her cup and kiss it, covering her mark with mine.

"Do you want to go out for a drink afterward?" I blurted it; Veronica blinked with surprise.

"Thanks, hon, but I can't. I've got an appointment." She took up her cup. "Maybe another time."

"Maybe we could go see a movie?" I trembled in my extended position, but I held it.

She dropped her eyes. She said, "That would be lovely," but her voice hesitated, as if her foot had halted midstep while her body veered in another direction. The moment was fragile and uncomfortable, and it united us as if by touch. Veronica raised her eyes. "I could do it this week?"

We met during a windy, trash-blown day—cold, but with a bright, triumphant sky. The movie was about a middle-aged woman, a former teacher, on a binge of young boys and drinking in Mexico. "It's supposed to be wonderful, hon." We sat in the back, eating candy and popcorn. A crazily smiling woman with hot, besotted eyes and shoulder blades like amputated wings talked to the camera about being "on vacation from feminism" with a sultry blond acquaintance who'd "never heard of it and never had to."

"Me and my aunt on vacation in Arizona," whispered Veronica. "I was sixteen. She got drunk and danced with a truck driver who called her 'a whore.'"

I stared at her. She faced the screen as if she'd addressed it, not me.

"'Are you a whore?' She just smiled and nodded."

The ex-teacher and her friend went to the hotel swimming pool; men churned the water as they swam toward the blonde, heaving their dripping, longing selves up onto the tile beneath the reclining chair where she lay, oblivious as a custard. "I don't have that nonchalance," said the ex-teacher. "I don't have that beauty. What I have is desire. And there's great purity in that." She turned from the camera to gaze at the sleeping loins of a sloe-eyed boy in wet bathing trunks, then cut back to us with a pop-eyed "Here I go again!" grin.

"Purity," whispered Veronica, "as in unalloyed."

I looked at her. She ate a fistful of popcorn.

The ex-teacher walked with a Mexican man on a cobbled street at sunset. She had on a short skirt, and his hand was up so far between her legs that she was nearly walking on tiptoe. "Your name means fish," he said. She smiled. *Feesh.*

"Duncan," whispered Veronica, "both halves."

She talked in and out of the movie, as if its enlarged characters were fragments escaped from her head and willfully acting out on their own, assuming the perfect narrative forms they were denied in life. It was like somebody in a church repeating and affirming the minister's sermon in noises and half syllables. The Mexican man fucked the teacher so hard that her head slammed against the wall; I whispered, "Me in Paris. Both halves." And I could feel Veronica smile before I saw it.

By the end of the movie, Veronica had stopped whispering. Her feelings, grown too broad for words, were strong enough that I could feel them running, sinking, rising, and again running in an ardent fluxing pattern. The ex-teacher stroked the cheek of a beautiful teenager who didn't bother to look at her. All the feeling in her face had sunk into her jaw and mouth in a heavy expression of appetite and pain— except for a tiny spark in one of her deserted eyes, which held aloof, amazed to find itself on this brink and wanting to stay conscious enough to savor it. Then the spark fell in with the rest and went out. Sick and feverish, the woman ran across a beach like an ostrich with no plumage, pinwheeling her arms ecstatically. Print appeared on the screen, saying she had disappeared in Juárez and was presumed dead. She ran and pinwheeled nonetheless. Ugliness had broken through into beauty and flown into death with it, pinwheeling and joyous in its pain.

When we emerged from the theater, two men stopped us in the lobby to ask what we thought of the movie. They were stout and barrel-chested, with a damp, testicular air that was wounded and bellicose and craved to be loved. I could feel they wanted to look at me, but they didn't. They didn't address me, either. They were there to talk to the ex-schoolteacher, not the custard. They were there to preen before her and to acknowledge her; it was her show now. "I loved it," she said. "I loved her. I love anything that goes to the edge." She gave her baubled voice to them and they saluted her with their stout, barreled chests.

Then we went to have ice cream under a green-and-white-striped umbrella. A living sea of pigeons boiled and ate bread at our feet. I looked at them and for a moment the world became strange to me. Then I remembered it had always been strange. I had a dish of pistachio gelato and remembered that the first time I met a model, I didn't even know she was beautiful.

We went to the movies again the next week and several weeks after that. If we could sit alone in an isolated row, we talked our way through the story. If we had to sit where others could hear us, we didn't. Either way, we left the theater feeling like we'd been talking in tongues. Sometimes I would see men look at me, and at her, then withdraw their eyes in confusion. Sometimes their confusion would confuse me; sometimes I looked through their eyes and saw that Veronica and I made no sense together. But then I came back into my own eyes, and that kind of sense seemed stupid. It could never see the tenth picture. It couldn't even see past the first.

I went to more go-sees without being chosen; I was calm. My agent stopped calling me. I looked for another one. Instead of seeing Joy or Cecilia, I went to dinner parties at Veronica's apartment. She lived up a dingy flight of stairs, behind a door painted with green lead dissolving in rust and rot-speckled yellow. The door opened; a Siamese cat peered from a dark crack; lounge music issued out like an enchanted cloud and in it was Veronica wearing an antique lace dress. The enchanted cloud formed a face with pouting lips and heavy-lidded eyes that beckoned us past a small bed wedged sideways, a giant TV, and a window with cracked moldings propped up by a rain-warped book. Another cat leapt up on a rickety table and tilted its velvet triangle head toward the living room, where a table was draped with linen cloth and set with silver. I was introduced as "the Parisian gamine," then greeted by a small circle of dignified old men and appealing boys—clerks, proofreaders, and word-processing drones gladly transformed by the enchanted cloud, which traveled among them, touching them here and there with subtle scent and color.

"So anyway, it's the Korean War and these adorable soldiers are about to charge Pork Chop Hill, and the chaplain says, 'Let me tell you about another hill,' and suddenly we're at Calvary, and there's James Dean as John the disciple—"

They were talking about James Dean's debut on Catholic television, and Veronica led the conversation, directing it as if with a scepter made of cardboard and tufts of beaded netting, which, at certain moments, might burst into flame.

"—which was a superb choice. Just look at the old art. John is always slouching and bored."

Remembering, I hear Charles Trenet's voice traveling like sunlight over the surfaces of the earth, singing ("*heureux et malheureux*") and making beautiful shadows on the refrigerator or the prison-yard grass or a girl's quiet, crying face.

"Magdalen had goodness, whereas Margary was just the meanest old—she was in Anthony's last movie and she was just dreadful. The way she made that trailer shake from side to side! It took her four hours to do the mascara on one eye, and that was after the false eyelashes!"

"Faye Dunaway played the maid in *Tartuffe*, a walk-on really, but I picked her out in a *second*."

"I don't want to read this nonsense where every other character is depressed. I want murder and they catch the killer and life is delicious."

Heureux et malheureux—and life is delicious. Laughing sunlight plays with the shadows of trees, grasses, and birds in the heat-rippling air. The music plays. My father sits in his chair.

"—as we flew along past him, pussies to the wind—"

"—the snow all magical and pure and the lights . . . the lights . . . well, anyway. Rosalyn died. And—"

"—then Gielgud spent five glorious minutes putting on his gloves. I could simply have screamed with pleasure."

I think of my father because their signals were as elaborate and ardent as his, but theirs were received and passed along a living circuit, growing stronger and more affirming with each pass. I tried to feel superior, but I couldn't. In that apartment, beauty and perfection belonged to Veronica and her guests in the form of a glimmering mirror ball hung high above their heads. They could never reach it, but still they guarded it like fierce elves with lightning-quick rapiers that they drew with a jolly bon mot. Before this guard, I felt wordless, slow and shy, aware that the currency of my sex was worthless here. It made me even more shy to realize that they tolerated my awkwardness, and might even have been kind about any attempts at opinion and wit I might've but did not make.

"I'm so glad Veronica finally found a good girlfriend," said George, a fatherly fellow who walked me home one night. "She really needs some female companionship—especially since the Travesty is finally over. Hopefully for good this time."

"I never met Duncan."

"Better for you—a very nasty man. If she gets back together with him, I don't know if I'll be able to stay friends with her."

One night, I went with Veronica and two boys named Thomas and Todd to see three legendary actors in Noël Coward's *Blithe Spirit*. According to *The New Yorker*, it was "like watching three old foxes at play," but that was not the case; the male lead ("He looks like an old tortoise!") bumbled and periodically fell asleep, so that his costars had to shout their lines in his ear in order to wake him. The bored boys, punchy and tired of jokes at his expense, began ecstatically to joke about Veronica's vagina. To my amazement, she joked with them—so loudly that an usher rolled down the aisle with a flashlight in his fist. He leaned over us; the male lead woke with a start and blurted, "Be quiet—you're behaving like a guttersnipe," which caused Veronica and the boys to become so hysterical that we were thrown out. We made quite a procession up the aisle (Veronica, Thomas, and Todd waving and throwing kisses), out onto the street, and into a taxi, where Veronica got into a screaming fight with her friends about an imagined insult to the driver, and I slipped out at a stoplight in Times Square.

"Typical fag hag," said Cecilia. "I wouldn't be bothered." I shrugged. We were sitting in a fashionable cheap café with huge graffiti on the walls, yellow and orange and shaped like squared shock waves. Cecilia wore mesh fingerless gloves and a torn black lace blouse. So did a boy across from us.

When I met Veronica at work, we didn't speak of it. We barely spoke at all. A few nights later, Veronica switched to the graveyard shift. We saw each other fleetingly at shift changes; she looked at me with a pursed expression that said, Of course, this is what our relationship has been all along and that's fine with me. I returned her look, indifferent as a child who, done with the milk, drops the carton on the ground. We said hi.

The path goes up a steep ridge bordering a sharp drop. The wind rises. A small waterfall explodes with white water. My thoughts fly up and briefly float before sinking and spreading like squid ink on the ocean floor. Dark balances and weights the light. On the dark bottom of the ocean, a wicked girl is covered with black slime and snakes and surrounded by ugly creatures staring at her with hate in their eyes. She thinks they are staring at her because she is so beautiful. She doesn't know she is as ugly as they are. Sweat runs in gobs down the sides of my body, down my back and belly. My fever is rising.

"You should get a job at Ted's place when he opens it," said Cecilia one afternoon over little sandwiches. "The clientele there would be much better, and you'll be visible to the right people at a restaurant of that caliber."

I remembered a slim white arm and bristling hide and

pieces of pie on cream-colored dishes. Unbearable sweetness and sadness funneled into my mouth through a straw; broken feelings tried to be whole. A door of stainless steel swung open on a bright kitchen. "I could work in a restaurant," I had said. And I could. Even though I had no experience, Ted said I could start the following week.

I left my temp job before I started in the restaurant, and a week of days lay before me in sweet blank chunks. I went to movies by myself. I went to museums by myself. I went for walks. On one walk, I ran into George and stopped to talk with him. When I mentioned Veronica, he said, "We don't see her anymore, not Max and I. She started up with *it* again, and suicide is simply not something I want to watch, thank you very much."

It was late autumn and bright, and there was a delighted feeling in the air. A girl with magenta hair walked by in a tiny black skirt and leopard-print boots, swinging her slim hips with delight. George and I stopped to watch her. She smiled.

"Is Duncan really that bad?" I asked. A bilious look came into George's pale eyes.

"Yes, he is that bad. He's the kind of man who pretends to desire a woman because her desire tweaks his vanity—even when he knows he could . . . and she knows—" The bile receded. "Well, it's not my business. It's sad, but there's nothing you can say to her. She goes right into 'hon' mode."

I said, "She hasn't got another mode." We said good-bye.

Still, I called Veronica to tell her about my new job. She congratulated me. She said we must keep in touch. I told her about running into George.

"Oh, don't believe that old bitch," she said. "I only saw Duncan a few times for coffee. George is just using that as an excuse. He's a misogynist, you know."

"George?"

"I was shocked, too. But we had a fight and he said some things that were totally unforgivable."

"But a misogynist?" What does that word mean to her?
I wondered.

"Absolutely."

She asked if I'd like to meet for coffee. I didn't want to,
but I said yes. I guess she didn't want to, either; she canceled at
the last minute.

The following months were an oscillating loop of dreams—
brilliant and blurred, like a carnival ride at night, lighting up
and going dark as its cars toss and churn. From a distance, it is
beautiful, even peaceful. From inside, it rattles and roars and
roughly yanks you by the neck. I ran from dining room to
kitchen with my hands full of plates. The dishwasher creaked
and loosed gusts of hot steam, the kitchen boys yakked in Spanish, and the cook spun out plate after plate of flawless food. I
ran back through great vases of gaudy flowers, wild ginger and
birds-of-paradise with gaping orange beaks. Gorgeous people
leaned over succulent plates, gobbling. Earrings flashed and
jiggled on jawbones; an eloquent hand drew a lovely emotion
out of air; hot eyes fired rounds of arrows at a naked breastbone. Delicacy, roughness, mincing intelligence, and raw, rampant stupidity ran together in the pitched jabber. Back in the
kitchen, a radio played sequined songs and the Mexican boys
scraped everything off the plates, mashed it up, and washed it
down the garbage disposal while the boy at the dishwasher did
a butt-bumping dance with the boy mopping the floor. I gos-
siped with the other wait and bus persons about actresses in the
dining room and who was fucking whom as we snatched extra
plates of calamari, tuna tartare, bilberries, and lemon cream.
At closing, we all piled into a sagging taxi with its seat propped
up by oily black springs and got out at a club, where I leaned into
a wall of canned music and tongue-kissed a waiter as handsome
as Jamie until I passed out, only to wake up alone, slumped on a

cold banquette. After three days, I pulled myself out of this slop, put on fresh makeup, and went to a new agency, where I met a woman with powerful shoulders and flat buttocks dressed in a tight leopard print. She looked at my pictures, frowned, looked at me, back to the pictures, looked up, and burst out, "But you're Alison Owen! What are you doing in these awful pictures?"

Her name was Morgan Crosse. She had unmoored eyes and a voice full of force. I told her what had happened in Paris. It made it more real to describe it to someone who knew what it meant, and I began to cry. She said not to worry. She said I could destroy Alain. She said she'd get me a voodoo doll, which I would stick with pins every day for thirty days, then put in the freezer, and I'd be fine. Soon, I was standing in Central Park, bitterly cold in fluttering underwear. A stolid girl smiled uncertainly as she held the light-blinded eye of the reflector, and the camera saturated me with brilliance. Then I was sitting in an overheated trailer, talking with Pia about David Bowie and Ezra Pound while Ava nibbled cold cream from a jar and mechanical windup stylists tortured our hair. At a magazine party, I sat at a table with the most famous model of the year, a seventeen-year-old whose laughing face was a fleshy description of pleasure, satiety, and engagement that engaged at one decibel again and again. Photographers pitilessly filled her with their radiant needles until she was riddled with invisible holes and joyfully pouring radiance out each one. As an afterthought, a photographer turned and photographed me. My picture would appear later in a magazine society page. In the photo, I was sitting next to the young writer who had briefly occupied the chair next to me when it was vacated by a columnist. He sat down to ask me if I'd ever seen Modigliani's paintings. "Because you're like a beautiful Modigliani painting," he said. "You should go see the exhibit at the Metropolitan." I waited for him to ask me to go with him, but he didn't. He just looked at me a long moment. He had intense eyebrows and hazel eyes with bright changeable streaks glowing emberlike through the solid color. His name was Patrick. He gave the impression of a fast current that you might ride on, laughing. We talked about nothing and then he got up and left. I waited a very pleasant moment before getting up, too. Six months later, his friends would ignore me and sting me with weapons made of the finest jealousy and gossamer contempt. A woman writing a book on the history of troll dolls would look at me and talk loudly about the trivial nature of beauty and fashion. A short actress would turn her back on me while I was speaking and put her arms around Patrick. I would break a wineglass in a hostess's bathroom and walk on it until the splinters were unseeable. I would change my mind and guiltily mop the glass with a wet towel. "Alison?" Patrick would pound on the door. But that night, he proudly introduced me. That night, I said, "I'm a model," and it came out shy and shining at the same time. People smiled and parted, and allowed me to enter the social grid.

I slip, fall, and muddy my knee. The sky beats on my umbrella; the wind tries to take it from me. "Come on, rat face," said a photographer, "give me a little hope." My dream loop flies. I walk and pant like an angry wolf. Faces and scenes rapidly bloom, one out of the other, making a living mosaic that fed me and starved me, freed and captured me at once. And deep within the bright swift-changing pattern is the darkness and emptiness of my apartment, where my phone rings and rang. It was, is, Veronica. "Duncan is dying," she said. "He has it. He has AIDS."

We met in a neighborhood bar, a dark rectangle filled with jukebox songs.

"You might not have it," I said. "Some people still think women can't—"

"And you believe *that?*"

"I don't know. But everybody says they don't know how infectious it actually is."

"If I don't have it, it'll be another miracle at Fatima."

"I thought that maybe, him liking boys, you didn't actually do—"

"We did *everything*, hon. All the time. It was like *Histoire d'O*." Veronica sat very erect as she said this, and I saw a flash of pride in her wide, alert eyes. "He liked boys, but he liked me, too. Well, perhaps *liked* isn't the operative word, but . . ."

A song of betrayal came out of the jukebox like a flare. The faces in the bar suddenly appeared rigid, locked in shapes of willed happiness more terrible than pain. A young waitress danced at her station, anonymous and graceful in the warm light of the clanging kitchen. We hadn't spoken for nearly a year. I was almost sixteen years younger than she was. We did not belong together. I reached across the table and held her hand. "I like you," I said.

The wind is strong now. I'm afraid it will pick me up and throw me off the ridge. I picture falling, breaking on tree branches and cracking my head on the rocks below. I picture a tree branch falling on me and pinning me. How long would I lie there before someone found me? Night would come. The softness and greenness and moving stillness would make an immense fist and it would close around me. Bugs would come. I would die. Animals would come. Bugs and animals would eat me. I would rot and disperse. The dispersed flesh would travel down into the ground in tiny pieces, burrowing in the dirt, deeper and deeper. I would cease to be an I and become an it. It would get eaten by bugs, come out their assholes, and keep going. It would come to the center of the earth. The heat and light would be like hell for a human. But it would not be human. It would go on in.

In the bar that night, Veronica talked about Duncan angrily, tenderly. He denied he had AIDS, preferring to think he was losing his life to a tropical fungus he'd picked up years ago in South America. Stripped of his beauty, still he sat upright, bolstered by pillows and glittering desperately. It was a Catholic hospital and fierce comedy manned the battlements as nuns and doctors flapped in and out with prayers, pronouncements, and facial tics as they overacted to Veronica's wisecracking sound track. She and Duncan giggled at Sister Dymphna Drydell ("I kid you not"), who "warbled like Spring Byington" while glowering "like Bette Davis in *What Ever Happened to Baby Jane?*" They flirted with a handsome black-haired doctor, and refused to cooperate with the one who used the term *fag*. They earnestly stammered at the one who stammered, even when he stammeringly told them that Duncan had maybe a week to live. "And Sister Drycrotch, with eyes of the purest psychosis, trills, 'It's not the end, but a beautiful beginning.'" The enemy rattled at the gate; comedy pulled down its pants and gave it the moon.

Then Duncan remarked, "Well, I've always known something was wrong." He'd known for years.

"His whole family knew," said Veronica. "His sister told me in the waiting room. She smiled and said, 'You must feel so betrayed! Oh, oh! You must feel so . . . so—'" Veronica made her voice high, hysterical, and false, then cut it back to her inflected deadpan. "I've had Thanksgiving with them almost every year for the last six. I sent Duncan's niece a birthday present a few weeks ago—a beautiful French wooden pull toy, a red dog with blue eyes, playing the xylophone." She shrugged.

"What did you say?"

"To whom, hon?"

"Well, Duncan."

"*Say* to him?" She took a long drag on her cigarette, put it out, and looked at me, puffing herself up like the Red Queen about to open her inhuman mouth and strike. But halfway up, she lost heart and sank back. "There was nothing to say. He cried. He kissed my hands. He said he was sorry over and over again. When he was finished, I couldn't speak. I got in bed with him instead."

I felt my head jerk in disbelief.

"Not to make love, though I felt like it for an instant. We just held each other. His chest felt so thin, it was like his heart was coming through it."

Sister Drycrotch, who opened the door to announce that visiting hours were over, did not try to hide her dismay.

"You see, hon," said Veronica, lighting another cigarette, "I knew, too. Of course I did."

Two entwined trees with roots that break the ground form a lumpy cradle half on the path and half hanging out over the ridge. I squat between them, umbrella over my head. I drink big mouthfuls of water. I look down into the canyon at the treetops, vast and textured, twisting and moving like sea grass under an ocean of air and mist, full of creatures I can't see. Veronica raises her wand; it bursts into flame.

I imagine being in a hospital bed, holding my dying, unfaithful lover in my arms. I imagine feeling the beat of his heart, thumping with dumb animal purity. Once, when I was working in Spain, I went to a bullfight, where I saw a gored horse run with its intestines spilling out behind it. It was trying to outrun death by doing what it always did, what always gave it joy, safety, and pride. Not understanding that what had always been good was now futile and worthless, and humiliated by its inability to understand. That's how I imagine Duncan's heart. Beating like it always had, working as hard as it could. Not understanding why it was no good. This was why Veronica got into the bed—to comfort this debased heart. To say to it, But you are good. I see. I know. You are good. Even if it doesn't work.

 The rain has dissipated into a silent drizzling mist. The air feels like wet silk. Veronica lowers her wand. I get up out of my squat; in the canyon below I see dozens of ocher-colored trees swathed in mist. I think, They are so beautiful. I think, The disease is spreading. The flame of Veronica's wand arcs across a gray expanse and goes out. My fever abates. I climb the ridge, heading toward the top of the waterfall. I approach the broad path that will take me farther up the mountain.

Duncan died. A year later, Veronica tested positive for HIV. Our friendship continued even though there was no obvious reason why it should. Sometimes I would admit to myself that if she had not called me when Duncan was dying, I would never have seen her again. I would admit that if she'd tested negative, I would have let the friendship lapse. I'd admit that I was embarrassed to be seen with her, that duty and pity were all that joined us. I'd admit, too, that she was the only one I could trust not to reject me.

 I'm sure she had these thoughts. "She felt sorry for me," I'd imagine her bitterly telling an imaginary person. "I was a good listener." Then I imagined her expression draw inward as she considered that no, that was not all there was to it. But the imaginary Veronica did not admit that to the imaginary person. Instead, she drew on her cigarette, smiled ironically, and said, "Of course, she was a darling girl"—leaving the person to wonder what existed between the first two statements and the third.

 I told a makeup artist about Veronica once and he said, "She's a model hag; it's obvious. She wants to suck on your life." Deftly and precisely, he perfected my eyebrows with a tiny brush. "She wants to be invited to the party."

"That's okay," I said. "She's invited."

But she wasn't.

I worked regularly, not constantly. I went to bed at a decent hour. I didn't drink too much. I showed up on time. I was polite to clients and stylists. As I was no longer the girlfriend of a feared and hated man, my relations with other models were warm and dull as a hair dryer's drone. I did not let anyone grab my crotch, not even a famous photographer who snickered sideways when I found him banging a fifteen-year-old on a makeup table. (His butt feral, hungrily clenched, and spangled with mauve glitter from a tube the girl had crushed with the heel of her hand; perhaps it was the same glitter she wore on her eyelids as she gloated from the cover of the magazine I was supposed to be on.) I was a shop girl, not a poet. In an inexplicable way, I savored my ordinariness, my affinity with the office girls and waitresses I had briefly moved among. My livid past still lingered about me, but faintly, like the roar inside a seashell, and my longing for it was a dull arrhythmic spasm, or murmur, in the meat of my functioning heart. Sometimes, in certain pictures, I thought I could see this hollow phantom world tingle in the air around me, making you want to look at the picture, sensing something you can't see. In these pictures, I was what I had once longed for: a closed door you couldn't open, with music and footsteps behind it. I was holding Ava's hand, but I was turned toward Pia, and the fire of her eyes was reflected in mine.

I took the train to see my family almost every month; I brought them magazines with my picture in them. In Paris, I had sometimes torn pages out and sent them across the rumpled sea, but

I'd never seen a reaction to them. My mother looked at my image as if she were looking at a wicked little girl come to scornfully show herself to her poor mother. There was love in her look, but with such jealousy mixed in that the feelings became quickly slurred. It was what my mother gave me, so I took it and I gave it back; I reveled in her jealousy as she reveled in my vanity. Reveling and rageful, we went between sleep and dreams right there in the dining room. Silent and still, we attacked each other like animals. My father coughed nervously, pointed at my most mediocre picture, and said, "Well, this one's right nice." Daphne said, "Yeah! This is great." But as she turned the pages, she vibrated with the words she did not say but which I heard anyway: This is meaningless! And shallow! And false! My mother tossed a magazine down with a snap and said she had to go to the grocery store. Daphne went with her. Sara looked up and said, "But why didn't they put you on the cover? You're prettier than she is." But there was no kiss in her eye now. She was still working at the place for old people, and when she got home, she went down into the basement and stayed there.

Daphne, on the other hand, had gotten a scholarship to Rutgers; she had wrapped herself in a ribbon of *A*'s while working as a barmaid at a place where students drank and puked amid roaring jukeboxes and pinball machines with streaming globule lights. When she talked about her classes and her job, she strutted and threw off little scrappy airs that said, How'd you like to try that, Miss New York Model? And my parents looked at her with a pride they could not quite feel for paper copies of their prettiest daughter tingling with an air of Europe and statutory rape.

Still, I tunneled back to my life, happy to be away from them, yet safely attached. One night after a visit home, I lay naked with Patrick on my lopsided mattress, drinking wine and half-hearing my neighbors' pop songs come through the wall, and I would talk to him about my family.

"What I love about you is that you're so beautiful and still so real," he said. "You care about things."

"How could I not care about my own sister? She's the only one who's even half on my side, and she's been totally cheated by life."

"Why don't you have her come visit you?" asked Veronica. "We could take her to the theater, show her a good time. Who knows, she might consider moving here. I'll tell her, 'If I can do it, you can do it!'"

And so I did. It was summer and the apartment smelled of ripe foliage and rotten drains. When Sara arrived, I pulled the mattress off the box spring and we flipped a coin to decide who would sleep on which. (I got the mattress.) Then we went to meet Veronica in an ornate café lit with white lamps and candles that dripped and pointed with trembling witch fingers. Classical music, rampant and riven with dainty feeling, announced and upheld the display of cakes, which were swollen with sugar and cream. Veronica and Sara talked warmly about the eccentrics they worked with and their weird ways. In Veronica's baubled words, her bland nest of disaffected temps became a snappy sitcom where people suffered, strove, and lost and yet emerged with rueful grins wrinkling their eyes, ready for the next episode. And Sara told her own stories, about valiant old ladies and tough, salty aides as the candles slowly dropped their fingers into baroque heaps of dust-covered wax. We went to see *Vampire Lesbians of Sodom* and then ate dinner in Chinatown.

It was late when we left the restaurant through a swinging stream of plastic beads. The potholed street steamed with warm garbage and the chemical discharge of air conditioning. We walked around moldy cardboard, mashed fruit, fetid porridge, and crumpled vegetables still green and breathing on the pavement. An off-duty cab roared up; we shouted and waved our arms, but it sped away. We stepped past a fish with gelatinous, death-webbed eyes, each stiff red-speckled scale like a stone that for a short magic time had rippled through water as flesh and now was turning back to stone. "Pee-U!" cried Sara, and pinched her nose. But the stench buoyed us and filled the air with energy. Another off-duty cab roared up; Veronica stepped in front of it, tilting her hip, pointing her toe, and lifting an invisible skirt. Dark eyes flashed through the blurred wind-shield; the driver lustily hit the brake. As we climbed in, he smiled, newly awake and grateful, into his rearview mirror. "It never fails to stop a vehicle of some kind," purred Veronica.

"Veronica is great," said Sara as we dragged the mattress off the box spring into the center of the room.

"Yeah," I said, and meant it.

My sister wanted to meet models, and so the next day we had lunch with Selina, an ex–cover girl attractively worn at twenty-four. I had prepared her for Sara, but still I was afraid that on sitting down, each would look across the table and see the enemy. But that didn't happen. They got along. They dis-cussed reincarnation, phobias, and nightmares: the psychic who told Sara she was antisocial because she had once been an African noble put to death by the tribe for her refusal to kill a beautiful animal; Selina's recurring dream, in which she discov-ered herself as a child, shrunken like a mummy, eyes tightly screwed in permanent sleep in the baggage rack of a high-speed jet.

"Your sister is so spiritual," she said to me later. "You could say anything to her and she'd talk back to you."

"I don't know if she's spiritual, but she's certainly lovely," said Veronica. We were back eating cake amid candles and heaped wax. "She's got to move here; it would change her life. She—" A soprano voice floated from the sound system and unfurled, shimmering. Veronica put down her forkful of blond cake.

"What is it?"

"This aria," she said. "It's from *Rigoletto.*"

"Oh," I said. "I think my father has that on record."

"I saw it with Duncan. Years ago."

"Oh." She had not mentioned Duncan for months; I had almost forgotten him. "It's beautiful," I said uncertainly.

"It's a love song. Only I can't remember what it's called now." Her skin shone, like an eye might shine with tears. "We loved each other, you know. I know that must sound sick to you after what happened. But there was love there."

"I don't understand," I said slowly. "But I believe you."

"Nobody understands. *I* don't understand. My aunt was the only person who got it at all—my aunt! That dismal old bitch who once said to me, 'It's all about self-hate, isn't it?' She said, 'It must be terrible to lose someone you love.' And it is."

I thought of my father lost in his own house, his own family, his own chair. "I'm sorry," I said.

The singer opened wide her voice, like passionate hands, like arms of light.

"He wasn't a cunt," she said. "I'm sorry I ever said that." Her voice tried to open, to come free of its rococo shape. "He was a Ganymede, a beautiful boy. Royalty in disguise." Her voice broke free—the terrible freedom of shapelessness and grief. Anguish flooded her eyes. "The *'Caro nome.'* That's what it's called." Tears ran down her face. I looked away, as if she were naked. I didn't know what else to do.

When I was a young child, my mother told me that love is what makes the flowers grow. I pictured love inside the flowers, opening their petals and guiding their roots down to suck the earth. When I was a child, I prayed, and when I prayed, I sometimes would picture people not as flowers but as grass—plain and uniform, but also vast and vibrant, each blade with its tiny beloved root. By the time I moved to New York, I had not prayed for many years. But there was a soft dark place where prayer had been and sometimes my mind wandered into it. Sometimes this place was restful and kind. Sometimes it was not. Sometimes when I went into it, I felt like a little piece of flesh chewed by giant teeth. I felt that everyone was being chewed. To ease my terror, I pictured beautiful cows with liquid eyes eating acres of grass with their great loose jaws. I said to myself, Don't be afraid. Everything is meant to be chewed, and also to keep making more flesh to be chewed. All prayer is prayer to the giant teeth. Maybe sometimes there is pity for the chewed thing, and that is what we pray to. Maybe sometimes there is love.

Veronica said she and Duncan had loved each other. She said her parents loved her, too. My parents would say they loved each other, if you asked them. Patrick and I had loved each other, or at least we had said so.

I met Patrick for drinks after I left Veronica. I told him about how *Rigoletto* had come on the sound system and how her proud voice had broken.

"That's so touching and poignant," he said. "Is she a model?"

"No. I met her when I was temping."

"That's even more poignant," he said. "The poor girl."

"She isn't a girl," I said. "She's forty."

"My God!" He gripped the table and flung himself back against his chair. "That's not poignant; that's tragic!" His eyes flashed.

I drank up his flashing eyes. The day before, he had knelt naked between my spread legs, streaked eyes fluxing. Light flooded the room. Feelings of tenderness and devouring streamed through and lit his varicolored eyes. With a soft sound, he took my foot in both hands and bent my leg as he brought it to his mouth to kiss my instep, sole, and ankle.

He took a great gulp of strawberry frappe. His eyes flashed more faintly; he looked at his watch. We went to eat at a fancy place with four of his friends. We had precious dinners on big white plates, huge glasses of wine, and sweet-colored cocktails. Thick mirrors on each wall increased us. Bright music played and made pictures of abundant brightness: lips and teeth, soft breasts saronged in silk, warm skin, cut figs, wine and sunlight. The founder of a tiny magazine talked about writers who were supposed to be good and were terrible. The film critic for the tiny magazine talked about a bitchfest between a director and a writer whose story he'd adapted. The troll biographer denounced all that was shallow and vulgar. I listened to them and thought of a photographer who habitually held his arrogant head turned up and away from his body, as if pretending it wasn't there. His pretense somehow accentuated his hips, his thighs and butt, and made it impossible not to imagine his asshole.

A short actress with sleek black hair looked at me and said, "Thinking hard?"

"No," I replied. But I was. I was thinking of myself presenting my body without bodily reality, my face exaggerated by makeup and artificial feeling, suspended forever on an imaginary brink, eyes dimmed and looking at nothing. I thought of Duncan dancing in a dark place that glinted with hidden sharpness, his face set in curious determination. I thought of Veronica with her penny loafers and her fussy socks. But my thoughts were naked, and I had no words for them.

"You are too thinking about something," said Patrick. "I can hear you."

"I was thinking of things that don't seem to go together but do. Only I can't say how."

"Can't connect the dots?" asked the actress in a barely audible voice.

"And I was thinking about Veronica."

"Your friend with AIDS?" asked Patrick.

166

There was silence filled with quick-running currents. The actress turned abruptly away. Softness and apology rose from her shoulder and came toward me. Talking resumed.

Later, Patrick and I fought about his friends as we stood on the sidewalk in the spilled watery light of an openmouthed bar. I turned to walk away. He grabbed my elbow; I turned away from him and for a ridiculous second we pivoted around each other. A table of drunks near the bar's blurry window burst into laughter. I turned toward him and he banged into me. The table applauded.

"Come on," he said. "Don't be angry now. Let's go where there aren't any friends."

And he took me up and down two twisty streets to an office building with a blank-faced door and a back stair that led up a hot stairwell to a tar roof illuminated by a tin lamp clipped to a wire strung between two chimneys. On the roof was a rough stone bench made bluish in the angled light, a matching table, wooden planters ragged with roses, and cage upon cage of purling gray pigeons. There was an unlit candle on the table and a rain-warped book with its pages stuck together. The tin lamp wobbled slightly in a low wind and the pigeons wobbled with it.

"What is this?" I asked.

"A life raft in the sky. Come look."

The pigeons moved like dark water at our approach—soft and rolling, with little tossing plaps.

"The janitor of this building keeps the birds—his brother owns the building, so he lets him. I know the janitor and he lets me come here if I sort of pay him."

The pigeons purled like dark water, evenly stroking a dark shore. The burning roof released its acrid tang. Grainy light poured up off the city, reached into the sky, and sank back with a darkish milky glow. Patrick took off his shirt and spread it on the mattress. Smiling, I sat on it. He scooped up my hips and, with hands on either side of my wakened spine, used his thumbs

167

to open my body. Wave after wave reached the soft dark shore. An hour later, Patrick left ten dollars flapping under a corner of the milk crate.

A month later, he left me for the black-haired actress, whose shoulder had apparently apologized ahead of time. He told me after a torpid dinner, while I was trying to pull him down onto the bed with me. Frowning, he refused to come. I stopped pulling. He came and sat and told me. He had not slept with her yet, he said. He didn't want to disrespect me. His sense of honor shocked me; I lay in a state of dull shock, letting him kiss and stroke my hair until he left. He stroked me like he didn't want to leave. He stroked me like the pigeon sounds reached for the shore, again and again. I lay there, hearing those sounds for a long time after he left.

When I finally sat up, it was two o'clock in the morning. The apartment was dark and someone outside it was moaning. The gate on my window made a shadow window of gray diamonds on the floor. I thought of the shadow bars of a prison window striping an upturned face, one eye unstriped. I felt for the phone. I didn't expect Veronica to be in; I just wanted to hear and speak into her answering machine. The electronic bleat of the phone rippled and rose like a stair into the night sky, each step a bar of light. I saw myself and Sara, two tiny girls, climbing it step by step, each helping the other.

"Hello?" said Veronica. She had been sent home early and had just made herself a nightcap.

I arrived at her apartment moments later. She opened the door in a flowered floor-length gray gown with a yoke of lace on the breast and furry pink slippers on her feet. She gave me a mug of cocoa and white rum. We sat in front of the mumbling TV, and Veronica rapidly changed the channel as we talked.

Patrick and I had nothing in common, but he could hear me thinking. He was smarter than I was, but most of what he said was dumb. His friends were horrible, but I wanted to please them. I loved him, but I kept planning when we would break up. *Heureux et malheureux.* I would be with someone else and someone else and then someone else.

"Frankly," said Veronica, "it's hard for me to see this as a problem. You should enjoy it while it lasts. I'll never get laid again, and if I do, I'll likely infect him."

On the screen before us, faces cycled past—human, animal, monster, human.

"Veronica," I said. "What was it like between you and Duncan?"

"Like? Haven't I told you? Essentially, it was male-female relations. We enjoyed the same things—film, the arts." Human, monster, animal. The silhouettes of lions walked the African delta with alert ears. Veronica lighted another cigarette. "If you mean deeper, it's hard to explain. Together, we were able to express something in ourselves that was buried—I don't quite know what it was, but I've been thinking. It sometimes felt like I was something he needed to knock down over and over, and I would always pop back up. He needed that and so did I, the popping back up."

"He hit you?"

"No, hon, I'm speaking metaphorically. Anyway, then we would step back and crack a joke and laugh, and everything else would fall away. And we'd just laugh." She filled her lungs with fiery smoke, then let it go. "It was a narcissistic game maybe. But still, when you go through that with someone, it can feel like something very profound has happened between you. And it has, actually. That person's your partner, and there's honor in it."

I didn't understand. I glanced at the TV. Nature workers were filming a dominant lion killing a rival's cubs in order to protect his gene pool. Three terrified cubs watched him knock their sibling on its back.

"Nature," said Veronica. "How dreadful." She changed the channel. Human beings smiled over drinks. She changed the channel.

"Anyway, fifteen years ago, there was a precursor to Duncan, this beautiful man I met when I was traveling in the Balkans. He didn't speak English, so we couldn't understand each other, but for the week or so we were together, it didn't matter. Sometimes this look would come into his eyes, and I would feel the same look in mine. All this awkwardness and phony smiling and pidgin English—all of it was just for the times we got to that look. I remember this one time we made love. We were up in the mountains and we did it literally on the edge of a precipice. He turned me around so we were front to back, and if he'd let go of me, I could easily have gone over."

She changed the channel. Small paws resisted the big snout, then fell as the jaws came down. The lion squatted and ate. She changed the channel. Human beings kissed.

"I remember this tiny figure on the side of a mountain down below, someone in a field of something blue, filling a basket. Then rolling green, and the sun, and the sky going up and up. It was the most erotic experience I ever had."

One of the Siamese cats walked across the band of TV light and paused, its ears in fine bestial relief against the brilliant screen. There were only three cats by then. Veronica had already started finding homes for them through a service at the Gay Men's Health Crisis.

"I've done things that looked self-destructive all my life. But I wasn't really being self-destructive. I always knew where the door was. Until now."

The nature workers scared the lion away and scooped up the remaining cubs. Veronica turned off the television. She invited me to sleep over. She gave me a flannel nightgown imprinted with violets and green ribbons. The print was faded from many washings and there was a ragged hole in one elbow; it was so unlike Veronica to own such a decrepit item that I thought it must be from her childhood. As I slipped it over my head in the bathroom, I inhaled deeply, imagining ghost scents wafting off the gown. Childhood smells: silken armpit, back of the neck, fragrant perfect foot. Adolescence stronger, more pungent, heavy with spray-can deodorant, then secretly, defiantly rank. An adult snow cloud of soap and bleach, and the ghosts still whispering through it. The gown was tight across my shoulders; its sleeves went just past my elbow and its hem just past my knees. I smoothed it lovingly and left the bathroom, ready to get in bed and put my arms around Veronica; I imagined us together in our flannels, cuddling until we woke.

But as soon as we lay down, she said, "Good night," and turned on her side. I stared at the ceiling and listened to her snore. My heart said, Where am I? Where am I? Where am I? I remembered myself in bed with Daphne, and how I would've ground my teeth if she'd put her arm around me. I thought of the young Veronica, held on the edge of a cliff in the arms of a stranger she never had to know, embraced like a beloved child and penetrated with the force of one adult to another. That person did not want the reassuring arm of a sister. She did not want to cuddle.

I fidgeted until the day came through the blinds. One of the cats approached; I reached to touch it and it recoiled as if it were shocked. I got out of bed and softly walked the apartment in my ragged gown. The cats stared, lemurlike. The furniture slowly groaned awake. I went to a window and slit the blind with a finger. I watched people and cars pass in a trance of fixity and motion. Now the diamonds on my floor would be filled with light and gently moving. Now there would be no prison bars. Now I could go home.

I got back in bed and lay close enough to Veronica to feel the heat come off her. The week before, I had heard a man who had AIDS interviewed on TV. He said that on top of dying he constantly had to comfort his well friends, who were terrified that he was dying, and that it was exhausting to have to do that.

I'm not terrified, I thought.

My father stormed across the living room floor. "Do you know what that son of a bitch is doing to his family by going on a television show?"

I'm not terrified.

We breakfasted at a place that served a full English tea on mismatched tables. Our table slowly became a jumble of flowered plates piled with sandwiches and cakes, flowered cups and pots of tea, and red jam in a porcelain pot. We were waited on by severe middle-aged women who wore their dowdiness as if it were a starched uniform. Veronica leaned back in her chair and joked with them about girdles.

"My mother used to say, 'If he asks you what kind of underwear you have on, you tell him, "It's up to my chest and down to my knees and I've got panels where you don't need panels."' And that's actually what hers was like! Mine, too, until I could physically fight her about it."

"What was your mom like besides that?" I asked.

"You need to know *more*?"

Veronica said her mother spent hours putting makeup on every day, then came down the stairs crying because it was all wrong. She abused laxatives for so many years, she eventually lost bowel control and had to keep emergency towels in various locations around the house—little hand towels she'd neatly fold up and then forget. Veronica's father would find them and hurl them on the dining table. There were showers of tears and furious Kabuki scowls. Her mother's condition got so bad, she couldn't go out for groceries. Because her father was an agoraphobic, he couldn't do it either unless the perfect opportunity popped up in his drive-to-work plan.

"They would fight about who would go, until we were down to two frankfurters and a can of peas. Then they'd send me and my sister out across this huge intersection with our little red wagon. They'd be watching us from the window, waving."

"How old were you?"

"Ten and eight. We'd get back and they'd accuse me of

stealing—'skimming off the top,' my father would say. My sister was no fool—she began telling on me before they would make the accusation. *I* was no fool—I took the hint and started stealing."

The waitress brought us an ashtray. Veronica thanked her with a zesty simper.

"Do they know you could get sick?"

"Sort of. I mean, I told them. My mother said, 'You've always been a hypochondriac.' My father screamed, 'You're just trying to get attention,' and hung up." She shrugged. "Not enough sandwiches to make a picnic in that family."

For the first time, it occurred to me that the unsaid things were not so bad after all. For the first time, it occurred to me that my parents had hidden their hate and pain out of love.

"Perhaps," said Veronica, "perhaps that's why I've always felt it's my destiny to find respite, at the end of my life, in a safe, beautiful dwelling. It doesn't have to be an actual house. It could be an apartment, or maybe a cottage."

"I could see you in a cottage," I said. "With flowers growing up the side."

"Flowers on the side! I'd love that!"

"You could wear galoshes and make jam."

"I could! It's not too late—I'm in great shape! Who knows, I may *not* get sick. I could double-shift a few years and make enough to pay for a cottage near the ocean."

The red jam in its porcelain pot was like a viscous jewel in the sun. I imagined Veronica in her cottage, among flowers and fallen petals.

"But you know, Alison—you shouldn't listen to the things I say about my parents. You know me, I'll say anything for a cheap laugh. They weren't so bad."

"No?"

"No. My mother had a beautiful voice and she sang to us almost every night. She put on plays with us when we were little, wrote songs for us to sing. When we went to bed at night, she would say, 'Here are all the people who love you.' And she'd name everybody, every cousin, every great-aunt. She built a fence of protection with those names. And my father would come and stand at the door and watch over us all." She smoked and exhaled, making a tiny redness on the wet butt. "I can still see him standing there." She smiled and put out her cigarette.

There were small flowers sprouting on bushes growing along-side the path. They were a flat tough red that paled as their petals extended out, changing into a color that was oddly fleshy, like the underside of a tongue. They grew on clay red branches, slick and shiny in the rain, and they had tough red-tinged leaves. Against the gray sky, they were startling, almost rude. Not the right flower, I thought. Veronica had been startled enough. She needed silkiness and softness.

Patrick came back to me at a party. It was a benefit given for an AIDS relief organization. Lots of rich fucks milling, and me standing there. Before I saw him, I saw a black supermodel named Nadia, a woman known for her arrogance and mean-ness. "Oh no," muttered a magazine editor, "here comes Miss Big Bitch." But, like everyone else, he watched her move through the room. She moved like a queen inside a twittering entourage that functioned like a parade float of feathers and papier-mâché. She started conversations, then turned her back on them. She threatened relationships with a look. She made everyone either an extension of her or invisible. Her movements expressed a blistering scorn, which perversely electrified her beauty and made it even greater than it might otherwise have been.

I looked at her and saw her avenging the German woman who walked alone on the street with her arms wrapped around her torso, staring with hollowed eyes. I heard her say, Is this what you people really want? Is this what so awes and impresses you? *This?* All right, then, I'll give it to you.

"You better be careful," I said to the editor. "Secretly, I'm a big bitch, too."

That's when I saw Patrick. Warm with borrowed anger, sex, and pride, I crossed the room, borrowed raiment flowing. It sometimes takes a while for people to notice that borrowed things don't quite fit, and so for the moment they do. He smiled, his expression sweet and broad, and flicked his head, casting off nervous feeling as if it were sweat. We bantered and joked, circling, gliding around each other like animals getting ready to play. We kissed against the wall, and in a closet, and finally in the bathroom, like people on soft-core TV, me on the sink with my haunches up.

When we came out, Nadia had moved on and the air of the room had changed, like the sea in the wake of a great wave. All the little creatures and shells still stirred, fitful and chaotic. An oyster sweating in his cream-colored shell was talking into a microphone about something nobody could hear. A laughing blond bit of seaweed rolled against a scudding black-haired pebble and they slid down the wall, laughing. Patrick said, "Honey, let's go," and we swam for the door.

On the street, everything was rushing and corporeal, and the sky was soft blue, with small salmon-colored clouds. We went into a deli and wandered giddily among the rows of cans and bottles, wrapped pastel sponges, and a flashing orange cat. Tiny pictures that had smiled at us as children smiled at us as adults: a tuna wearing sunglasses, a laughing green man wearing leaves. We got potato chips and juices and went back out under the soft, glowing sky. A taxi shuddered to a halt and took us into its creaking dimness with a slam. A song came out of the radio, bouncing like balls of colored candy on a conveyor belt. "One more shot!" Bounce bounce! "Cos I love you!" The city rolled along, breaking against our driver's stalwart hairy neck.

"I have something for you," said Patrick. Smiling, he held out his bunched fist.

"Hmm?"

He smiled and opened his hand. I saw my wadded underpants. I blinked. The world opened its mouth and laughed like it was a baby being tickled. I'd forgotten to put them on when we were leaving the bathroom; he'd seen them come out my pant leg and fall on the deli floor. The cat flashed past; the green man laughed. We laughed, rolling around in the taxi, kissing. The city rolled along beyond the clouded bulletproof plastic that protected the driver with its hinged pocket for the wadded fare. It was stickered with advertisements for clubs and bands, and the stickers were doodled on with ballpoints and the radio drew its doodles on everything. Oh Miss Big Bitch, even you are overlaid with doodles and radio songs.

"I love you," I said.

He held me close and kissed me and his body said, Yes, and here we go.

He was still with the black-haired actress and her articulate shoulder. That was all right. If the entire world was going to open its mouth and laugh, there was certainly room for her. She could be in the world and I could be in the laughter that came rolling out and bounced away. There was room.

Once, I arranged for Patrick to come to my apartment right after a visit with Veronica; he arrived a few minutes early and so the two met.

"That's the woman who has AIDS?" he asked incredulously. "That's outrageous!"

"Why do you say that?"

"Because she looks like somebody's maiden aunt! How on earth did this happen to her?"

"She *is* somebody's maiden aunt, you idiot. Not technically a maiden maybe, but . . . it doesn't matter anyway."

"I know it doesn't matter. I'm not an idiot. But you know what I mean. She doesn't look like somebody who'd get AIDS from sleeping with a bisexual guy." He took my hand. "Alison, you're so sweet and human and you don't even know. You weren't friends with this person before she got sick, were you?"

"She's not sick now. We were friends. We were good work buddies."

"But you know, most people, when something like that happens, unless it's a really tight relationship, they run. That's when you *became* her friend."

"So what? I don't think I should get a medal for acting decent," I said.

Later that night, Patrick said, "That woman's face was so bizarre. Veronica, I mean. She was just vibrating with bizarreness."

I have not spoken to or seen Patrick for over twenty years. Still, on the mountain, I answered him. "Yes," I said. "She was bizarre. She was in pain and she was all alone. That can make a person bizarre."

But the thing was, I hadn't always acted decent.

Veronica was alone because her friends left her. She said they left her because she was sick, but I don't know what they would've said. She said, "They all told me, 'Don't sleep with him!' But I did, and now they're all angry with me. They want to think they're right, because if they can think they're right,

they can think they won't get sick." She shrugged. "I can understand that. It's idiotic. But I can understand."

The first New Year's Eve after Duncan's death, she was
alone. When the next New Year's Eve came, I decided I would
take her to a party. I examined every invitation I got, looking for
a Veronica-safe zone. There were two that I set aside: One was
a party on the Upper West Side; hosted by a magazine editor
named Joan, it was in honor of a New York filmmaker who'd
directed a movie called *Show Tunes.* Joan was an anomaly in the
fashion world. I remembered her, fat, smart, and keen-eyed,
peering over tiny square glasses placed on the end of her dis-
cerning nose as she scanned a martini menu. I imagined her
and Veronica drinking martinis together.

The other possibility was something called the Motorcycle
Party, at which, said the hostess, guys would jump over naked
girls on their hogs. I knew one of the naked girls; she looked perfect in photographs, but in person she had drunken, filmy eyes
and grainy skin and a hard little drum of a belly with a button
like a curled toe. I'd told her about Veronica once and she'd said,
"It's so great of you to stand by her. It's great and it's brave."

It was not brave of me to go to the movies with her. But it was
brave of me to invite her out that night. I'm embarrassed to say
it. But it's true. I was afraid to go out with her for New Year's. I
had to be brave to do it.

My cab arrived outside Veronica's apartment at 9:00 p.m. She
fluttered and waddled down the walk in a chiffon gown and a
black leather jacket. Her head was square and determined
above her waddling softness. Her smile gathered power with
each step. "I'm so glad we're doing this," she said. "Otherwise,

I'd have put on my leather chaps and walked the streets." I thought, I'm doing something good—a thought that was round with wonder and shy conceit.

The party was in a spacious apartment alive with ease and goodwill. People smiled at us, tilting their heads as if they were looking deeply, then deepening their smiles as if to show they were delighted by what they saw. The guests were old, young, and middle-aged people wearing good-quality clothes without fussiness or too much care. There were children, too, and they ran around holding spangled streamers high above them. Someone played show tunes on a piano, loosely, his big bald head erect and radiant.

"My God," said Veronica. "I don't deserve this party."

"Oh stop." But I wasn't sure I deserved it, either. I didn't see any other models. I didn't see anyone I knew. I looked for Joan and found her in a large room, sitting before a fire burning in an enormous hearth. She radiated warmth, and I wanted Veronica to feel it. But when they were introduced, Veronica seemed to shrink into something small and hard. Joan responded by withholding her warmth. Her fat body became imposing as a fortress and she peered out of it with hard, watchful eyes.

"How long have you known Alison?" she asked.

"Years. We worked together."

"You're a stylist?" she asked doubtfully.

"A proofreader," I said. "From where I temped once."

"I see."

The dull conversation went on, becoming subtly hostile without anything hostile being said. Joan's soft cheeks gradually hardened and I began to hear Veronica's voice the way she must've heard it: stilted, shrill, willed into garish rococo shapes. We were joined by a friend of Joan's, a busy-eyed little man who said he was a literary agent. In the middle of answering a question from Joan, I heard him ask Veronica what she did.

"I write. I paint. I've done some acting."

Her voice was so unctuous that for a second I thought she was affecting it to mock him. Then I saw her false, pleading smile.

There was a pause. His eyes filled with scorn and the pleasure of feeling it. He raised his chin. "Really," he said. "How *interesting.*"

I ran for the hors d'oeuvres table. I thought, If she wants to act weird, it's not my problem. I won't baby-sit somebody sixteen years older. But when I looked again, she was standing alone, the same terrible smile fixed on her face.

"Oh, I'm fine, hon," she said. "Somebody just came up to me and said, 'Who invited you here?'"

"They might've really wanted to know," I said hopefully. "Sometimes people ask you that as a way of placing you."

Her smile became more terrible. I could smell her sweating.

A man approached. "Excuse me," he said. "I'm about to leave and I just wanted to tell you that it's been a delight to be in the same room with you. You are just so pretty."

"Thank you," I said.

"Just so pretty," he repeated. He turned to leave, and in passing, he put his hand on Veronica's shoulder. "And you ain't bad yourself."

"Thanks for the bone," she said.

His retreating head flinched.

"Let's get a drink," I gasped.

After that, Veronica was more relaxed. Biting someone had probably taken a lot of tension out of her jaws. Now I had it and could calm it only by drinking. I wandered in and out of bland conversations and my heart beat, Where am I? We sang "Auld Lang Syne." We yelled "Happy New Year." When I turned to Veronica, she kissed me, and for an instant I knew where I was.

We left the party in a cheerful mood. A cab even stopped when we hailed it. But as soon as we were inside it, I did not want to be with Veronica anymore. I wanted to be at the Motorcycle Party, wandering through the crowded rooms by myself, watching strange haughty faces reveal themselves. I didn't want to hear Veronica say weird things to people. I didn't want to worry about her happiness. I didn't want to be judged because I was with this strange, badly dressed, badly made-up woman. She was talking and talking about how a little girl at the party looked exactly like her niece. Light rose and fell on her face, harsh, then soft. She will soon be very sick, I thought. And she isn't going to have much pleasure in the meantime. The cab stopped at a traffic light made brilliant and fiery in the cold. Clumped people with gentle, expressive faces leaned against the wind. Frail special dresses stuck out from under the women's lumpen daily coats.

"Veronica," I said, "I hope you don't mind, but I think I'd like to go to this other party by myself. I hope you don't feel insulted. I just feel like being by myself."

I dropped her off at her apartment. She kissed me and said, "Happy New Year." I remember it as though I'd shoved her from the car.

It wasn't always like that. One night, we went out to dance. She had said, "Just once I'd like to go to one of those chic places to dance. Just once." So I found one that had only just stopped being chic and we went. She wore a red jacket that had been fashionable five years earlier, a lacquered hide with gold buckles, shoulder pads, and trick pockets. She wore it defiantly. She wore it as if to say yes, it was ugly, yes, it was tasteless, but right now only the forceful character of tastelessness and ugliness could help her shake her booty one last time. She danced the same driven way she moved in aerobics class— leaping and kicking with manic propriety. As if to show a disbelieving someone, once and for all, what she could really do. But with each repetitive movement, she seemed to wind more deeply into a place where she didn't have to show anybody anything, a place where there was no propriety. I looked up; on crude stages, fat men in wigs haughtily, expertly danced. Hot colored lights crashed down around them in waves. Sirens went off and clown horns honked as they danced in the face of death and in the face of life. The music blared gigantically, as if it were propelling a baby into the outrageous world and bellowing with shock at what it saw. The queens danced and Veronica danced, and their dancing said, World, kiss my fat middle-aged butt.

The narrow path winds against the mountain. It is surrounded by thick, dripping vegetation, and the foliage seems hostile, gluey, weblike, and humming. I remember my mother reading to us, her arms warm and glowing in their fragile nimbus of hair; the jaws of the nature-show lion; the cub's helpless paws. The camera crew filmed the lion eating the cub's guts, then scared him away. Or shot him. They let him eat one for the TV show, then scooped up the others.

I don't know what I said when I danced. Probably nothing. Probably "I'm a pretty girl, I'm a pretty girl, I'm—"

Veronica began to cough. She ran a low fever. She fell during an aerobics class and began to pour cold sweat. I yelled at her about seeing a doctor.

"My main problems are yeast, perpetual herpes, and hemorrhoids," she said. "The first I can take care of at the drugstore, the second they can't do anything about, and the third I'm not going to some swinish doctor about."

"Why not if you can get them removed?"

"Hon, don't be naïve. I'm not going to some clinic on Broadway with a red neon arrow that reads 'Hemorrhoid Removal—Strictly Confidential,' where they'll core me like an apple and I'll be expelling bloody rags for a week. I know I'm going to die soon, but I'd rather it not be like that."

"Then get your lungs looked at," I said sulkily. "Or get something for the fever."

Eventually, she did see a doctor, but she pronounced him a bastard and wouldn't go back.

"I had to wait for hours in a roomful of men with sores on their faces, and there was this one dreadful woman who sat on the edge of the couch like she had a boil on her ass. She went in before me and came flying out like a witch on a broom. Then I went in, and the doctor, who, of course, was a heterosexual with the face of a drunk pig, went on this self-congratulatory rant about how she'd complained about being in a room with AIDS patients. 'I told her to get the fuck out,' he said. 'I don't need her; nobody needs her.' Like I'm supposed to think he's so great."

"Don't you agree with him?"

"Not really. Of course she doesn't want to be in a room with AIDS patients. Who would? I told him—I said, 'Sir, I have AIDS, and I don't want to be in a room full of—'"

"You don't have AIDS yet. And I thought you said she was dreadful."

"They were both dreadful," she snapped.

I sighed. "Look," I said. "I know it's shit. But you've got to decide if you want to live or not. Because if you do, you're going to have to start fighting for your life."

"Yes, I know, hon. I'm just not sure it's worth it."

"Okay. Maybe it's not. Probably it's not. You've got insane parents and your sister is useless to you. You're lonely and you have a crummy job. And you're not going to beat the disease whatever you do."

Veronica stared like I'd slapped her out of a crying jag. At least I'd refrained from telling her she looked like shit.

"But even if you live only five more years, even if you live only two more years or one year, if you use that time to really . . . to really . . ." I fumbled, embarrassed.

She looked at me, sorry for me.

"To really find out who you are and care for yourself and . . . and forgive yourself—I mean—I don't mean—"

"I'll let that pass," she said softly.

"I *don't* mean forgive yourself for getting sick. I mean caring for yourself." My words were wooden and trite. I had gotten them out of articles in health-food magazines. I did not know what they meant any more than she did. Still I said them: "I mean loving yourself."

"I understand what you're saying, Alison." Veronica spoke gently. "I think it's lovely. But it's just that it's . . . it's not my personality."

"Okay. But then there's the physical stuff. If you don't like that doctor, there's others. There's herbs, there's acupuncture, there's yoga. There's GMHC, there's Shanti, there's support groups—women's groups, too. Medicine won't cure you, but it'll ease the pain. It'll let your body know you're caring for it, loving it. I know it's corny, but—"

"I don't have insurance."

I stared. "But I thought you got insurance a while ago."

"I did, but it lapsed. It was lousy insurance anyway."

I was speechless.

"I tried an acupuncturist a year ago. I can't say it did much for me, though he was awfully nice. He talked about the organs and how they relate to different emotions. Lungs are sadness; liver is anger. He said my main weakness was my small intestine. Would you like to guess what emotion that's related to? Deep unrequited love. The small intestine! Who knew?"

Sometimes I had contempt and disgust for Veronica. It would come on me as I lay alone in bed, drowsy but unable to sleep. I would picture her with one of her false smiles or arranging her cat coasters or adjusting her jaunty bow tie, and I would fill with scorn. I didn't try to fight it. I let it snort and root. Why had she been involved with someone like Duncan anyway? Someone who let her be called an old fish in public and then went off holding hands with the guy who'd said it. She wanted to be a victim. Probably she even wanted to die—she'd said so herself. *Most people, when something like that happens, they run.* Of course they did. It was horrible. People like Veronica dragged everyone down; it was paralyzing to be confronted with such pain. Especially since she'd chosen it for herself. How could anyone respect a person like that? She'd made choices. She'd made choices!

"You made choices," my mother said to my father. "If you're not happy with your life, you can choose to make it different. That's what I did. I chose to come back to you, and I can choose differently."

A Jazz Age band was on loud and jumping. The TV was on, too, and Sara was hunched up in front of it, doing a crossword puzzle with one hand pressed against her ear to shut out the jazz.

"Choices! Choices! What choices do you make when you're fifty years old? What choice did I have then with a baby to feed and another one coming and another one after that? I had to take what they gave me!"

His voice was pleading, but his rumpusing music mocked us all. Sara made a fist of her ear-blocking hand, muttering curses and gripping her hair as if to tear it out.

"She also means choices inside yourself about how you handle things," I said. "Like you can let the people at work upset you or you can—"

"Fuck!" shouted Sara, and stormed up the stairs.

"Sara, you do not talk that way!" shouted my mother.

"I do too and so do you!"

"Choices inside you! Do you think a human being's a fun house with something behind every door?"

"Yes!" I said, laughing.

"Maybe in the New York City fashion world they are! But not here. Not here. Oh, Lordy."

When I came back the next month, he was reading aloud from a book about queers and the awful things they did. According to this book, all men had the potential to be gay, to fuck anything, all the time, and they got better only with the influence of women. "These guys don't have to be that way!" he cried. "They have a choice!"

"I thought you didn't believe in that."

"I'm not talking about 'inner choices'! I'm talking about behavior! I'm talking about reality!"

Sara quietly ate her dish of ice cream. My mother rolled her eyes.

Veronica quit temping and took a full-time job with excellent insurance. She joined a support group for women with HIV. She quit smoking. She found a doctor she could tolerate. She double-shifted for a year and bought a large and expensive co-op. She filled it with heavy furniture and blinds, which made her rooms quiet and dim as an aquarium.

I moved into a bigger apartment, too, with high ceilings and casement windows and a bar down below that was full of music, faces, and sweet-colored drinks. As soon as I did, work fell off. I was supposed to be in a swimsuit spread, but I stood next to a girl with big boobs and a butt like a mare, and the photographer said, "You look like her twelve-year-old sister!" During an evening-wear shoot, a client suddenly appeared with a tape measure and held it to my hips and said, "Look at this! We can't have this!"

"Crazy bitch!" said Morgan over sushi. But then she paused, chopsticks poised over a slice of fish shaped like a lovely tongue. "Were you about to have your period, by any chance?"

It's Alain, I thought. Finally. It has to be him.

Morgan arranged for me to meet a photographer named Miles. Miles was an eccentric who'd made his reputation working with slightly unusual girls ten years earlier. He'd been recently taken up by a maverick designer whose tiny lace skirts and flowered chenille leggings were everywhere; there was a sense that his face was going to pop noisily out of the background at any minute.

I had drinks with him and a sixteen-year-old starlet named Angelique, a tiny Hispanic girl with a narrow body that made me think of a salamander in a column of fire. By way of greeting, she bit me on the cheek, then on the arm. When she went to the bathroom, I asked Miles if she was crazy. "No," he said. "She's just a scared little girl trying to take on the world. But she does bite. She told me once she bit through a box of Kleenex when she couldn't sleep."

Miles was a tall, rangy person who wore red plastic sunglasses and carried his bald head the way a certain kind of truculent person carries his butt—high, proud, and glandular. He wanted to know the most embarrassing thing I'd ever done, the sexiest thing, the cruelest thing. I told him and he said, "She's telling me the truth. That's lovely!" Angelique frisked like a puppy. "I never tell the truth!" she said. "I know you don't, darling," he replied, and took her picture with a small Polaroid camera.

We spent the night going from bar to bar. Wherever we went, Miles took Polaroid pictures of whoever was in front of us; a well-dressed middle-aged woman with wild eyes and a tough shiny nose; a sleek redhead in a T-shirt with a hairy grinning rat on it; a very blond man in a black shirt and thick black glasses, standing ramrod-straight and looking weird on purpose. I noticed Miles didn't choose anyone too fashionable or too beautiful. He was going for real. The real women tried to look sexy. But there was uncertainty at the bottom of their eyes. Miles threw their pictures on the table with our drinks. I looked at a picture of a woman in a suit. Her clothing was rumpled; her forehead and nose shone with splotches of abnormal light. She was smiling like she believed "fun" was something that could be grabbed and held, and she was still trying very hard to grab it.

"Why do you do this?" I asked.

"I like to see people have some fun."

"This woman doesn't look like she's ever had fun in her life."

He regarded the picture. "Probably not. But she's trying, and that's what's interesting to me." He held up the camera and took my picture. I made the ugliest face I could. Angelique put her arms around me. She said, "I want to marry you," and bit me.

At the end of the night, we had to walk a block to find a cab. Angelique ran ahead of us; when we caught up with her, she was flirting with some Hispanic men on a public bench. They were rough-looking and wore shabby clothes; they had unshaved faces and meaty shoulders just starting to go round. But they were still full of sex, and one of them was handsome. Angelique darted around them like a drunken little bird twittering in Spanish. They were so smitten that they didn't notice Miles taking pictures. Angelique put her arms around the handsome one and made as if to kiss him. Miles took another picture. One of them did notice, and he glanced at us, frowning. "Pose with them," Miles said to me.

"No." I moved away.

"Okay," he said. "Come on, Angelique, quit kissing the criminals."

Heat shot through each man on the bench and brought all of them to their feet. Angelique started talking, her voice quick and supplicant. The handsome one snapped at her; she stepped back.

"You call me a criminal?" said one of them. "I'll fucking kill you."

"I was only kidding," said Miles.

"You're nobody to kid with me, faggot."

"Look, why don't you—"

"You've got AIDS, don't you, faggot? Go home and die, faggot."

We walked down the street and they followed us, yelling at Miles's aggrieved butt of a head.

When we were in the cab, he said, "So that's what they're saying in the street—'You've got AIDS.' That's the worst thing you can say."

"That didn't mean anything," said Angelique. "They were just barking."

"They didn't want to be used," I said.

There was a silence and in it I knew Miles would not work with me.

"But that was okay, wasn't it?" he asked. "That wasn't too scary, was it?"

"No," said Angelique. "That was fun!"

That night, I dreamed I was in Paris, posing for a magazine cover. The studio was filled with people—René, Alana, Simone, Cunt Face, every drunk bitch and bastard from rue du Temple. And sliding among them, bending and flattening his body like a snake, Alain showed his white flattened face. There was no movement in his eyes now. They were still and empty as a waiting grave. The photographer was furious, but there was nothing he could do. Alain smiled and disappeared. The crowd milled. The photographer cursed and pinched me.

So I left my body and went to a place more empty than a desert, a place that seemed to stretch into forever. In it shimmered thousands of veils and masks and personalities, each as still as a statue and waiting for someone to step inside them and make them live. Quickly and lightly, I stepped from one to the next. Pleasure zipped across my surface like a water bug.

But under the surface, something heavy pulled and twisted. It pulled and twisted because it did not want to take these shapes. It pulled me back into my body and twisted my face off my head. But it was okay. No one noticed; the camera flashed. I smiled and woke up thrashing, like I was trying to throw off a great blanket of darkness.

Hungover and haunted, I went to the next day's go-see. Grainy light fell on the bent heads and shining hair of a dozen wan, yawning beauties. The booker opened my book and closed it. He said, "Honey, your look is dead." Once again, I thought, Alain. He had entered my world through my dream and poisoned it for me. I knew this was absurd. But I thought it anyway.

That night, I showed Patrick the Polaroid Miles had taken of me. My eyes bugged out. My hands were claws. My mouth was open so wide, my cheekbones seemed to pop off my head and my discolored tongue stuck out as far as it could go. My throat was a mass of wet redness.

Patrick looked at it for a long time. "It really is heinous," he said finally. "It's the throat that does it. It looks substantial—like there's something trying to get out."

Veronica said she hated the people at the office and that they hated her. She said she was forced to work with men who said filthy misogynistic things and that no one would listen to her complaints. She was terrified they would discover her illness, fire her, and cancel her insurance. Yet she worked double shifts, putting in sixty-hour workweeks because she was behind in her taxes.

I thought she was wrong. I thought if they knew she had HIV, they would treat her better. "They'll be more understanding if they know," I said. "They'll go easy."

"Nonsense," she snapped. "They'd circle for the kill."

She'd left her support group by then because, she said, the women were all stupid cows and the moderator was a condescending queer.

"One day, I made the mistake of being vulnerable around them—if you can't be vulnerable with cows, then who? I told them what was going on at work, all of it. I said I felt like God hated me, and the snotty faggot said, 'Oh come on. I know you're bigger than that.' I said, 'My fucking God! How big am I supposed to be?' And the cows just pursed their detestable lips. No wonder men hate us. No wonder."

Finally, the moderator told the group that he was writing a book on women with AIDS and that they were going to be part of it. Veronica found this outrageous, and she tried to unite the other women against him. One of them snitched on her and she was asked to leave the group.

During the same week, her sister called and told her to stop sending presents to her niece. "She says whether I'm sick or not, I need to live my own life and stop trying to glom on to the child. She said once I *scared* Sunny on the phone. Of course she wouldn't tell me how." Veronica sat straight, her smoking hand quivering with rage. "She talks like I'm going to contaminate her." Rage filled her eyes with streaks of yellow bile. "She talks like I'm going to *eat* her."

She fought with people at work, until no one would partner with her anymore and she had to work alone. When she and I went to the movies, she accused the people behind her of kicking and screamed at the people in front when they asked her to please stop talking. She fought with people in our aerobics class for getting too close to her on the mat. Once, she fought with the instructor during class. We were on our elbows and knees, pulsing one leg at a time up toward the ceiling. "Hold that pelvis firm!" shouted the instructor into her mouthpiece. "Pretend your favorite person is behind you, holding it very firmly!"

"Excuse me!" Veronica's voice rang through the room, rising over the music. "Excuse me!" The instructor turned. Veronica was already on her feet, eyes crazy with rage. "One," she said, "that was a very rude remark. Two, my favorite person is dead."

I argued with my father about choices. I made fun of him when he talked as if he didn't have any. But when I talked about Veronica with Daphne, I argued the other way. Daphne lived in Hoboken with her boyfriend, Jeff. She was almost done with graduate school. She had grown steady and a little plump and her eyes had an expression of gathering power. Her kitchen had blue wallpaper and smelled of garbage and lilac. We sat in an oval of sunlight and drank mugs of honeyed tea and talked as if we were walking around the block at Christmas.

"She acts like a demented bitch," I said, "and I want to tell her that, but I can't. I don't know how I'd be if I were her. People say you have a choice about how you act. But it seems like she really doesn't."

"What d'you mean? Of course she does. It's horrible that she's got AIDS. But she's got a choice, just like everybody else. You can be her friend, but you can't help how she chooses to handle what's happened to her."

"But sometimes I get this picture of what it's like inside her. I picture inside her being like a maze that's really small and dark, full of roadblocks and trick doors. I picture her twisting around and around, wanting to go forward and not being able to find the way. Like a bee that's banging on the screen door—

you open the door and you wait for it to go out, but it just keeps banging on the screen."

"But she's not the bee," said Daphne. "She's the person who built the maze."

I wished my father had been there right about then. He'd have said, "*You* don't build anything! You come up out of the ground like a tree and that's what you are! You're not the one who made it!"

But I said, "Is she? Even if she built it the way it had to be when she lived with crazy parents?"

"Yes, she still did it. Everybody does. You create these strategies—"

Discussing and describing things we didn't understand, we walked around a winter block in a sunny kitchen, past little girls dancing on green chairs or sucking up milk shakes in a warm car smelling of mother and vinyl; of Mother's bare shoulder in her sleeveless blouse with its piercing half circle of sweat. *You're just too good to be true. Can't take my eyes off you.* We walked and walked against the impassable membrane of our understanding. *Good to be true.* We pressed against it until we could press no more. *Eyes off you.* We returned to the kitchen and finished our tea.

On my way back to Manhattan on the train, I remembered that lying in bed with Daphne six years earlier had been like lying in a hole with a dog. The memory was flickering and far away as "heaven" had once been. It flew past me, like the shabby old houses and cars and discarded bathtubs flew past as the train gathered speed, then plunged into a coruscating black tunnel. I dozed in the droning car. I felt like a discarded bathtub sitting out in a yard with sun shining on it. I felt good.

· · ·

Patrick and I broke up. We had a fight about something I can't even remember. There was a break in the yelling and I said, "Maybe we should just stop seeing each other." And he looked up with gratitude and relief. We were quiet for a while. He asked me if I wanted to walk a bit and I said yes. We walked for about an hour, not saying much of anything. At the end of it, we were done and it was okay.

I saw other men after Patrick. They were important to me at the time, but now I can't remember why. Maybe there was a demon in my pants saying, Do it with this one! No, don't do it with that one! I did it with one named Chris, a thirty-five-year-old former model with the touching face of an unformed boy. His blond hair fell in his eyes. He wore pastel jackets over white pants. I lay awake at night thinking about him. When we kissed, I felt hope and joy. When we fought, I cried. Now the things I remember most viscerally about him are the way he smartly tapped his packets of artificial sweetener against his saucer, and that he left most of his food on his plate. He was very thin and when you first looked at him, he appeared much younger than he was. His eyes were young. But there was rigidity in his mouth and neck and chest and it was old, very old. One night in a café, I said something and he leaned toward me with tenderness in his eyes. For a moment, his rigidity trembled, trying to move with the feeling; then it was gone.

Years later, when I was lying in my bed crying because my life was broken, Chris came to me as powerfully as in a waking dream. He was leaning toward me, full of tenderness. He did not tremble. His mouth was not rigid; it was alive and firm, and his neck was supple. His chest radiated warmth that was more loving than erotic. My heart was comforted, my mind calmed. In life, we had parted coldly. Afterward, we didn't speak. We didn't even look at each other. Still, I believe that somehow he came to me.

There were several others. I lay awake thinking of them, too. I leapt into their arms, laughing, and covered their necks with kisses. I told them secrets and stories from my childhood. I told them I loved them. Now I can't think why. Perhaps it was simply that, in each case, I was the woman and he was the man. And that was enough.

In the winter, I began to get catalog work rather than fashion assignments. It was dull, and I knew that one day soon I would want to find something else. But I was not bitter or afraid. I was twenty-five years old and I was stronger than I had been in Paris. I waited, alert and listening.

In the spring, Daphne got married in someone's back-yard. There were children running around shouting. There were two-colored tulips and slim trees with heavy bunches of white flowers. While Daphne and Jeff made their vows, a child cried, "There's a daddy longlegs!" and Daphne laughed under her veil.

In the summer, Sara moved to a Newark bedsit with an aide from the old people's home. He was a tall, handsome black man with loose, gangling limbs, and he almost wordlessly loaded Sara's cardboard boxes of things into his car. One rau-cous night at the bedsit, Sara put her hand through a window-pane; he made a tourniquet and took her to the emergency room. "He thinks quick and he did the right thing," said my father. "He might not be so bad." But then he drove off with the car, leaving Sara without any way to get to work. After a few weeks, he brought the car back with a smashed windshield. Sara moved back in with my parents and went to school to learn court reporting.

In the fall, I got a job with a photographer named John. He had a small, tense body and a large head that craned around like something on a turret. He asked me if I was from San Francisco. Because I was wary, I said no. Halfway through the shoot, I recognized him.

A night or two later, we met for coffee in a large café. It was raining; the shadow of a dripping little branch shivered happily on the lit pane. John hunched forward over his thick white cup, warming it with his hands. He said I should go to L.A. There was more joy there, he said, and he had connections to music video work. I said, "I'm not one of those idiots who thinks she can be an actress." He said, "This isn't acting." I said, "I don't know anybody there." He smiled and raised a hand off his coffee cup. He had a fleshy, emotional hand. He said, "You know me."

In a surge of headlights, the grain of the window glass became suddenly visible. Its lines were fine, glowing and curved in shape. They joined the glistening shadow branches and made a phantom web dripping with wet, senselessly beautiful light.

"Can you help set things up for me?" I asked. "Can you help me find an apartment?"

I love you, said John's eyes. I love you, said the set of his lips. I love you for a little street girl who'd take off her clothes if you gave her a glass of wine and told her she could be a model. But that's not what I was. Thrilled and trembling, the phantom web filled with surges of traveling light. Yes, he could help me. Of course he could.

And he did. He found a cheap apartment for me in Venice Beach. I had money to pay for both places for a time. If it didn't work out in a year or so, I could always come back to New York.

"I'll see you off to the airport," said Veronica. "I'll wave my handkerchief. I'll run alongside your cab waving my handkerchief."

"Oh no, that's all right."

"Only joking," said Veronica sharply. "Don't worry."

. . .

My new apartment was a small two-story with EL SERENO misspelled on its stucco front in worn-out cork. John took me to flea markets to shop for furniture: a polka-dot shag rug, an orange sectional couch, a red Formica table with matching chairs. He took me to lunch and sometimes to dinner. I told him about Paris and everything that had happened there. He told me about Gregory Carson, who'd folded his agency and gone back to Texas to run his father's oil business. He told me I would have to learn to drive but that until then he would take me to jobs whenever he could. He said, "I got you into this mess, after all."

My first video was for the comeback effort of a middle-aged trio of overweight guys with big beards. They played a song about hot girls; I rode in a pink car with two other models in tiny skirts, fighting crime and showing up obnoxious people. My big scene came when, fists on hips, I stopped a barroom bully by planting my gold-heeled foot on the bar, my skirt riding crotch-high. The bully's eyes popped; he back-flipped out of the frame. Fists on hips, I bounced as if my crotch were the steed I'd ridden in on, humpty-hump! By catwalk standards, it was clumsy and crude, and at first I hated doing it. But then the clumsiness became fun. One of my gal partners stepped on the hand of a fallen villain; the other twirled a toy gun and blew on it with lush lips. The band wandered in, sharing a bag of potato chips.

I went home in a taxi that cost one hundred dollars and walked the peopled gray beach behind El Sereno, feeling my aloneness. It did not feel bad. It felt like something hidden was slowly becoming visible. I thought of Joy, Cecilia, Candy, Jamie, Selina, Chris. They fell away from me like empty potato chip bags thrown from a car. Even Patrick. He was good, I thought, but now he's finished. And I pictured throwing away an empty milk shake container. These thoughts and images scared me. I could not believe I was really like that. I thought of Veronica.

Here there was a change. Veronica did not fall away or seem finished. She seemed to go on forever, all the way down into the ground. I asked myself why and was answered immediately. Her pain was so deep that she had become deep, whether she liked it or not. Maybe deeper than any human being can bear to be.

I went back to New York just before Christmas. The piss-elegant city wore salt-stained winter clothes and soiled jewels, its colors stunned and mute in the cold. People who passed me on the street looked like acquaintances whose names I would remember presently. I went to dinner with Selina and to a party with the naked motorcycle girl. I thought, I will not throw them away like empty bags.

Christmas came. My father's music boasted of fatted abundance, and so did the tree, the scented candles, the stockings, and the stuffed toy sheep my mother had dressed in red Santa suits she'd sewn. Fear was still in the house, as was the sadness and the unsaid things. But happiness had come and dazzled its eyes. Daphne was pregnant. Her breasts and belly were just starting to swell and her skin was plumped and rosy. Sara's eyes had wakened. My mother bloomed. The decorations, which had looked sad and weak to me, now looked like offerings carried in my family's arms. I saw my family, exhausted but still hopeful, walking with arms full of offerings down a long road, giving without knowing why to something they couldn't see. Amid their giving, my video was a trinket, but it was a trinket everyone enjoyed. My father watched it again and again, smiling and expanding inside. For this was no flat picture in a magazine—this came with music! His daughter was punishing bastards to music and bouncing around like a girl nice enough to be a little clumsy. Even when he stopped watching, it stayed on the TV, mutely rewinding and replaying, becoming part of the tree and the stockings and the Christmas sheep.

"How's Veronica doing?" asked Sara.

We were setting the table with the holiday silver from my mother's side of the family, and that boasted, too.

"She's okay."

"Did you see a lot of her this visit?"

"No. I didn't see her at all."

"Oh."

Of all the people I had spoken to about Veronica, Sara was the only one who didn't know she had HIV.

I flew back to L.A. just before New Year's Eve. I had dinner with John. I said I felt bad about not seeing Veronica but that it was painful to be around her. "You can't talk to her about it because she won't listen to anything anybody says. But you can't ignore it, either, because she acts so awful that you always have to remind yourself that she can't help it, since she's sick. *And* her parents were crazy, *and* they abandoned her. Et cetera."

He agreed that I had to take care of myself, and that she had choices.

I went home and took a hot bath. My mind talked and talked. I got in bed. The darkness of the room grew over me. Just before I curled into it, I started awake and thought, Where am I? Then I sank back to sleep as if slipping into black water.

Under the water, I saw two naked little boys tightly bound and hung upside down. One of them was dead. His rectum had been torn open and gouged so deep that I could see into his belly. Something white moved inside him. The living child sobbed with terror. "He has AIDS and now I have it," he sobbed. "I'm going to die." I put my arms around him and tried to hold him upright, but he was too heavy. I said, "I'm sorry you have AIDS," and the insipid words were loathsome, even to me. In a fury, he bit me; I dropped him and ran, terrified he would give me the disease. Veronica rode past in a cab; I was in the cab telling her about the boys. "And then he bit me," I said. Her eyes grew wild and she bit me with razor teeth. I jumped out of the car and ran. I woke up and a voice inside me said, You will go to hell. Silent and still, the room roared over me.

The next day, I called Veronica. The phone rang a long time. I was about to hang up when she answered. She sounded as if my voice had called her from a dark place she'd barely been able to pull herself from. As if my voice was a familiar but puzzling and distant sound, significant in a way she couldn't quite remember.

"Oh, hon, hi. Do you need anything?" she asked. She sounded exhausted and hoarse.

"What do you mean? Are you all right? You sound terrible."

"I'm not all right, hon. Not at all."

"Have you seen a doctor?"

"No. I'm too weak to leave the apartment."

A voice in my head said, This is real.

"Veronica," I said. "I want to see you. I want to help. I can get a flight tomorrow."

"You don't have to do that, hon."

"Please," I said. "Let me come. If you really don't want me to, I won't. But I want to."

She didn't answer for a long moment.

"Hello?" I said.

"You don't want to stay with me, do you, hon?"

"No! I mean, unless you want."

"No, I really don't. I'm a very private person. You know that. But if you stay in your own place, I'd love to see you. If it doesn't put you out too much."

"Veronica," I said, "I love you."

She didn't answer.

. . .

On the plane, I sat next to a fat old woman who'd come on board in a wheelchair. She wasn't crippled, but she was too sedated to walk. She was flying to see her son, who had just been shot. He was unconscious and would likely be dead by the time she arrived. Her grief fanned out from her, huge and tender. She did not try to display it or hide it. Her name was Suzanne Lowry. I listened to her talk about her son, and I talked to her about Veronica. She said she was sorry. It didn't sound like politeness. It sounded like her grief was big enough to take in my lesser grief. We talked about small things. She told me what she was knitting. We snorted over the airline food. She talked about an article in *Ebony*. She asked, "Do you read *Ebony*?" She was black, and when I said no, she said tartly, "Well, you should."

She was in shock, and because she was heavily medicated, she kept dropping her knitting needles and her silverware. I had to cut her airline food into pieces for her. I poured her half a cup of water and she trembled so that she spilled it on herself anyway. The stewards and stewardesses rolled their eyes behind her back. They didn't know about her son. They weren't able to see her grief. They saw a fat old lady who kept screwing up, and they thought it was funny. One of them caught my eye and smirked, like I would think it was funny, too; I gave him such a look that he blanched and turned away. But the others kept giggling. I wanted to march down the aisle and make them stop. But I pictured myself, skinny and prissy, shaking my finger and acting the good girl. I wasn't the good girl. The old woman couldn't see them anyway and would have had to put up with my climbing over her so that I could be the good girl.

When I last saw Mrs. Lowry, she was being wheeled through the airport by personnel. I held up my hand in a static wave, but she no longer saw me. She probably forgot me as soon as she got off the plane. But I still remember her. For a long time, the memory confused me. I would recall the soft feeling between us as something precious—and then I would see it as worthless. My feeling had not helped Mrs. Lowry, and her feeling had not helped me. Veronica was dead, and most likely the son was dead, too. The flight attendants had laughed behind their hands. But still I remember the feeling, like a trickle of water in a dry riverbed.

Veronica flung open her apartment door and stepped into the hall with the rakish pose of a cabaret emcee. She had lost weight, but she was not emaciated. Her undyed brown hair was cut close to her head. As I came closer, I saw the glitter of sickness in her eyes. We embraced, her head against my hard shoulder, her heart speaking to my belly with muffled, desperate joy. She was burning up and damp through her clothes. I looked over her head, and saw the last Siamese cat staring at me with a look of flat terror.

I took her to see her doctor. She'd apparently had a bad reaction to AZT, compounded by a respiratory infection. She'd started smoking again, which had probably provoked the infection. She stopped taking the medication and quit smoking. She rested at home. I brought her takeout. In five days, she was well enough to go out. We went for brunch in a restaurant decorated with blue chinaware and animals that crouched on blond wood shelves. We ordered eggs and red flannel hash, and it was placed before us in squat blue pots.

"You always told me I should let my hair go natural," said Veronica. "It looks good, don't you think?"

Yes, I did.

"The barber in my building did it. He asked me what I wanted and I said, 'Whatever you think would look good at a funeral. I am dying, after all.' Scared him, I think. Goodness, this hash is delicious."

She said she never felt better. She asked about Venice Beach and the video shoot. We talked about her visiting me out there. She apologized for being "hysterical" on the phone.

"You were sick," I said.

"I really think it was the AZT," she said. "It made me psychotic. I literally broke into several people, all arguing with one another. Some of them wanted to live; some wanted to die. I was awake, but I saw it like a dream. It was me, attacking a woman who was also me. A third woman—also me, natch—came to her rescue and stopped me. But the one I had attacked defended me; she understood why I'd done it—she understood completely. But the third—well, that part, I can't remember. Do you think I'm crazy?"

"No," I said.

"I knew you'd understand." She sounded genuinely relieved. "You're probably the only person I could tell."

It was Sunday afternoon and the restaurant was crowded, its rooms full of pleasant talk. There was a table of gay men sitting across from us, and I was drawn by their ease and companionability. My attention hovered on them for a moment, receiving the affected, elegant lilt of their voices with vicarious enjoyment. Then my reaction swerved sharply. Their voices sounded contorted, tortured into fluted curlicues. They seemed to reflect base souls trying to hide their baseness under the thinnest of pretensions—and then to exaggerate the pretense, as though it were something great. They all talk like that, I thought. You can always tell a fag. And Veronica is just like them. She talks just like them.

Mortified, I divided like Veronica in her sick-vision. Shut up, I told myself, shut up!

"After I got off the phone with you, I decided I wanted to live," continued Veronica. "All of me. I got up the next day at five-thirty in the morning and made myself go out to the deli on the corner for poached eggs and toast. No wonder I was so weak—it was the first real food I'd had for days. It was so good,

Alison, I can't tell you. I felt life coming back into my body. It was still dark outside and I had this wonderful feeling of safety and warmth. I loved watching the countermen setting up, filling the sugar dispensers, putting out all the little creamers. I flirted with them and they flirted back, even though I looked like hell."

Her voice was the same bitterly inflected instrument I had just despised. But now there was hope in its center, and that subtly made it sweeter. The sweetness didn't go with the habitual hard showiness of the voice, and the incongruence gave it a wobbly, unprotected quality that pierced me. I love her, I thought. I love her.

But then she said something with such force that a tiny bit of spit flew from her mouth and landed on my hand. I jerked it away as if I'd been bitten. There had been no thought or even feeling behind it. It was pure reflex. For a second, the conversation stopped. Then Veronica changed the subject. There was no sweetness in her voice.

We left the restaurant and took a walk down Seventh Avenue. The sun gave everything a glow that crackled in the stark cold. Hungrily, I took in the aging patchwork of buildings, the rhythmic pattern of traffic, the people, walking with miraculous order and civility. I had no hateful thoughts. I enjoyed our walk.

The next night, I went to see a play with Veronica, her old friend George, and David, a boy George was dating. When I heard George would be coming, I was surprised—the last I'd heard of him, Veronica had called him a "misogynist." But when I arrived at the restaurant before the show, my surprise evaporated. The two men were wearing suits and ties; Veronica wore a suit, too. The men were leaning slightly toward her, their faces expressing pleased alertness, as if they were courtiers in the presence of a queen known for her extraordinary wit and didn't want to miss the slightest nuance of her royal demeanor, let alone her words. They were lavishing this attention on Veronica like praise, ensconcing her in their regard as if it were flowers. They knew she was sick and they were very likely afraid they were about to get sick, too. But their bodies did not speak of this. They sat erect and open, as if the best of life was ahead of them. They gave their courage to the sick woman so that she would be upheld.

When George stood to greet me, I surprised him with a full embrace. He and David complimented me on photos they had seen, not mentioning that they hadn't seen any for a while. They asked me about Nadia again and again. Veronica drank soda water, but the rest of us shared bottles of wine. We talked about films, books, magazines. Veronica and George quoted lines from *All About Eve* back and forth intermittently. ("I heard your story in passing." "That's how you met me, in passing.") We had big desserts and then piled into a cab as if we were wearing capes and carrying walking sticks. ("I told my story in bits and pieces." "That's how I met you, in bits and pieces.")

When we got to the theater, I went to the bathroom, leaving the others in the lobby. When I came back, I saw them before they saw me. George was talking to Veronica, his back to me. David was behind Veronica, looking over her head at George. He was taller than George and I could see his expression clearly. He looked bewildered and scared. I thought, He is even younger than I am. Then he saw me looking at him and smiled brightly. We all went to the play.

But when I got in bed that night, the hate came on me again. With no conversation or pots of flannel hash to dim it, it came big and loud. Gnawing and terrified, it ran back and forth in erratic diagonals, exuding grotesque visions: a handsome gay man, a hairdresser I'd just had dinner with—hate made his teeth and nose pointy and foregrounded like a dog's snout. It squeezed him together with the flute-voiced men at the restaurant and with Duncan in Central Park, pulling his ass open, his body reduced to a dumb totem with a single meaning. And with Veronica, her ugly face, her proofreader's kit—her rulers, her box of colored pencils—her prissiness, which denied the shit of the world and so drew it down upon herself.

Sweating, I twisted in my bed. I thought: I tried to be so liberal, so free. I lied to myself. Those men were always about death. And Veronica chose them. That's why she's dying.

I sat up and turned on the light. I saw myself in the mirror, disheveled and shrunken, my head looking strangely small on my long neck, my eyes remote and ashamed. So this was who I really was. I wanted to blame my father, but I couldn't. This was who I was. I thought of David's face in the theater, the way he'd smiled when he saw me looking. I thought of Mrs. Lowry, the way she'd tartly said, "Well, you should." I thought of the rivulet of hope and sweetness in Veronica's voice. Sadness brimmed; it bore up my hate like water bears ice and carries it away.

I stayed in New York for ten days. During that time, I saw no one but Veronica. "I told my aunt you'd come to visit me," she said. "And she asked, 'How much did you pay her?' I said, 'Dolores, would you listen to yourself? She's my friend. She came because she cares about me.'"

I arrived back in L.A. at night. John picked me up and took me to dinner at an all-hours place with a boiling dark air. He looked angry. He kept telling me I had to learn to drive if I expected L.A. to work out for me. I drank too much and took him back to my place. Maybe I felt I owed him. Maybe I liked him. Maybe the demon whispered, Do it with him! In any case, it didn't work out. He kissed me too hard and touched me with violent shyness. We rolled awkwardly on my sectional couch; it came apart and almost dumped us on the floor.

"You're so beautiful," he blurted.

"I'm not beautiful," I blurted back. "I'm ugly."

He reared away, frowning. He was taking it as an insult, and with reason. But it would not be taken back. "You're beautiful," he said angrily.

"No I'm not. I'm ugly."

He slapped me. I fell off the couch. He sat on the edge of it and held my shoulders. I could see in his eyes that his heart was pounding. "Stop saying that!" he said intensely.

"No! I'm ugly, ugly!" My voice *was* ugly.

He slapped me again. I tried to stop him. He held my wrists. Now we were really in it. The room was buzzing with the energy of it. "Tell me you're beautiful!" he said, coldly now. I wouldn't. "You're beautiful," he said, and slapped me again.

"John, please stop."

"Say you're beautiful."

But I couldn't get the words out. He slapped me until my ears sang. Finally, to stop the hitting, I said what he wanted to hear. He let go of me and sat back as if deflated.

"Don't you see?" My voice broke. I was nearly crying. "Don't you see how ugly I am?"

"No," he said quietly. "I don't." He crossed his legs and looked away.

I asked if he wanted a drink. He said no, that was okay. He said he was going to go but that he could tuck me in if I wanted. I said no, that was okay. I saw him to the door; we kissed quickly, on the lips.

We didn't see each other for a few weeks. Then I called him and asked him to drive me to a job, and things went back to normal. Except I didn't see anger in his eyes for a long time. I saw sadness.

. . .

When I told Veronica about John slapping me, she said, "Ooh, that sounds kind of sexy."

"Maybe if it had been somebody else. With John, it was just weird."

She didn't seem surprised that I'd said I was ugly, nor did she act like there was anything strange about it. I appreciated that.

I went to New York every month for the next six. When I wasn't in New York, I talked to Veronica on the phone. She complained about her doctor, her neighbors, her sister, people at work, people on the street, at the movies, in the store, and at the gym. She insulted David and fell out with George. She had a screaming match with the woman who lived above her, a "bitch" who walked on her hardwood floor in high heels, making a "murderous" noise. Her exterior became to me like a vast prickly thicket broken by patches of ice and tiny, weirdly pursed receptors built only to receive what they'd heard before. It was boring and ugly. You couldn't talk to it. I'm sure she knew I felt this way. But she didn't get angry. Probably she didn't dare. If she'd lost me, she would've had no one.

"I'm always the one to call," I said. "I'll wait for you to call next time."

"I understand, hon," she said. "You're setting your boundaries."

"I'm not setting anything," I said. "We can talk anytime. It's just that you never call me, and I don't want to bother you."

"I don't have anything to talk about except my new disgusting aches and pains. It's just depressing."

"I don't care if it's depressing. I want to know what's going on with you."

"It may not be too depressing for you, hon. But it's too depressing for me."

And so, when we met, I talked brightly about nothing and she let herself be drawn into bright nothingness. But I could see dark shapes moving behind her eyes.

Daphne's baby was born in June. They sent me a Polaroid of the delivery: a splayed leg, my sister's extruded red flesh, a bloody cord; life caught in the doctor's great mitt. My mother's head between the open leg and the far border of the photograph, grinning from ear to ear. Later, I balked when they handed me the infant, a girl named Star. But when I held her, it was like two opposite electrical poles lit up inside me and discharged twin bolts that met and joined. It was a small place inside me and far away, but I felt it.

That summer was moist and hot. The city exhaled, farted, and sweated through the bars of its concrete cage like a massive animal of flesh and steel, glass and bristled hair. It sent up a mighty stink to carry all the little smells that played in and out of it—flowers, dirt, cars, garbage, piss, and food. I called Selina and we went to see a band. They played in a modest venue, a dark and delicious place with a copious flow of strange faces and a bar of colored bottles lit up like the Emerald City. I drank and bit the rim of my plastic cup and lost myself in the music on the sound system. I had succeeded. I had become like this music. My face had been a note in a piece of continuous music that rolled over people while they talked and drank and married and made babies. No one remembers a particular note. No one remembers a piece of grass. But it does its part. I had done my part.

The sound system cut off. The band came onstage. The front man was rail-thin, with gaunt eyes and pale, pouchy cheeks. He carried himself like a dandy, but rawness hung off him like the smell of meat. He picked up his guitar; dandified feeling came out of it. They weren't good, but it didn't matter. The room was full of life that wanted forms to hold it, and it wasn't picky. Neither were we. We watched as if we were witnessing the preservation of a place in our collective heart—a place that had once been primary and that now had become so layered with auxiliary concerns that we no longer knew what it was or where it was. And now we felt it: secret and tender, and with so many chambers. Some were dark, with bats flying out. Some were speed, light, and joy. Some were tenderness and soft red flesh. Some had babies curled inside them. Some were the places where all the others mingled. I remembered standing on the street with Lilet, eating ice cream off a paper plate and bags of hot cashews. I remembered rooms of strangers and people dancing and a boy who said, "And then I fertilized it!"

Selina put her arm around me and I leaned into her a little. In a chamber of my heart was Daphne, her open leg radiating triumph and pride, and my mother's grinning face between her legs, a net of love to catch the baby when it came. In another chamber was Nadia, sailing like a ship, her scorn unfurled like silk sails. I saw the German woman from behind, walking alone down a dark corridor, almost disappeared. There was Sara, living in an enchanted shadow world only she could see. There was Veronica alone in her apartment, locked in full engagement with forces the musicians lightly referred to. The song said nothing about any of them, but they were part of it anyway.

I wished I could tell them all about this, tell them what I saw. But I wouldn't be able to find the right words for conversation. Even if I did, it wouldn't make sense to them, any more than my father talking of his favorite songs made sense to the men he worked with.

The music turned the corner of a darkly baubled wall. I imagined Veronica alone in the dark, waiting for the brute that stalked her to show itself in full. I imagined her horror at the small eruptions of death on her body—the sores, infections, rashes, yeast, and liquid shit. I imagined her holed up in the part of herself where all was still orderly and clean, insistently maintaining the propriety and congruence that had enabled her to get through the senselessly disordered world, and that was slowly being taken from her.

Even more than the others, I wanted to tell her this. I wanted her to know that even though she was dying, she was still included in the story told by the music. That she wasn't completely and brutally alone. The music raised its lamp and illuminated its own dark interior. I will tell her, I thought. I will remember and I will tell her.

I went to visit Veronica the next day. She put out a tray of brownies in special pink paper, fruit, and cheeses. Her breathing was labored; it must've been hard to go out for the food, and she couldn't even eat it. In her presence, what had been important and true the previous night seemed trivial. But it was what I had to offer.

"I thought about you," I said, "because the music was so dramatic and a little dark and—first, it reminded me of the story you told me about being on the mountain with that Balkan guy?"

She nodded, a little dazed, an eyebrow cocked.

"But also the whole event was trying to create this experience, this feeling that these guys were great because they were really dealing with something. Compared to you, they weren't dealing with shit. I don't mean just because what you're dealing with is bad, but because it's real."

Veronica's face went from bewildered to hard. "This isn't a rock song, hon," she said.

"I know, I—" I felt my face reddening. "I know it sounds stupid, but I just mean . . . I thought of you. I thought how strong you are and how much guts you have. You're the realest person I know. You are! Other people just write songs and strike poses and . . ."

Veronica turned and looked at the last cat. The gesture was more eloquent than any cutting remark. Silence fell, slow as dust. I realized I was holding my breath; with difficulty, I exhaled.

"Do you have a home lined up for her yet?" I asked.

"No. Not yet. I'm supposed to talk to someone tomorrow."

"I could take her," I said.

She didn't answer me. I thought, In a minute, I will leave.

"Do you remember the nun who tended Duncan in the hospital?" she asked. "Dymphna Drydell?"

"Sister Drycrotch?"

"Yes, well, Dymphna wasn't her name. It was Dorothea, but she said we could call her Dymphna if we wanted to. She was a lovely person. She sang to Duncan one night. She sang him a lullaby."

Outside, someone shouted; gray car noise went down the block. In a minute, I would leave.

"Don't think I'm angry with you, Allie." She was still looking at the cat. "I've never been angry with you."

"Why not?"

"I don't know."

I got up and sat beside her. Finally, she looked at me. Her face was stunned and drained. I put my hand on her breastbone. I felt her subtly respond. Shyly, I rubbed her.

The trail runs into a wide road on a high plateau overlooking the entire Bay Area. The rain is now a low drizzle. The fog is still very thick, but it is moving; to my distant right lies the ocean and the bony spangle of the Golden Gate Bridge. I lick my dry lips. I try to imagine myself connected to Veronica even now, but there is no weight to my imagining. I want to know who she was, but I can't because I didn't look in time. When I look now, I see a smile hanging in darkness. Then I tip over, pulled down by my own weight. I have the last of the water and tuck the bottle back in my bag.

I rubbed Veronica's chest and then I left. I said, "Call me if anything happens," and she walked me to the door. I hugged her and she said, "Wait a minute, hon." She took a ring off her finger and gave it to me. It was a handsome sienna-colored stone set in ornate silver. "It's a carnelian," she said. "Duncan gave it to me the second time we saw each other. He put it on my finger and then he kissed it." She put it on my finger. She squeezed my hand. She said, "Good-bye, sweetheart." And she smiled.

Three weeks later, Veronica's sister called to tell me that Veronica was dead. She had been found by the police, who had gone to her building when the neighbors complained about the smell coming from her apartment. She had died of pneumonia. "She died peacefully," said her sister. "She was watching television."

The last cat had still been in the apartment. Veronica had apparently torn open a large bag of cat food and left it in the kitchen so the animal wouldn't starve before someone found her.

I fold my umbrella and rest it against my thigh. I take off my gloves, put them on my other thigh, and look at the ring Veronica gave me. It is beautiful against my cold-bleached fingers. I try to draw from it some wisp of spirit, some faint echo of

Veronica's smile, her touch, her mad anger, a ghost of fiercely exhaled smoke. Nothing. I put the gloves back on.

Veronica was cremated. I went to New York for the memorial. The rented hall was filled with the coworkers Veronica had hated, including a supervisor. There were also a few temps I'd worked with five years earlier—among them the woman who had once called Veronica a "total fucking fag hag." When I walked in, they turned to stare at me. I wonder if I looked like Nadia to them.

"I knew she was sick with something," I heard the supervisor say, "but I had no idea it was AIDS. Somebody'd told me her boyfriend had had it, but she just never looked that bad to me."

I found George and stood with him. His face was puffy and his eyes sad. A former lover of his had been hospitalized, probably for the last time. He had not seen or spoken to Veronica since I had last visited her. I asked what had happened to the last cat. He said David had adopted it.

"Where is David?" I asked.

"He decided not to come, I guess."

"And you're the model!" A woman had my hand and was shaking it. She looked like Veronica in a mask of terrible happiness. "Hi, I'm Veronica's sister, June. I've been following your career, so exciting. How did you meet my sister again?"

George uttered a courtesy that sounded like a curse and fled.

"Oops," said June. "Did I say something? And there's my mother. We'd better keep it down—whatever *it* is!" She winked as she pointed to an elderly woman with a hive of dry bleached hair, who was standing a few feet from us. She did not look like the kind of person who would abuse laxatives in order to lose weight.

When I stood up to talk, I told how I had met Veronica. I said that she knew I had been in Paris before I told her; I said that when I was looking for a job as a secretary, she'd told me I had to be like Judy Garland in *A Star Is Born*. I said that once when I'd complained about a feeling of tightness in my forehead, she'd said, "No, hon, that's your sphincter." I said, "Veronica was very beautiful."

Then George told a story about a party Veronica had given years ago in L.A., where a faded pop musician had walked into the room naked. Everybody laughed. *"Naked?"* said Veronica's mother in a loud, querulous voice. "Naked!" she repeated. Everybody laughed.

The last person I spoke to before I left was Veronica's mother. I didn't mean to speak to her, but she grabbed my hand as I walked by. "You were my daughter's friend?" Her voice was made of dead, still sparking wires. I looked at her face, swollen under her hive of hair, and, for a moment, saw her daughter. Except that this woman did not have Veronica's armor of pain sculpted to look like sophistry. Her face reflected pain received with the simplicity of a child.

"Yes," I said. "I was her friend."

"Thank you so much for coming. I'm so glad to see Veronica had friends."

I was angry, but I just said, "She was a wonderful person."

And the old lady embraced me and pulled me close, where I could feel the full force of her pain and fear and need. My anger left me. Gently, I patted her poor back. I felt her quiet slightly. I kept holding her. I felt her subtly open, like Veronica's chest had opened under my hand. Emotion passed through me; Veronica seemed to move through her mother's body, swift and graceful as light. I held tighter. Veronica was gone. The embrace broke.

"I'm just glad she didn't suffer," said Veronica's mother.

I moved back a little. My anger returned in a bolt. I said, "She did suffer, ma'am. She had AIDS."

Veronica's mother did not change her expression. She just opened her mouth and moaned. She sounded like my mother when she fell on the concrete and the wind was knocked from her.

Veronica's father had not come to the service.

I sit on the wet ground. My cruelty had been pointless. My kindness had been pointless. I remember rubbing the small bones in the center of Veronica's chest. I remember her surprise at being touched that way, the slight shift in her facial expression, as if feelings of love and friendship had been wakened by the intimate touch. The subtle muscles between her chest bones seemed to open a little. Then I left.

I never should've touched her like that and then turned around and left, leaving her chest opened and defenseless against the feelings that might come into it—feelings of love and friendship left unrequited once more. I put my head on my knees. I fantasize giving Veronica a full-body massage, with oil, with warm blankets wrapped around the resting limbs. Drops of sweat would've rolled from my arms to melt on her skin. When I finished, I would've held her in my arms. Except she never would have allowed any of that. She only responded to the chest touch because I took her by surprise.

My mind distends from me, groping the air in long fingers, looking for Veronica. The air is cold and bloated with moisture; Veronica is not here. I draw back inside myself. Again, I try to imagine. This time, I can. I imagine Veronica lying on her couch, descending slowly into darkness, the electronic ribbon of television sound breaking into particles of codified appetites, the varied contexts of which must have been impossible to remember. I wonder if, at certain moments, a peal of music or an urgent scream had leapt in tandem with the movement of the darkness, and if so, what it had felt like. I wonder if Veronica's spirit had tried to cling to the ersatz warmth of the TV noise; I think of a motherless baby animal clinging to a wire "mother" placed in its cage by curious scientists. I imagine Veronica drawing away from everything she had become on earth, withdrawing the spirit blood from what had been her self, allowing its limbs to blacken and fall off. I imagine Veronica's spirit stripped to its skeleton, then stripped of all but its shocked, staring eyes, yet clinging to life in a fierce, contracted posture that came from intense, habitual pain. I imagine the desiccated spirit as a tiny ash in enormous darkness. I imagine the dark penetrated by something Veronica at first could not see but could sense, something substantive and complete beyond any human definition of those words. In my mind's eye, it unfurled itself before Veronica. Wthout words it said, I am Love. And Veronica, hearing, came out of her contraction with brittle, stunted motions. In her eyes was recognition and disbelief, as if she were seeing what she had sought all her life, and was terrified to believe in, lest it prove to be a hoax. No, it said to Veronica. I am real. You have only to come. And Veronica, drawing on the dregs of her strength and her trust, leapt into its embrace and was gone.

I stare at the clay dirt before me. I think of the great teeth; the lion cub torn to pieces in the adult's embrace. I imagine the methodical grind of digestion and blood. I imagine a moving black coil with white shapes inside it disintegrating in a grind of dirt, roots, and bones. I look up. Before me is a small tree with delicate orangy skin, its limbs, with dull sparse clusters of leaves and buds, arrayed like static flame. It plants its roots in the bones and the dirt and it drinks. I think of my sister's bit of flesh, red with triumph, and my mother's joyous head. I think of Veronica leaping into complete embrace, her love requited now forever.

After the memorial, I visited my family. While my mother and Sara were out, I asked my father to play *Rigoletto* for me. I told him I had a friend who loved a particular aria and that I'd like to hear it. "It's a love song," I explained.

My father was happy to play it for me. I rarely spent time alone with him, and I even more rarely showed any interest in the things he loved. I wasn't really showing interest now. I didn't want to hear his *Rigoletto*. I wanted to hear Veronica's *Rigoletto*, and it didn't seem possible to hear both. If my father had met Veronica, he would've liked her. But he would not have wanted to meet her. She had loved a bisexual and thus had done wrong. It wouldn't matter to him that she'd loved the music he loved, that she might've understood his sentimental passions in ways that I could not.

With self-righteousness and also a wish that he might know me, I talked to my father about Veronica. I could tell immediately that he didn't want to hear what I said but that, because he respected death, he would suffer it. This made me all the more determined to make him hear me. I told him of Veronica's loneliness, her idiosyncrasy, her love of order. I told him how kind she had been to Sara. I told him that Veronica, too, had despised the way people used words like *choices*. "It's terrible for anybody to get a disease like AIDS," I said. "But it seemed even worse for her. Because she tried so hard to be proper and dignified. She didn't want to be phony; she didn't want pity. She wound up being and getting what she didn't want. But at least she fought."

My father's face had the retracted look of a threatened animal—tense around the jaw, ready to bite. But he nodded to let me know he was listening.

I told him about sitting in the café with Veronica, listening to the aria from *Rigoletto*. "The sad thing is, I think she was telling me the truth. I think there probably was love between her and Duncan. But it got put together with a lot of other horrible stuff that both of them couldn't stop doing to themselves. So the love didn't help them. That's sadder to me than if they didn't love each other."

He didn't answer. Loud voices leapt up in declarative oblongs, then divided into fine, vibrant strands of delicacy and strife; father and daughter sang against each other. But my father didn't answer me. He didn't look at me. He said, "Now Rigoletto is talking to Gilda, his daughter. He's warning her not to leave the house. He says, 'It would be a good joke to dishonor the daughter of a jester.'"

He said this last phrase with relish, as if the idea of a daughter's honor was like a precious jewel to him, a jewel the world no longer valued (not even his own daughter!), and now here it was, celebrated and jealously guarded in *Rigoletto*. The *idea* of a daughter's honor, I thought bitterly, not the reality. In reality, he didn't honor me enough to answer what I'd said to him. I thought of telling him more, of forcing him to respond. But how could I insist that he face what I had failed to face?

"Now here's the love duet," he said. "The Duke has come to woo Gilda, only she doesn't know who he is."

I listened to see if this was the music I had heard in the café. I didn't recognize it. I imagined a vessel of fluted glass falling through the air, landing, and shattering. I had just said that there was love between Veronica and Duncan. But how could I believe Duncan had loved her, when he had been so careless with her life and his? How could I believe she even knew what love was? My thoughts faltered and will-lessly followed the music. No. People who loved each other would never treat each other, or allow themselves to be treated, with such indifference and cruelty. But even as I thought this, I felt, rising from under thought, the stubborn assertion of love living inside their disregard like a ghost, unable to make itself manifest, yet still felt, like emotion from a dream.

"Now Rigoletto's back," said my father. "And Gilda's gone! He cries out, 'Gilda! Gilda!'"

The words cracked his voice as they burst from his lips, more fierce and dramatic than the voice of the singer. The music rose in a great fist. He said it again, more quietly this time. "'Gilda! Gilda!'" I stared at him, shocked. His voice was full of emotion, but his face was rigid, his eyes glassy.

When I got back to L.A., I went for a job the next day. John drove me to it, hectoring me about learning to drive. In his voice I heard my father crying out. He laid on the horn and braked as a big white car cut us off, its rear end wagging. A blond child with a blurred face clutched a soft toy and waved at us out the back window. "Son of a bitch!" yelled John. We got slammed from behind and thrown forward. I grabbed the dashboard hard with one hand. John swerved the wrong way and sideswiped a white blur. Crashing and grinding rose in a great fist. Veronica came at me with razor teeth. I screamed. We swerved again and went off the road.

. . .

I came to strapped on a gurney in a white corridor of pain and intercom noise. My first thought was, I have AIDS. Then I remembered. A nurse came to check my vitals. "Is my face all right?" I whimpered. "Just bruised," she replied, and said they'd take me for X-rays soon. People moaned. People ran up and down the hall. I could not move my head enough to see them; there were only upside-down white backs flapping away. Five hours later, I was fighting with a technician who insisted on taking out my earrings before she did the X-ray. She yanked them out so hard, I thought she'd tear my ears.

"If you fuck up my ears, I swear I'll sue you," I said. "I'm a model and I can't have fucked-up ears!"

"Why not?" she asked. "You got a fucked-up head."

I had a broken wrist, a torn rotator cuff, and whiplash. Because I didn't have insurance, they let me go that night with a neck brace and a sling for my arm. They told me to wear the sling for three weeks or my rotator cuff wouldn't heal properly. But I was frantic for money. I persuaded a doctor to take my wrist out of the cast early, then took a hundred-dollar taxi ride to audition without the sling or the brace. Even the tryout hurt like hell. I got the job but broke down with pain in the middle of it. When I told them why, they felt bad for me, but they had to let me go anyway. I got paid for the whole thing. But my neck and arm were never right after that.

John had a concussion, a broken ankle, and two broken ribs. He had insurance, so they kept him longer. When I went to visit him, he said, "See? Didn't I tell you? You have to learn how to drive!"

Going back down the mountain, I see some bushes I didn't notice on the way up, even though they grow thick all along the edge of the path. They have twisted little trunks and limbs, dark red and wryly formed. I think of the devil sticking out his tongue of snakes; I think of Robert Mapplethorpe, triumphant, with a whip up his ass; I think of Veronica crying, "They're taking it all away." I hadn't understood her then. But I do now. They did take it away. Veronica's world is gone, campaigned against by people like my father, who saw his world taken away from him by people like her—I understand that now, too.

A lot was taken. But not everything. Not from Veronica, and not from my father, either. When we listened to *Rigoletto* together, he had not ignored me. He had sent me a signal through his music. A signal so strong that twenty years later, I finally hear it. I hear him crying out with grief for his daughter, who was taken away from him and violated by people he found alien and terrible. I hear him crying out for Veronica, too, another daughter taken and violated fatally. I hear him signaling a grief so private, I knew nothing about it, even though it hurt so much, it made him cry out.

On both sides now, devil trees escort me. I hear her. The sun has come out. I hear him.

I gave up on music videos and moved back to New York. Incredibly, Morgan was still able to get me work. But I was older and something had gone out of me. I arrived late for bookings and on two occasions slept through them. My arm had lost full range of motion, which put me off balance. I drank too much and took pills and played with heroin. The work stopped coming. John called me from San Francisco to say he was starting an agency there; I went.

The agency was up a narrow flight of stairs on a cold Mission District street, next to a taquería. Just before I went up the stairs, I spied a bag made of hot pink leather lying on the street with its gold clasp open. I thought I'd pick it up on my way out to see if it could be salvaged, but when I emerged, somebody else had gotten it.

The agency lasted a little over a year; then it became a modeling school (". . . opening the door for potential models to enter an incredible career—or to make a splash in any field"), and I found myself telling nervous teenagers with bad skin and longing eyes that they might be models. After a month of this, I began drinking every night with a washed-up local musician and a former Playboy bunny who'd had an unhelpful face-lift. After two months, I had a terrible fight with John because I'd told an especially hopeless girl not to waste her money. I ran out, slipped on the stairs, and dislocated my shoulder when I grabbed the banister, hoping to break my fall. John drove me to the hospital. At a particular intersection, I could see unshed tears shining on his sideways eye.

I went back to temping, but my skills were dulled and the injuries to my arm and neck had traveled into my hand, making typing impossible. I saw a doctor, who said the problem stemmed from my neck and that there was an operation that might fix it. Years later, I read in the paper that, in addition to ruining my neck and arm, he had gotten into trouble for trying to perform cosmetic surgery on a horse. By that time, I had discovered I had hepatitis. *Who wants to think about their liver or their hand?* Now I have to think of mine—all the time.

When I come to the waterfall, I see someone standing on the rocks abutting it, looking into the rushing water—a man wearing a yellow rain slicker. We say hi and I stand near him for a minute, watching the movement of the water. I say, "Those trees there." I point to a sick ocher tree visible in the canyon. "There must be something really wrong with them to make them look like that. But they're so beautiful—it seems funny the disease would make them beautiful."

"They're not diseased," he says without looking at me. "They're madrones. They lose their bark in the winter. It's normal." His voice is faintly peevish, as if he wonders what kind of person would see illness in a tree just because it's naked and ocher-colored. "It's the tan oaks that are diseased. Not the madrones."

"Oh!" I smile nervously. "But the color is so extreme; it's amazing."

"It's not that bright usually. The wet brings it out."

A month or two after Veronica died, I called David to see how her cat was doing. He said that she'd hidden under the bed for the first three days but had recently come up to sleep with him. The first time the cat came onto his bed was right after he'd wakened from a dream about Veronica. The dream had begun with David entering a mansion where a party was being held. The marble walls were veined with threads of purple, blue, and pink, and they were hung with paintings and treasures of all description. There were big windows draped with silk curtains and a skylight high above; the interior was full of light. In the center of the room was a live fountain, and guests were sitting around it. David was amazed at how beautiful they all were, how every detail of their clothes was perfectly done. Their faces were expressive, generous, and exquisitely intelligent. There was one woman he noticed in particular; even though he saw her from behind, there was something familiar about her. She wore a beautiful man's suit, tailored to fit her. On her head of gold-blond hair sat a fedora, angled rakishly. She was talking to two men, and even from behind, her poise and intellectual grace were visible. As if she could feel David's eyes on her, she turned to look at him. It was Veronica. She smiled at him, a dazzling smile he had never seen her smile in life. An elevator opened before her; she stepped into it and, still smiling, went up. When David woke, the cat was on his bed with its legs in the air, purring loudly.

When I got off the phone with David, I called Sara to tell her about it. I don't know why. When I finished describing the dream, I said, "And that's what Veronica was really like, under all the ugliness and bad taste. It's so sad, I can't stand it. She'd gotten so stunted and twisted up, she came out looking like this ridiculous person with bad hair, when she was meant to be sophisticated and brilliant. Like in the dream."

Sara was silent, and in the silence I felt her furrow her brow. "I thought she was sophisticated and brilliant, Alison. I thought her hair was nice."

Sara, the only one who saw Veronica the way she looked in her heaven. At forty-two she is now an administrator at the nursing home where she once worked as an aide. She was never married but she has a son, Thomas, who is autistic but also in the gifted program. She's proud of him, but it's hard. Daphne worries about her, sends her money. She worries about me, too, but I don't let her send me money. She has three children of her own now, and her money is not unlimited.

Of the three of us, Daphne was the only one who did well enough to tell a happy story about. A story of love between a man and woman, their work and children. There are other stories. But they are sad. Mostly, they are on the periphery. If we were a story, Veronica and I would be about a bedraggled prostitute taking refuge in the kitchen with the kindly old cook. If the cook dies, you don't know why. There isn't that much detail. You just know the prostitute (or servant or street girl) goes on her way. She and the cook are small, dim figures. They are part of the scene and they add to it. But they are not the story.

. . .

On the way down the path, I have to crouch, holding the trunks of slim trees and bracing my feet in their roots. My red umbrella is closed and hanging from my wrist. Mother, Mod, modern, mod-el. That last syllable soft and unctuous. I think of my mother dying, her mouth small and sunken, her nostrils large and black. The four of us clasped hands and made a circle around her, standing at her bed or kneeling on it. We held it all between us: the sweet milk shake in the warm car, the blanket in the lamplight, the green chairs, the bright blue waves of the swimming pool, the Christmas tree jeweled with color. One by one, we bent our heads to hear her words. To me, she whispered, "My most beautiful." Tears came to my eyes. She had never said the word *beautiful* to me as praise. "Mother," I said. "I love you." But she had faded again.

Later, I asked Sara and Daphne what she'd said to them. Each of them looked embarrassed. She'd said the same thing, of course. Each blade of grass is beautiful to the one who made it.

But there is another story, too. There is the story of the girl who stepped on a loaf of bread because she cared more for her shoes than for the flesh of her family. She sank into a world of demons and suffering. Her mother's tears didn't help her. The tears of a stranger did. In the fairy tale, a mother tells her daughter the story of the wicked girl who stepped on a loaf, and the innocent girl bursts into tears. Far away under the bog, the wicked girl hears this and for the first time begins to feel. Years later, the innocent girl is an old woman and she is dying. As she dies, she remembers the wicked girl and she enters heaven crying for her. The wicked girl is filled with remorse and gratitude so strong, it breaks her stony prison. She becomes a bird and flies from the swamp. She is tiny and gray and she huddles in a chink in a wall, trembling and shy. She cannot make a sound because she has no voice. But still she is full of gratitude and joy.

I sank down into darkness and lived among the demons for a long, long time. I became one of them. But I was not saved by an innocent girl or an angel crying in heaven. I was saved by another demon, who looked on me with pity and so became human again. And because I pitied her in turn, I was allowed to become human, too.

I come out of the ravine into the neighborhood. The sun is bright and warm even through the wet trees. A child is coming down the walk on his way home from school. He looks maybe eight years old. We are about to meet, when he turns to walk up a long flight of stairs leading to an enormous multilevel house. The air is prickled by wind chimes.

In the story, the gray bird feeds the other birds with crumbs until she has fed them an amount equal to the loaf. Then her wings turn white and she flies up into the sun.

The child mounts the stairs, his gaze fixed on the house. Even with his big eyes and the baby softness of his face, there is maturity and intensity in his gaze, a suggestion of private responsibility taken on willingly and with determination. Not my child, but a child—the future. My eye falls on a torn piece of foil in the gutter. The sun strikes it; an excited ghost leaps up out of it and vanishes in the air. I leave the canyon and walk down a street of shining puddles. I will get something to eat at the Easy Street Café and talk to my friend who works there. I will take the bus home and talk to Rita, standing in the hall. I will call my father and tell him I finally heard him. I will be full of gratitude and joy.

Acknowledgments

I want to thank Christobel Wigley, Mimi Fisher, Jennifer Egan, Dani Shapiro, Cindy Stephans, Yaddo, Ragdale, and MacDowell, with special thanks to Zoya Loeb for her astute reading, Knight Landesman for tactical assistance, and Ginny Robinson for advice and receptivity. Most of all, I want to thank Peter.

Permissions Acknowledgments

Mary Gaitskill is the author of *Bad Behavior, Two Girls, Fat and Thin*, and *Because They Wanted To*, which was nominated for a PEN/Faulkner Award in 1998. She received a Guggenheim Fellowship in 2002; she is now an associate professor at Syracuse University.

A NOTE ABOUT THE TYPE

This book was set in a version of Monotype Baskerville, the antecedent of which was a typeface designed by John Baskerville (1706–1775). Baskerville's types, which are distinctive and elegant in design, were a forerunner of what we know today as the "modern" group of typefaces.

Composed by Stratford Publishing Services,
Brattleboro, Vermont

Printed and bound by R. R. Donnelley & Sons,
Harrisonburg, Virginia

Designed by Pamela G. Parker